Lizzie Marshall's Wedding

EMILY HARVALE

Emily Harvale lives in East Sussex, in the UK.
She can be contacted via her website, Twitter or Facebook.

Author contacts :
　　www.emilyharvale.com
　　www.twitter.com/emilyharvale
　　www.facebook.com/emilyharvalewriter
　　www.facebook.com/emilyharvale
　　www.emilyharvale.com/blog
　　www.pinterest.com/emilyharvale

Also by this author:

Highland Fling

The Golf Widows' Club

Acknowledgements:

Thanks to my wonderful friends for their support and friendship, particularly Julie Bateman, James Campbell, Sherry Thomas, Rachel Taylor and Eileen Mills.

To Karina of Miss Nyss, for the gorgeous cover of Lizzie Marshall's Wedding. – www.missnyss.com

Special thanks to David of DC Creation, not just for building me such a fabulous website but also for designing my newsletter and all the other clever things he does; for always being at the end of a phone or email when technology gets the better of me and particularly for never getting annoyed when I say 'What's this button for?' for the thousandth time. – www.dccreation.com

To my Twitter followers and friends, Facebook friends and fans of my Facebook author page; it's great to chat with you.

And to you, whoever you are and wherever you may be, for buying this book – Thank You.

Best wishes,

Emily x

ISBN 978-1480124356

Print edition published worldwide 2012
E-edition published worldwide 2012

Cover design by Miss Nyss

This book is dedicated to Sylvester.
You made me smile every day. I miss you.

CHAPTER ONE

'Have *you* seen him, Becky?' Jess Shaw twisted in her seat and yelled across the café to her friend.

Becky Cooper ordered a cappuccino and a slice of coffee and walnut cake then joined Jess, and Susie, at their favourite table, next to the window; they liked to watch the world pass by as they drank their coffee and caught up on the latest news.

Not that much of the world *did* pass by The Coffee Cake Café; there wasn't really much "world" in the village of Beckleston. There wasn't really much news either, in the normal course of events but today wasn't normal – the Bedfords had moved into Beckleston Hall.

'No,' Becky lied, tugging off her scarf and almost threadbare, winter coat and dumping them on a chair already overloaded with her friends' coats and bags. She knew Jess was referring to Max Bedford; he was the only topic of conversation in Beckleston this morning it seemed, and just thinking about the man again so soon was making her cross. She slumped onto a vacant chair and sighed. This was one conversation she wasn't going to get involved in.

'Well, he's gorgeous!' Jess said.

'And he's spoken for,' Susie added with authority.

'No he's not!'

Susie grinned. 'Yes he is – by me.'

Jess tutted and shook her head. 'Yeah right! In your dreams perhaps.'

'Is he spoken for?' Doreen, the owner of The Coffee Cake Café asked as she hurried over and placed Becky's cappuccino and cake on the table, 'I heard he was divorced.'

Jess glanced around her then leant forward as if she had top-secret information to share. 'He *is* divorced – but not by choice. Apparently, his wife slept with some guy who was actually on his stag do at the time. Can you believe that? She sounds like a real tart. Anyway, Max wanted her to stay

1

with him but she dumped him and ran off with the engaged guy!'

'No! The poor love,' Doreen said, shaking her head sympathetically.

'He was heart-broken apparently,' Jess continued. 'Ever since, he's been going from one woman to another trying to get over her. The cow.'

'Well, he can get over me any time he wants – and under me –'

'Yes Susie, thanks, we get the picture!'

'And me,' Doreen sniggered. 'I could be one of those panthers.'

Jess' brows knit together. 'I think you mean cougars, Doreen.'

'Do I dear? Oh, that's a shame, panther sounds so much better. I'm sure you're right though. Enjoy your cake Becky love.'

She tapped Becky on the shoulder then scuttled back to the customer waiting at the counter. For a seventy year old, she was still very spritely.

'You're quiet today,' Jess said. 'Everything all right?' She watched Becky stab at the walnuts on the slice of cake, with her fork. 'Oh Becky! I'm so sorry. I'd forgotten what day it is. Here's me going on about Max Bedford and –'

Becky shook her head and a mass of luxuriant, brown curls fell about her face. 'Don't worry about it Jess. It does me good to think about something else.'

If she'd been honest, she would have said it would be good to think about anything else *except* Max Bedford, but she didn't. Her friends had helped her with too many other problems over the last five years for her to burden them with this latest one. Besides, they both seemed to think that Max Bedford's arrival was the best thing to happen in Beckleston since Queen Elizabeth the First had reputedly stayed at Beckleston Hall in 1573.

Becky still found it amusing that The Beckleston Inn had a plaque outside asserting that the Queen's horses had been

2

stabled there; the stables at the Hall having unfortunately – and rather mysteriously – burned to the ground just weeks prior to the Royal visit. Becky was fairly sure that the fire hadn't been at all mysterious, although she would agree that it was definitely unfortunate. Many wealthy aristocrats found themselves far less wealthy after the Queen had stayed with them, and some went to great lengths to try to avoid such a sojourn. Burning the stables was, she believed, Sir Robert Beckleston's futile attempt to do just that, because, according to the estate records, no horses were injured or any other item, damaged. But Sir Robert paid a heavy price for his efforts; the Queen stayed for longer than originally planned; he had to rebuild his stables at great expense and he lost his position as one of the Queen's favourites. Only his son's arranged marriage to a woman of great wealth, saved the Becklestons from total ruin.

'How are you feeling?' Susie asked, reaching out and gently squeezing Becky's left hand.

Becky shrugged. 'I'm fine,' she lied again.

'Then why the cake?' Jess nodded towards the towering, moist layers slowly being demolished into a pile of gooey sponge. 'We all know that the only time you splash out on coffee and walnut cake is when you need cheering up.'

'Oh!' Becky shoved the plate away from her. 'I needed something sweet.'

'You needed something to destroy, more like,' Jess said. 'You haven't eaten a mouthful.'

'Has ... has something bad happened?' Susie asked.

'Other than the usual, you mean?' Becky regretted it as soon as she'd said it. She hated moaning about her life; she knew there were many people a lot worse off than she. 'Sorry, I sound like a real whiner, don't I?'

'No! Life has treated you really badly – you deserve to whine,' Suzie said, squeezing Becky's hand again.

Becky shook her head. 'No I don't. Things could be a lot worse.' And, after meeting Max Bedford earlier, she thought things probably soon would be. 'At least I've got

Lily. I should be grateful for that.'

Jess and Susie exchanged concerned looks.

'What you need is a man,' Susie said, banging the palm of her hand down on the table to emphasise the point.

Becky almost spat out her mouthful of coffee. 'Are you mad? I can assure you, a man is the last thing I need!'

Susie shook her head. 'I disagree. Jeremy's been gone for five years today and I know he left you with a lot of problems and you've had to struggle to cope and to raise Lily, but she's almost five now – and this year she'll be going to school.'

'Er ... I don't disagree that she needs a man, but what has Lily going to school this year got to do with it?' Jess asked.

'She's growing up. Soon she'll be dating and off to uni and then she'll get married and Becky will be all alone.'

'Oh. That's true,' Jess agreed, 'and these things take time. It's not easy to find a man in Beckleston, as we all know – at least, not one who's single and below sixty. In fact, I don't think there are any.'

'There's the vicar,' Susie said.

Jess looked horrified. 'P... lease Susie! Not even Doreen would date him – and she's not picky.'

'I'd go on a date with him,' Susie said, twisting her long, blond hair around her fingers.

Jess raised her eyebrows and smirked. 'You'd go on a date with any man who still has his own teeth. Actually, does the vicar have his own teeth – or did he nick them from some unsuspecting horse?'

'Don't be mean! And I wouldn't. I've got standards, you know.... Hey! There's Max.'

'Where?'

Jess' head whipped round so fast, it was amazing she didn't suffer whiplash and even Becky found herself scanning the street outside.

Susie giggled. 'I didn't mean Max was *here*. I meant he's single – and he's perfect. He would solve everything.'

'But I thought you'd already bagged him,' Jess said.

4

'I had, but Becky's need is greater than mine.' Susie bowed her head graciously as if she'd made a huge sacrifice and given her friend the greatest gift possible.

Jess and Susie eyed Becky, smiling hopefully but Becky just looked dumbstruck and remained silent, glancing down at her half-empty coffee cup.

'Well?' Jess said, 'Susie says you can have Max, so what do you think?'

Becky sighed deeply and stirred her coffee. 'I think I spend too much time with a couple of complete and utter lunatics. Firstly, Lily isn't even five yet! I know time flies and all that but it'll be a good many years before she starts dating – if I have anything to say about it, and at least thirteen or fourteen before she goes to uni. I know she's very smart but she's not a child prodigy. Secondly, the vicar's teeth are his own, they're huge I agree, but they're his – and I agree with Susie, he's not that bad. Thirdly, as kind as it is of you to give him to me, Mr. Bedford may have other plans where romance is concerned, and fourthly, how many times do I have to tell you two, I DO NOT NEED A MAN! And certainly not, Mr. Bedford.'

'Oh you're just saying that because you're scared,' Susie said. 'That's okay, we understand. And we don't blame you. We would be too, in your shoes but we're not getting any younger and it's harder for you, with Lily and everything. You really do need to get back into dating soon or it may just be too late. Do you really want to end up like Doreen?'

Three pairs of eyes focused on Doreen as she leant on the counter, flirting with the postman. It had become a morning ritual and, although he was at least forty years her junior, she'd told the girls on more than one occasion, that age didn't matter.

'Morning handsome,' she said.

'Morning gorgeous. I've got a big parcel for you.'

'Ooh! I bet you say that to all the girls.' She winked at him and eyed him up and down.

5

'Only the girls who give me coffee and cake; I like a woman with nice buns,' he said, winking back.

Becky, Jess and Susie groaned quietly.

'Little does he know, she'd like to get more than a parcel from him,' Susie whispered, picking up her spoon and stirring the remnants of her coffee.

'I'm not sure who's worse,' Becky said.

'I'm not sure he's joking,' Jess added. 'I've heard he goes to that disco in Hastings. You know, the one where all the female divorcees go, on the prowl for young guys. No wonder they're called cougars.'

Becky shook her head and grinned. 'How do you know all this stuff?'

'I have my sources.'

'You're in the wrong profession. You should be a private detective, not a hairdresser,' Becky said.

'Hair designer extraordinaire, if you don't mind!' Jess beamed. 'I've decided to update my title. Anyway, that's how I get all the info. I've told you before; you'd be amazed what people talk about when I get my scissors out.'

Becky didn't mean to ask. She wasn't in the slightest bit interested, so she had no idea why she did, but she heard herself say, 'Who told you all that stuff about Mr. Bedford?'

'Oh, that was Connie Jessop. The Bedfords kept her on when they bought the place and she heard it from his mum. Or was it his mum's friend? Can't recall what she said. Anyway, someone at the Hall told her.'

'Oh, so it must be true,' Becky said sarcastically, flopping back against her chair. 'Everyone knows what a gossip Connie Jessop is; she never lets the truth get in the way of a good story. Mr. Bedford's probably happily married with six kids.' Although, for some reason, she didn't really think he was.

'Why do you keep calling him Mr. Bedford?' Jess asked. 'He's not your boss.'

'He's not my friend either. What do you want me to call

him?'

Susie sniggered and leant back in her chair. 'Play your cards right and you might be calling him darling.'

Becky's mouth tightened as she remembered what had happened between herself and Max Bedford just hours earlier, and her contempt was apparent. 'I may be calling him a great many things in the not too distance future, but I can assure you, *darling*, will not be one of them!'

An hour later, Becky, Jess and Susie were grocery shopping in Beckleston Stores. Like all the shops in the village, the Stores was privately owned and consequently carried stock the owners, Mary and Martin Parkes, knew was popular with their customers. Most of it could be purchased for less at the supermarket a few miles away but this didn't deter the villagers and, unlike similar stores in other villages, this one thrived.

It may have been because most of the population of Beckleston were retired and many of them didn't drive. There was a bus service but few could be bothered with that when the Stores stocked everything one could need, albeit for a few pence more. For Becky, Jess and Susie, Beckleston Stores was simply convenient; they all lived within a ten minute walk.

'We're having chilli,' Becky said, 'so I just need an onion and some rice. I forgot them at Sainsbury's the other day.'

'Shush.' Jess placed a finger over her lips. 'Don't mention Sainsbury's in front of Mary and Martin.'

Becky laughed. 'They know we don't live on the few items we buy in here every few days, Jess.' She lowered her voice anyway. 'They know we go to Sainsbury's.'

'Yeah. I always feel guilty though. Weird isn't it?'

'What's weird?' Susie asked. She'd been flicking through the magazines and tossed "Glamour" into the basket as she spoke.

'Wishful thinking?' Jess said, raising her eyebrows and

nodding towards the magazine.

Susie pulled a face. 'At least there's hope for me; I'm not the one with pink and blue hair.' She flicked her long, blond tresses over one shoulder and stuck her chin in the air.

'You'd better watch where you're walking or you may trip over your own ego,' Jess sneered, 'and there's nothing wrong with pink and blue hair: it's colourful – like me'

Becky smirked. 'Stop it you two. You're behaving like children. That reminds me, I want to get Lily a comic. I think I've got everything else, so I'll grab one and we can go.'

She dashed across to the magazine section and bent down to look at the children's magazines and comics. She picked one with a free gift and was about to stand up when she heard a male voice she recognised.

'"Fifi and the Flowertots" – a little young for you isn't it?'

Becky's eyes shot to the face of the man towering over her and she almost stumbled backwards but Max Bedford reached out and grabbed her arm, gently pulling her to her feet.

'This is the second time I've had to stop you from falling flat on your back today. It's getting to be a habit. Tell me, do all men have this effect on you or is it just me?'

She saw the corners of his mouth twitch and had to summon all her strength, for a second time that day, to stop herself from slapping his face. Even his eyes seemed to be mocking her, and she shrugged her arm free of his hold, took a deep breath and clenched her fists, screwing up the edge of the comic as she did so.

He glanced towards the mangled comic, 'Unless ...' his brows knit together and a serious expression replaced the look of mockery. 'Is that why you couldn't read the sign?'

Becky's mouth fell open in astonishment. He had already abused and manhandled her once today, and now he seemed to be saying that he thought she may have reading difficulties.

'Yes! That's precisely why I couldn't read the sign,' she snapped. 'Down here in the country we don't get a lot of time to learn our letters. We're all too busy bowing and scraping to the incoming, would-be gentry. Tell me, were you born an arrogant twerp or do you practise?'

Max's eyes scanned her face then a huge grin spread across his lips. 'I practise.'

Becky wasn't quite sure what to do next. Once again she'd lost her temper with this man and once again, he seemed to find it amusing. She wanted to make some cutting remark to wipe the smile from his face but the only thoughts that seemed to enter her head were, how kissable his lips looked; how lustrous his blond hair was and that little gold lights seemed to twinkle in his green eyes when he grinned.

Jess and Susie raced to Becky's side; they'd seen Max come in and heard the exchange between them.

'Everything all right Becky?' Jess asked.

Max raised his eyebrows and still grinning said, 'And these must be the Flowertots, Fifi.' He glanced from Becky to her friends and the grin turned into a friendly smile, exposing perfect white teeth. 'Very pleased to meet you. I'm Max Bedford.'

'Hi. I'm Jess and this is Susie. Pleased to meet you too, Mr. Bedford. We saw you earlier this morning ... buying a paper ... in the Stores.'

Becky watched her friends almost visibly swoon.

'Please, call me Max.'

Jess smiled then glanced at Becky. 'You didn't tell us you had already met Max.'

Becky tried to avoid her friend's eyes. 'I ... I forgot.'

'Ah, forgotten so easily, I'm cut to the core.'

He didn't look cut to the core, Becky thought. He seemed to be enjoying himself immensely – at her expense.

'I'm sure you'll recover,' she hissed, and headed to the counter to pay.

'Not until we meet again, Madame Fifi.'

Becky could hear the laughter in his voice and she spun around to face him. She knew she should have ignored him, but there was just something about his attitude that made her see red and for some reason, she wanted him to know that she'd had a good education.

'How charming,' she said as calmly as she could, 'I've progressed from a children's comic character to a fictional 19th century French prostitute. What next I wonder?'

Max raised his eyebrows, clearly surprised but still grinning he said, 'I'm impressed. Your reading has come on in leaps and bounds in such a short time, although, I think that was Mademoiselle Fifi. But no. I was actually reminded of my mother's poodle, Madame Fifi; she too, had curly brown hair, chocolate brown eyes, and her bark was also far worse than her bite.'

Becky felt as if her body had transformed into an active volcano as anger bubbled up inside her. 'A poodle! Now you're calling me a dog!'

'I'm not calling you a dog. I'm merely saying you remind me of her. You seem to have similar temperaments. It's actually a compliment. I was very fond of that dog.'

The volcano erupted. 'I have never met such an arrogant, conceited, rude, obnoxious ...' Words failed her. She was already being repetitive.

'Twerp?' Max offered.

'Pig!' Becky shrieked.

'So ... does that mean dinner is out of the question?'

Becky took a step forward but Susie grabbed her arm and without a word, handed Jess the shopping basket and almost dragged Becky from the Stores.

Jess paid a rather flustered Mary Parkes for the shopping, threw Max a cursory nod and dashed out after them.

CHAPTER TWO

'I see what you mean about not calling him darling anytime soon,' Jess said when they were safely back at Becky's. What the hell was all that about and why did you lie and say you hadn't seen him, when we were in the café earlier? You obviously had.'

Susie handed Becky a glass of red wine. 'Are you okay? I haven't seen you lose it like that for years.'

Becky was sitting on the sofa in front of the fire, her legs curled up beneath her and her head resting in her right hand. She took the glass and gulped down the contents then held the glass out to her friend. 'More please.'

Susie refilled it but not before she glanced across at Jess, Becky noticed.

'I'm okay. I'm sorry about what happened and I'm sorry about lying. I don't know why I did. It's just ... oh I don't know. He made me so cross this morning and then just now, when he laughed at me, I ... oh, it's just today, that's all. I got some more bad news yesterday and this morning, I went for a walk to try to think, and that man started shouting at me and grabbing me and –'

'What do you mean he shouted and grabbed you? When? Where? Why didn't you tell us?' Susie was clearly horrified.

'What bad news?' Jess asked.

Becky's head was splitting. 'I'll just get some pain killers then I'll tell you.'

'I'll get the pain killers, you stay put – and slow down on the wine.' Jess was back in less than a minute and she handed Becky the tablets and a glass of water. 'With water, not wine.'

Becky swallowed the tablets and sighed. She rubbed her forehead and closed her eyes briefly. 'Okay. Yesterday, I got a letter from my solicitor. It seems one of the creditors is no longer prepared to accept monthly payments and they're going after the full amount. That means the whole thing comes tumbling down and I'm back to square one.'

'What? They can't do that! They all agreed to accept reduced amounts and monthly repayments. They can't just change their minds and go back on it,' Jess said, stunned by Becky's news.

'Apparently they can. This creditor has been taken over by another company and its lawyers have said there is no signed agreement. I was sure I got all their agreements in writing, but this one must have slipped through somehow. The terms were that all creditors must agree, so this could make the whole thing void or something. You know what banks are like, and most of the creditors are banks. I don't really understand it but my solicitor said it's true, although he'll do what he can – which will mean more costs and ...' Becky shook her head and fiddled with the stem of her wine glass.

'Oh God, Becky,' Jess said, 'just when you think things are getting better something comes and knocks you back down. Why on earth didn't you tell us?'

'I think I was trying to pretend it wasn't really happening and, I suppose, part of me was hoping my solicitor would come back to me on Monday and say it was all a mistake and the agreement still stands. Besides, you've heard enough of my problems to last a lifetime. And then, of course, it's the anniversary today. To be honest, I thought if I started telling you, I'd end up crying my eyes out and might never stop.'

Susie sat down beside Becky and put her arm around her. 'You should have told us. We'd have cried with you. That's what friends do, and then, we'd have tried to think of a way to deal with this.'

Becky smiled half-heartedly and tried in vain to stop the tears welling up. 'I don't know what I'd do without you two – and I mean that. Sometimes, I can almost understand why Jeremy felt he had to do what he did; why he felt so hopeless, and if I didn't have you –'

'No!' Jess snapped. 'Don't you ever say that. It's only

money and nothing justifies what he did. Nothing ever will. He had you, and he should have talked to you. Instead, he deceived you then left you in the lurch and you've spent the last five years trying to pay off his debts and deal with the grief. I know you loved him and I know he's Lily's dad and everything but he was still a bastard! Don't ever say you understand it and don't ever say you feel the same!'

'Jess, don't,' Susie said, hugging Becky tighter.

Tears rolled down Becky's cheeks. 'It's okay Susie. Jess is right. And I'd never do it. I couldn't leave Lily. Sometimes, even I hate Jeremy, especially when I think what he spent all that money on. But gambling's a sickness, an addiction, like alcohol and drugs and he just couldn't stop.'

'Then he should have got help. I've said this before so there's no point in going over it, I know, but it wasn't just his life he gambled away, it was yours and Lily's too and I'll never, ever, forgive him for that.' Jess strode towards the kitchen. 'I'll get more wine.'

Becky grabbed a tissue from the box on the coffee table and wiped her eyes. 'I was really beginning to think things might be improving and that this year would be good, until I got that letter yesterday. I didn't get much sleep last night, as you can imagine. It was hard enough trying to sort it all out the first time around. I just don't have the money. If they void the agreement, I could lose everything. That's why I went for a walk to think things through – and what happened? I met that bloody man! It's like it never rains but it pours.'

'What happened with him, Becky?' Susie coaxed.

Becky shifted uncomfortably. Even thinking about him irritated her. 'I was walking across the fields towards the pond. I know I shouldn't have been, without permission, but it's second nature to me to go there when I'm having a bad time. I could hear someone shouting and I saw a figure in the distance, near the house but I'd forgotten the new owners moved in on Thursday, to tell you the truth and I thought it was Bill Jenkins, doing the garden, so I waved back and went on. When I got to the pond, I couldn't believe my eyes. It was empty!'

'No!' Susie said, clearly shocked.

Jess reappeared with another bottle and refilled their glasses and Becky waited until she'd sat down before continuing.

'There's a sign up saying to keep away or something. I didn't really get a chance to read it. The next thing I know, Max bloody Bedford is racing towards me, yelling at me to get away from there and threatening me, saying I'm risking my life! He was like a madman. I'm not really sure what happened next, I think I may have had a funny turn or something because it felt like the ground had vanished from beneath me and I was falling. He grabbed me, picked me up and marched off with me then unceremoniously dumped me on the old witches' oak, tree stump, without so much as a by-your-leave.'

'Wow!' Susie said. 'Actually, that's sort of romantic, and rather sexy – in an odd way.'

Becky and Jess glared at her.

'You've been too long without a man, if you think that's romantic.' Jess shook her head in disbelief.

'I said, sort of! I think it is romantic to be swept off your feet, especially by someone as gorgeous as Max Bedford – and he did save you from falling, so that's romantic too. What happened then?'

Becky sipped her wine and cast her mind back to that morning. She could remember it all so vividly.

'What the hell are you doing?' Becky had snapped.

Max Bedford set her down on the witches' oak tree stump and stepped back, glaring at her. 'Saving your life,' he said, clearly displeased. 'Can't you read? This is private property and that area is dangerous. You could have been seriously injured – or worse!'

'Don't be ridiculous! The pond's been there for centuries

and it's perfectly safe. I've swum in it hundreds of times.'
She stood up and smoothed her clothes with one hand,
trying to regain her composure. She was shaking with anger
and surprise.

'So you come here often do you?' he said sarcastically.

Becky tilted her chin up. 'All the time.'

'Well, perhaps in future, you'd be good enough to ask.
I'm Max Bedford and my mother, Margaret is the new
owner of Beckleston Hall. And you are?'

She met his eyes then watched as he looked her up and
down, his brow creasing just a touch as if he found her
discomforting to look at, or unpleasant; like something the
cat had brought to him. She felt her temper flare.

'I've lived here all my life and the moon will turn to
cheese before the day dawns when some jumped up,
London banker can tell me where I may or may not go!'
She could feel her cheeks burning as she stepped forward to
pass him but he stood in her way.

Their eyes held for a moment then she saw his mouth
twitch.

'You did say banker, didn't you and not ...' he said, a
grin spreading across his face.

Becky was astonished. 'Yes,' she said still furious, 'I did
say banker – but it's not what I meant.'

She was even more astonished when he burst out
laughing.

'Actually, I'm neither one,' he said. 'Well I hope not
anyway. I didn't catch your name.'

'I didn't throw it. Why have you drained the pond?' She
gave him what she hoped was an unpleasant scowl.

He didn't seem bothered. 'It leaked and it was
dangerous –'

'A natural pond can't leak,' she interrupted, still
scowling.

'I assure you it can – and it did. Are you going to tell
me your name?'

'No! What have you done with the ducks?'

Again, his eyes travelled the length of her body then met hers and once more, she saw the corners of his mouth twitch.

'We've eaten the ducks,' he said.

Her mouth fell open in horror. 'You ... you bastard!' she shrieked. Tears welled up in her eyes and, without thinking, she pushed him out of her way and ran as fast as her legs would carry her, even though they felt like jelly.

'Oh my God!' Susie said when Becky had finished her story. 'Was he serious? Have they eaten the ducks?' Her startled eyes darted from Becky to Jess and back again.

'No! Um ... I hate to tell you this,' Jess said, a rather contrite look on her face, 'but Paul came in for a haircut the other day and he said something about the Bedfords employing him to empty the pond because it was leaking. I know it sounds ridiculous but it's true. The roots of the trees in the copse have caused all sorts of problems apparently. Paul's cutting some of them back, putting some special lining or something in the pond then refilling it. He did say the surrounding ground had become dangerous and liable to collapse and they'd had signs put up, just in case anyone went there. They were worried about kids and –'

'Bloody hell Jess! Why didn't you tell me?' Becky's eyes opened wide in disbelief.

'Sorry, I should have, but I didn't think you'd go there, not until you got to know the new owners anyway and, to be honest, until you mentioned the ducks, I'd forgotten about it.'

'So ... he really did save your life then,' Susie said, a wistful look in her eyes.

'Possibly ... I suppose. But that doesn't make him a hero in my eyes. And what about the ducks? Where are they then?'

'Um ... Paul said they paid to have the ducks moved to a temporary enclosure. They'll be brought back when the work's complete.'

Becky shook her head and sighed. 'It would have been nice to know that Jess. No wonder he thinks I'm the village idiot. I really believed him when he said they'd eaten them.'

'Why were you so cross with him anyway?' Susie asked. 'It's not like you to jump down someone's throat like that. I hate to point this out but ... you were, technically, trespassing you know,' Susie saw Jess glare at her. 'Sorry! I'm just saying.'

'I know. You're right of course,' Becky agreed. 'It was just the wrong place at the wrong time. I was surprised; I was upset; I was angry and, after getting that letter yesterday and him being a banker ... he is a banker, isn't he? Someone said he was, although he seemed to be saying, he isn't, I think. Anyway, we all know they're not at the top of my "favourite people" list.'

'They're not at the top of anyone's,' Jess said. 'So, he doesn't know who you are?'

'Apparently not. There's no reason why he should and I had no intention of telling him after the way he behaved.'

'When he was saving you from falling into a dangerous mud-hole, you mean?' Susie said. 'I understand completely why you're so angry with the banks Becky, but it's not like you to take it out on people who're not directly involved with Jeremy's debts. Perhaps you overreacted slightly?'

Becky frowned. 'Perhaps, just a little. It all happened so fast. As I said, I was already upset because of the letter and today being the anniversary, and I'm missing Lily terribly – I can't wait for her to get back from Jeremy's parents' tomorrow. I suppose, when I saw the empty pond and I thought he was telling me I couldn't go there anymore, it was the final straw. But he really is arrogant and ... there's just something about him. I honestly don't know what it is.'

'And the Stores? Why did you get so angry then?' Susie asked.

'Because he was laughing at me! And then he called me a prostitute and a dog!'

'I don't think he did,' Jess said. 'Not from what I heard anyway. I think he was just messing around. He wasn't being nasty or abusive or anything and you could tell from his gorgeous smile, that he thought it was all a big joke.'

'Well I couldn't! I didn't find it the least bit funny – and I don't think he has a gorgeous smile!'

'Oh Becky,' Jess said, refilling their glasses, 'maybe, next time you see him, you should explain –'

'No! I don't care what he thinks. Okay, perhaps I did overreact but there is no way I'm going to tell that man anything and I'm certainly not going to apologise, so don't even think about suggesting I should. He'd probably just laugh at me anyway. Oh God! I wish I could start today all over again.' She buried her face in a cushion.

'Don't worry about it – and I wasn't going to suggest you apologise. You could just tell him that you both got off on the wrong foot or something. He seems to have a good, if somewhat odd, sense of humour. I can't see him holding today against you. He was still smiling when I left the Stores, so that must be a good sign.'

'Smiling or laughing?' Becky said, peeping over the cushion.

'Does it matter? Either way, he thought it was funny. I'd only be worried if he'd looked angry and believe me, he looked far from that.'

'Did he ask you out for dinner?' Susie said, 'When we were in the Stores, he said something about assuming dinner was out of the question.'

'I think he was being sarcastic,' Jess said.

'Of course he was,' Becky said. 'As if someone like Max Bedford would want to go out to dinner with me – even if we had met under better circumstances.' And for some reason, the thought of him not wanting to take her out, made her angry with him all over again.

CHAPTER THREE

Max decided he rather liked Beckleston, as he strolled up the drive towards Beckleston Hall, and no one was more surprised by this fact than he, especially as he'd only been in the village for two days.

When he'd arrived on Thursday, to make sure his mother's move went smoothly, he'd only intended to stay until Sunday but here he was, on a bright, cold Saturday afternoon, with the sun slowly disappearing behind the centuries-old trees, seriously considering staying on for a week or so.

He could go back to London on Monday to arrange things for his absence; that wouldn't be a problem. And the more he thought about it, the more the idea appealed to him. The last time he'd taken any time off, he remembered, was two years ago, when Lizzie hurt her foot and she was still, technically, his wife. No point in thinking about that though, that had nothing to do with the present.

His mother didn't need him, of course, she was perfectly capable of looking after herself, and they'd retained Connie Jessop and Bill Jenkins, so it wasn't as if she'd be completely on her own. Her life-long friend Victoria was around too. She lived just a few miles away and had helped coordinate things prior to his mother moving in. Nevertheless, he decided he would stay.

Strange really, because when his mother had called him, just a few months ago, and told him that she wanted to buy a Tudor Hall House in an East Sussex village, more than fifty miles from London, he'd wondered if she were losing her faculties. But now that she'd moved in, it seemed the most natural place for her to be; almost as if she belonged there.

Max's mind wandered back to the conversation they'd had when she first told him she intended to buy the Hall. Being an only child, and his father having been dead for several years, he spent a fair amount of time with her, and he hadn't noticed any deterioration in her memory or her general appetite for life. In fact, she probably had a larger network of friends than he, and frequently went to the theatre, art galleries and lunch with them. She'd even been to Rome and Paris with friends recently, so the mention of her wanting to move to a village, miles from London, came as quite a surprise. When he saw the village and the house, for the first time on the internet, he had serious worries. The village was small; the house was huge.

'I'm not losing my marbles, Max and your inheritance is safe, as you well know,' Margaret Bedford said when he questioned her about it. 'I just fancy having a place in the country and this is exactly what I want.'

'I couldn't care less about the inheritance, as *you* well know, and I'm all for you having a country house but this isn't a house, Mum, it's a stately home! And one that needs a fair amount of refurbishment, by the look of it on the agents' website – possibly even some structural repairs.'

Margaret tutted. 'I admit it's rather large for just me but I was thinking that I could employ someone and we could run art courses there. Maybe even have country house weekends. You know how the Americans love that sort of thing. And weddings; it would make the perfect wedding venue. It would be any bride's dream to sweep down the central staircase. It's beyond magnificent Max – at least, it was ... '

'Mother. Why do I get the feeling there's something you're not telling me? Have you already been to see it? What do you mean by, "was"?'

'Ah. A slip of the tongue, darling. I hadn't meant to say that. But let me tell you Max, here and now, I mean to have the place and there's not a thing you, or Gerald Merriton, can do to stop me.'

Max was surprised by his mother's attitude. She could be stubborn, he knew that, but she always listened to advice both from him and the family solicitor, and friend, Gerald Merriton. The fact that she'd made up her mind before getting their opinions, was a new path for her to take.

'We could have you committed,' Max joked.

'Just you try it, my boy.'

'Seriously, Mum, why are you so set on the place? And do you really want to start a new business venture at your age?'

'What's my age got to do with anything? I'm fitter than many people half my age and I've still got my wits about me. As I said, I'll employ someone ... several people actually. I think it'll be fun. Please don't try and talk me out of it. I've made up my mind. I'd like you to come and have a look at it with me though. Get an idea of what needs doing and such.'

'Of course I'll come and look at it, but I hope you don't expect me to start doing d-i-y. That's really not my forte.'

'God forbid! The phrase, "do it yourself" isn't even in your vocabulary, these days, is it Max? Although, when you were young, you and your father built a boat, I seem to remember.'

'We did; it sank. The aeroplane nosedived and the car crashed. I learnt early on that there are certain skills I just don't seem to have.' He grinned mischievously and ran his long fingers through his unruly, thick, blond hair.

'Hmm! I seem to remember that you learnt early on that there are certain skills you *do* have; like making money and getting girls to fall in love with you. I believe that had more to do with you abandoning the tool-shed than any doubt in your own abilities.'

'I believe I simply found better uses for my hands.' He sprawled on the sumptuous sofa, still grinning.

'And look where that finally got you. Would you like some tea?'

'I'd love some.' He watched his mother head towards the kitchen. He would have offered to make the tea but he knew she wouldn't let him. She liked to maintain her independence.

She stopped in the doorway and half turned back to face

him. 'By the way, I've been meaning to say for some time, I prefer your hair like that, not slicked back as it was when you were at the bank. You've made a few changes since then.'

'All for the better I hope.'

Margaret ambled into the kitchen, filled the kettle then switched it on. 'Speaking of Lizzie, have you heard from her recently?'

Max shifted uncomfortably. 'I didn't know we were speaking of Lizzie. I thought we were speaking about a money-pit in some East Sussex back-wood.'

'Beckleston village is not a back-wood, I can assure you darling, and the Hall, I think you'll find, rather than being a money-pit may well turn into a money-spinner. Your father said I could always spot a sure thing.'

Max couldn't argue with that. He'd heard his parents' rags to riches story enough times to know it by heart. His mother had been the financial genius and his father was smart enough to know it, and follow her lead.

Margaret Bedford had persuaded her husband to invest his meagre earnings, first, in stock and later in property and they'd made a killing from both, often when others were losing money hand over fist.

Royston Bedford often told his son, it was his mother's brains that had got the family where they were and it was his mother's brains that Max should consider his best inheritance. The fact that Royston had worked on all the properties himself and turned crumbling wrecks into little palaces enabling them to sell for many times the price the Bedfords had paid, Royston himself, considered of little importance.

Margaret returned with a tea tray, full, as usual of cakes she'd baked, and bearing the teapot she had used for afternoon tea, for as long as Max could remember.

'Well, have you?'

'Have I what, Mother dearest? And when are we to venture on this expedition to the back-woods?'

'Don't take that sarcastic tone with me, my boy. And don't think you can avoid the question by changing the subject. Have you heard from Lizzie recently?'

'Funnily enough, I have. And, unless I'm very much mistaken, my dear ex-wife has told you the good news too.' He took the cup of tea she held out to him and grabbed a chocolate éclair from the tray.

'Use a plate, Max.'

He grinned, taking the plate she handed him and bit into the éclair. 'Delicious as always, Mother.'

'Thank you dear. So ... is it ... good news?' Margaret put her cup to her lips and waited, eyeing her son over the rim.

'Yeah, I think so. It is as far as Lizzie's concerned, and Jack's a really nice, if somewhat too easy-going for my liking, kind of guy. I think they'll be happy together. I hope so. She deserves to be happy.'

'And you? Don't you deserve to be happy too?' She sipped her tea.

'I'm very happy. This chocolate éclair is so good I may have to have another.' He winked and grinned at her.

'I'm serious Max.'

'I know you are. Don't worry about me. I'll admit it's taken me a while, but I'm over it – and I'm over her. I have no one to blame but myself, anyway.'

'That doesn't make it any easier darling. I didn't think Lizzie would be getting married again so soon after your divorce. I'm not going to pretend it wasn't your fault, because we both know it was, but I hate seeing you unhappy.'

'I'm not. Honestly. I'm really not.'

'So, which woman are you currently *not* being unhappy with? Or is that plural?'

Max smirked. 'Okay, so I see a lot of women. I tried the marriage gig and it didn't work. I'm in no hurry to try it again. And, we've been divorced for two years now, Mum, so Lizzie's hardly rushing things.'

'I still can't believe how that all came about. Fate really

23

does play the strangest games.'

'I don't believe in fate. That implies we don't have free will. I think we make our own choices and hope it turns out for the best. Sometimes it does, sometimes it doesn't.'

'Well, that's as may be but you're not getting any younger Max. Don't you think thirty-seven is a little old to be playing the field? I'd like to have a house full of grandchildren in the not too distance future.'

Max shot her a look of horror but his smile belied his expression. 'Good God, Mother. I sincerely hope you're not referring to your, soon-to-be, country pile. That place must have at least twenty bedrooms by the looks of it. It'd take me years to fill that with my off-spring – if I didn't die from exhaustion first.'

Margaret beamed at him. 'Twenty-five, to be precise. You'd better get busy, son.'

'You'd better find me a wife with good child bearing hips then, Mother.'

'You're more than capable of finding your own wife Max, and from the amount of women who seem to fall for your, I'll admit, abundant charms, you're not lacking in choice.'

Max leant back against the cushions. 'Finding them's the easy part. Wanting to keep them seems to be the bit I have trouble with.'

'That's because you haven't met the right one yet. I confess, I did think Lizzie was the one, but even she couldn't keep your eye from wandering. I don't know where you get that from. Neither your father or I so much as looked at another person – well, not in that way at least.'

'That's because you were perfect for one another – and you were lucky.' Max sat up and helped himself to another chocolate éclair. 'And why would Dad want anyone else, when you make such delicious cakes?' He winked.

'I'll admit, it was very lucky your father and I met when we did, and believe me, you don't know quite, how lucky. But that's what I'm saying. It was fate. The perfect man came along at the perfect time. The perfect young woman is just waiting for you Max – in Beckleston, perhaps.'

'Yeah right. Can you really see me being interested in a country bumpkin from an East Sussex back-wood? I don't think I'll find any Cinderellas living there, Mum.'

'You might be surprised.'

Margaret Bedford was sitting at her desk in the window of the Morning Room in Beckleston Hall, writing yet another list, when she spotted Max walking up the long drive. Something about his demeanour had changed since they had arrived in Beckleston just two days ago and as she watched him saunter towards the house, she wondered what had caused it.

Max had made no bones about the fact that, in his opinion, the purchase of Beckleston Hall was a mistake and had repeatedly found obstacles which should, he had said, make her change her mind, but she had stood firm and, ultimately, seeing that he couldn't dissuade her, Max had done everything in his power to make the purchase go smoothly. And Max had considerable power and, it seemed, a great many contacts.

Royston, Max's father had been the same, she remembered, watching her son, but in a slightly different way. He'd had an outward, physical strength and rugged determination and did things himself to overcome obstacles and achieve his goals.

Max was physically strong too, and determined, but there was something in the way he held himself; in the way he spoke to people and interacted with them. He didn't need to do things for himself; others were only too willing to do them for him. And, over the last few weeks, a great many people had done a great many things, for him.

Obstacles over planning questions had been overcome. Issues with the Title Deeds had been quickly sorted out. Workmen had been found at short notice. A wildlife shelter had even been found to look after the ducks whilst the pond was being drained and repaired and all, it seemed, without Max lifting a finger or experiencing a moment's concern.

Several times though, he had asked whether she wanted to go ahead, hoping she had changed her mind. But she and Beckleston Hall had history and, although she wondered whether she should share her past with her son, she wasn't sure he'd understand. He had loved his father deeply and might feel that her wanting to return to the Hall was, in some way, a betrayal, so she'd decided to retain her secret. But she was determined to have it and this, Max did understand. He too had come to expect that, if he wanted something, he would get it and the only time that he hadn't, was when Lizzie had left him – and refused to go back.

'You're looking very pleased with yourself,' Margaret said as Max entered the Morning Room from the terrace, via one of the French windows.

He bent down and planted a playful kiss on her immaculately coiffed, silver waves. 'Am I? What are you doing in the Morning Room, Mother, it's almost three in the afternoon?' He grinned and sat down on a chair next to her writing desk.

'Very droll, dear. Yes you are. Did you find anything of interest in the village?'

'As a matter of fact, I did. Tell me, why is this called the Morning Room but there isn't an Afternoon Room or an Evening Room? And why is the Drawing Room called that?'

Margaret peered at him over the rim of her glasses. 'The Drawing Room is where the ladies used to "withdraw" to whilst the men smoked their cigars after dinner but as to the rest, I have no idea. What did you find in the village?'

'I'll have to find some local toff and ask them.' He leant back in the chair and put his feet up on her desk. 'Is a parlour, like the one in gran's old house, called a parlour from the French parler, because people used it to talk in – or gossip about the neighbours, in gran's case?'

Margaret raised her eyebrows. 'Probably. Don't put your feet on my desk, Max. The soles of your shoes are muddy.'

He put his feet back on the floor. 'Sorry.'

'I don't think there are any local toffs left around here to ask. Why the sudden interest in the names of rooms anyway?'

'Pity. I suppose, because you have so many rooms called different things. As incoming would-be gentry, I feel I need to find out. Shall I ring for whatshername to get us some tea?'

Margaret put down her pen and twisted in her seat to face him. 'Shall you what? Would-be gentry. What on earth are you talking about, Max?'

He grinned. 'Nothing, Mum. Don't mind me.' He got to his feet. 'Would you like some tea? I'll go and put the kettle on. Remind me, is that the scullery or the kitchen, I need?'

'What you need, my boy, is a clip around the ear.'

His grin turned into a beaming smile. 'I think I nearly got one today. In fact, I think I nearly got one, twice. Oh ... and I've decided I'm going to stay on for a week or so, if that's okay with you.' He strode across the room without waiting for an answer. 'If I'm not back in half an hour, send someone to find me. God alone knows which room I'll end up in.'

Margaret watched her son march into the hall, with mixed emotions. She was pleased that he wanted to stay but also slightly anxious. Max rarely took time off and whilst he had initially offered to, to help her settle in, he had seemed almost relieved when she'd told him there was really no need, since Victoria would be popping over regularly. So, why the sudden change of heart, she wondered, and what had he meant by that remark about almost getting a clip around the ear? Had someone threatened him in some way?

Even as she thought it, she dismissed it. People didn't threaten Max. Even at school, he had never been picked on or bullied and he certainly wasn't the type to get into fights.

27

He could defend himself though, if the need ever arose. His father had made sure of that.

Royston Bedford had been born into the streets of London's east end, in the days when it was wise to know how to defend yourself. His father had taught him and, although Max had been born into a very different street – there weren't many gangsters in Esher in Surrey – Royston had taught Max.

So what had he meant? He seemed amused by it, whatever it was and whatever it was had happened twice. He wasn't joking then, he really had found something of interest, in the village – or someone, and with Max, that could only mean one thing – a woman. She found herself hoping that it wasn't his usual type but someone a little more like Lizzie.

CHAPTER FOUR

More than five hundred miles away, just outside of the village of Kirkendenbright Falls in the Highlands of Scotland, Lizzie Marshall stood in the kitchen of Laurellei Farm, her bed and breakfast, and, as usual, when she had something on her mind, she was baking.

'All I'm saying is it's weird.' Lizzie's best friend, Jane Hamilton passed her a mug of coffee then dropped onto the chair next to the Aga.

Alastair, Lizzie's black Labrador, immediately sat up in his basket and rested his chin on Jane's knee.

'Why?' Lizzie said using the back of her hand to push a strand of wavy brunette hair out of her eyes.

'Why? Because Max is your ex-husband, that's why! I know you're still friends and I know Jack likes him – which is also really weird in my opinion, but that's beside the point – you can't have your wedding at your ex-husband's house!'

Lizzie took the dough she'd been mixing, and slammed it down on the table. 'I don't see why not! Although, it's not his house anyway, it's his mum's, and I don't think it's at all weird that Jack likes him; Max is a really lovely guy.'

'And I'm sure hundreds of other women agree with you – okay – I won't get on my "Max is a womaniser" soapbox, but come on, he was your husband and Jack's your fiancé – it's weird!'

'It isn't! Lots of ex's get on really well together. What's weird is why I listen to you when I know how much you dislike Max!'

After a few seconds of silence Jane said, 'Are you going to beat that loaf to death?' She gave her friend an apologetic smile. 'I don't dislike Max; okay, he's not on my Christmas card list and I wouldn't trust him with my sister, if I had one, which I don't, but this isn't about whether I like Max or not, this is about you getting married to someone you met whilst you were still, officially, married to Max. There are hundreds of places you could have your wedding. Why choose your ex mother-in-law's house?'

Lizzie took a deep breath but didn't answer.

'And why does every conversation I ever have with you about your love life, end up giving me a headache?' Jane reached down for her handbag and took out some aspirin.

Lizzie smiled, despite herself. 'You and me both. Chuck me a couple of those please.'

'There're not sweets,' Jane joked, getting up and handing two to her friend. 'Have you discussed this with Jack? Wait, what am I saying? Of course you have. Oh my God. He thinks it's okay doesn't he?' She sank back onto the chair.

Lizzie beamed. 'As a matter of fact, he does. We discussed it yesterday evening, although not for long; we had other things on our minds.'

Jane tutted. 'Yeah, like sex you mean. I don't know how you two cope with being so far apart all week. I'd go crazy if Iain and I were apart for longer than a day!'

'It's tough, I'll admit, and I think we both had trust issues at the beginning, after everything that happened but ... well, we love each other and the week just seems to fly by. Besides, we chat via webcam every day, so it's not too bad.'

'Yeah. That would only make it worse, for me though. To see him and know I couldn't touch him – that really would drive me insane.'

Lizzie giggled and put the dough back in the bowl, covering it with a damp tea-towel. 'That's because you're sex mad, and it wouldn't take much to drive you insane anyway – you're more than half way there already.'

Jane stuck out her tongue and tossed her copper coloured hair behind one shoulder, with a flick of her hand. 'Takes one to know one. So ... you're seriously going to do this. Have the wedding at Max's mum's, I mean.'

Lizzie pulled out a chair and sat at the table. She picked up the coffee Jane had made her and cradled the mug in both hands. 'I think so. I've seen pictures of it on the web and it looks spectacular. Margaret says it needs some work but she's hoping it'll be ready by the summer. And it just makes sense. All my family live in either Kent or Sussex, Mum and Dad will be home by then. All Jack's family live down that way – and so do yours, comes to that. It seems easier to get everyone together down there than it does to make them all come up here. Besides, I'm not sure grandma and grandpops would be able to make the journey, and if I want anyone at my wedding, it's them.'

'I agree it makes sense to have it down south, what I don't agree with, is the venue. There are dozens of fabulous places you could have it. Herstmonceux Castle, Bodiam Castle, Leeds Castle –'

'You seem obsessed with castles. I don't want a castle. I just want a place large enough to accommodate the main wedding guests. Beckleston Hall has twenty-five bedrooms and we won't need anywhere near that amount but it will mean we'll have privacy. I don't want to go to some hotel where others will be staying. I ... I just want to make sure that it'll be okay with Iain. He will be able to take the weekend off from the farm won't he?'

'Of course he will! It's busy in the summer but then, it's always busy so I don't think it'll make much difference. Are you inviting Fraser too?'

'Of course. That's what worries me. Iain usually leaves Fraser in charge when you and he go away. Would he be able to organise things so that Fraser could come too?'

Jane nodded. 'I'm sure he would. One of the farm hands would be fine just for the weekend. Do you want me to check with him?'

'Please. If it's a problem, I'll have to have a rethink.'

'Are you planning to do something up here too? I think the village will be a bit put out if you don't. They're hardly likely to want to trawl all the way down south, if you were planning to invite them all anyway, which I'm assuming you're not.'

Lizzie shook her head. 'No. We're saying that the wedding down south is just for family – which is true, it is; you, Iain and Fraser count as family but we thought we'd do something up here too, maybe have a celebration at Dougall and Isabel's, like you and Iain did. That way, no one will feel left out.'

'Good idea. You don't want to start a feud. I'll make some more coffee. Jack and Iain should be back any minute.'

Lizzie watched Jane make the coffee. She'd known her friend wouldn't like the idea of the venue for her wedding but it was *her* wedding, and whilst her best friend's opinion was important, this was one time she felt she could ignore it.

She and Max were friends – good friends – and nothing would ever change that. The fact that her fiancé, Jack, had since become friends with him, was an added bonus.

They'd bumped into Max one night, when Lizzie had taken a couple of days off from the bed and breakfast and had gone down to London to be with Jack. They'd gone to the local pub, The Black Swan – or The Mucky Duck, as it was affectionately known by the regulars – and Max was there.

It was awkward at first, Jack was, after all, the reason she'd finally decided to get a divorce from Max, ending their separation once and for all, but he wasn't the cause of the break up, so there was no reason for animosity between them.

Max and Jack hit it off, and since then, they often met up after work for a pint or two.

Jane thought it was weird and said so, frequently.

'Wakey, wakey,' Jane said, putting a fresh mug of coffee on the table in front of Lizzie, 'you were miles away. Planning the big day?'

Lizzie shrugged. 'Not really. I was actually just thinking how pleased I am, that Jack and Max have become friends.'

'Yeah well, it's all very lovely I'm sure, but if Jack asks

Max to be his best man, I'm having the lot of you certified.'

Lizzie grinned. 'No need to worry on that score, Jack's already asked Phil.'

'Thank God for that! Of course, it would have been just as bad if he'd asked Ross. We could have had a reunion of all the players in "The Stag Party Farce" as I like to think of it. That really would have been fun.'

'Well, now that you mention it ... '

'No! You've got to be kidding. Don't tell me that woman's going to be a bridesmaid! I'll kill myself, here and now.'

'No!' Lizzie giggled. 'But she will be at the wedding. Don't look like that. She's Ross' wife and Ross is one of Jack's best friends.'

'Yes and we all remember how that friendship turned out, don't we? Mind you, it all worked out for the best. Ross got her and you got Jack. God, even thinking about that again, is making my head spin. Tell me, how is the delightful Kim? Do we know? Do we really care?'

'Honestly Jane, you're dreadful sometimes. Of course we care ... not much, but we care, mainly about Ross though. Actually, I think they may be having problems. I don't know for certain but Jack did say something along those lines. I think he was meeting Ross for a drink last Thursday to talk about it – which reminds me, I didn't ask him how it went. I must do that.'

'Yes, and then phone me and tell me all about it ... speaking of which,' she leant back in the chair and peered out of the kitchen window, 'here come the boys.'

CHAPTER FIVE

'Good morning Becky. How are you today? Looking forward to seeing Lily I don't doubt. What time are they bringing her home?' Mary Parkes hardly stopped for breath.

Becky's head was aching. She and the girls had drunk a little too much wine the night before and she felt as if the top of her head had been sawn off and her brain was exposed to the elements. The wind and rain hadn't helped and the ten minute walk to the Stores had seemed like a ten mile hike.

'I don't feel too bright, to be honest, Mrs. P. I think I may be coming down with something,' she lied. She seemed to be getting rather good at lying recently, she thought. Perhaps she'd learnt it from Jeremy. He'd lied to her for years.

'I hope it wasn't from your upset yesterday with Max Bedford. I don't think he meant any harm, dear. You know what men are like. Talk without thinking, that's their problem. He seems such a nice man. So handsome too, and as rich as Midas, so I heard.'

'Croecus,' Becky corrected.

Mary didn't seem to notice. 'Bit of a one for the women though, by all accounts.'

Becky almost felt sorry for the man. He'd only been in Beckleston for a few days and already there were rumours flying about like vultures over a wounded animal. He could take care of himself though, she was sure of that.

'You'd better be careful around that one dear,' Mary was saying.

'Why?' Becky asked, immediately wishing she hadn't.

'Why? Well, because he's got his eye on you dear, that's why.' She smiled as if she'd just given Becky good news.

'Don't be ridiculous! Sorry, Mrs. P., I didn't mean to snap at you. I can assure you though, Mr. Bedford is not in the least bit interested in me.' She grabbed a pint of milk, put exactly the right money on the counter and headed towards the door. She didn't like where this conversation was going.

'Really? Well, for someone who isn't interested, he's been asking Martin rather a lot of questions about you.'

Becky stopped in her tracks, although she hated herself for doing so. She knew that was exactly what Mary Parkes wanted her to do.

'Not that Martin told him anything, of course. You know what he's like. He changes the subject in the nicest possible way. You ask him what time it is and he says we're lucky to be having good weather! No need to worry dear; all Max got from Martin was that everyone in the village likes you. Mind you, he could always ask someone else I suppose...'

'He's probably asking questions about everyone. He and his mother are strangers after all. It's only natural that they should try to glean some info from the village ...' she almost said gossip but that was unfair. Martin wasn't a gossip, only Mary. She saw Mary's eyes narrow and continued, 'from the village ... in general. He's probably been in Doreen's café asking about you.'

The expression on Mary's face was priceless and for a second, Becky forgot her headache. She knew that, as soon as she left, Mary would call Doreen and ask her. It wasn't that Mary Parkes – or the other gossip, Connie Jessop – were bad or nasty people, they just liked to talk. Unfortunately though, they liked to talk about people, and if there was nothing nice or true to be said about someone, Mary and Connie saw no harm at all in making something up.

'I must dash. Lily will be home this afternoon and I've got a few errands to run before then. Have a good day Mrs. P.'

'What? Oh yes Becky, thanks, you too. And give little Lily a hug for me. No wait,' she scurried from behind the counter, grabbed a bar of chocolate and shoved it in Becky's hand. 'Give her that, and a hug.'

'Thanks Mrs. P.'

No, Becky thought as she headed home, pulling her coat collar up in an attempt to shield her face from the driving rain, Mrs. P. wasn't a bad or nasty woman.

The wave of water, took her completely by surprise. One minute she was hurrying home, the next, she was drenched from head to foot with dark brown, muddy, freezing water.

A mixture of shock and the cold took her breath away and, as she finally gasped for air, she swallowed a scrap of sodden paper. She managed to spit it out but it made her wretch and her eyes watered with a surge of pain.

'Shit! I'm so sorry,' someone shouted from a Range Rover that had pulled to an abrupt halt, just yards ahead. 'I didn't see the puddle. Are you okay?'

Becky wiped mud from her eyes and tried to focus. She saw a man of at least six feet tall with thick blond hair, dashing towards her.

'Y... yes,' she stuttered through chattering teeth. 'J... just, a little w...wet ... that's ... You!' Recognition dawned.

'We meet again Fifi,' Max said, grinning through a curtain of torrential rain. 'Here, get in the car and I'll give you a lift.'

'No thank you! You've d...done quite enough already.' She was freezing and it felt as though her coat weighed ten tonnes.

'Don't be ridiculous,' Max said, half lifting, half pushing her into the passenger seat before she had time to resist. He shut the door and dashed to the driver's side. By the time he sat beside her, he too, was saturated. 'We look like a couple of drowned rats,' he said grinning broadly.

'Sp...speak for yourself,' she hissed.

'Where to?' He revved the engine.

'This is st...stupid. I only l..live a few m...minutes away.'

'In a few minutes, you'll have caught pneumonia. Now, where do you live – exactly?'

'R..Rosemary C..Cottage. St..straight ahead.' He was right, she thought. She could hardly feel her hands and her feet had gone numb ten seconds ago.

Max sped off, arriving at Rosemary Cottage in less than a minute.

'Th...thank –'

He was already out of the car and opening the passenger door. He helped her out but her legs seemed to crumple beneath her. In one swift motion, he swept her up then he carried her to her door.

'Key?'

'N...not locked,' she said, still shaking, but not from the cold. This was the second time he'd carried her in his arms since they'd met less than twenty-four hours ago, and she found it very unsettling.

Max gave her a quizzical look then tried the door. He seemed genuinely surprised when it opened. 'Not very security conscious.'

'It...it's a village.'

His raised eyebrows seemed to indicate that wasn't a good reason, as far as he was concerned but he said nothing.

'You c...can put me down now, p...please.'

'You need a hot shower. Where's the bathroom?' He glanced at the stairs and headed towards them, not waiting for an answer.

'I c...can manage!' Even Becky heard the note of terror in her voice.

'Of course you can. Don't worry. I'm not planning to undress you – or get in with you.' He smiled down at her as he reached what he believed to be the bathroom door and he gently stood her on her feet keeping one arm around her waist. 'Unless ... '

His eyes held hers and for one moment, she forgot where she was and that she was freezing to death.

'Only joking. I'll go and put the kettle on. You sure you're okay?'

She wasn't sure of anything but she managed to nod.

'Yell if you need me.' He turned and jumped down the

stairs three at a time.

Becky watched him go then closed the bathroom door. She stripped off her clothes and dropped them into the bath then got in the shower, leant against the tiles for support and turned the water on. It took a few minutes for her to feel her feet and hands again and her skin started to tingle as the warm water brought her back to her senses.

She washed the mud from her hair and face and was mortified to see three more scraps of what looked like newspaper, on the shower floor. They must have been in her hair, she realised, wondering what she must have looked like. It was bad enough that her coat had seen better days, without her being covered in mud and slivers of newspaper – doing a passable impersonation of a scarecrow.

It was almost twenty minutes before Becky made her way tentatively downstairs. She was hoping he'd left but he was standing in the kitchen, his torso bare, nursing a mug of coffee. She felt herself blush as her eyes took in the sight of his toned, tanned body.

'I hope you don't mind, but my clothes were soaked. I was dripping on your floor.'

He nodded towards the sink where he'd wrung out his shirt and jumper and she only now realised that he'd got out of the car without putting a coat on.

'N...no,' she said, still stuttering, and not because she was cold. 'I can put your clothes in the tumble dryer and ... you can have a shower too... if you want.'

He grinned at her. 'As tempting as that is, I'll pass ... this time round. I'll get soaked again going back out, so I'll wait till I get home thanks.' He handed her a mug of coffee. 'It's hot. I made it when I heard you coming down the stairs. I'm guessing milk, no sugar.'

'Thanks,' she said, taking the mug from him, their fingers briefly touching and their eyes meeting for a split second.

Becky looked away. Guessing or did you ask Doreen? she found herself wondering.

'I'd better run,' he said, putting his mug on the counter and grabbing his clothes from the sink. He tugged his jumper on over his head but screwed his shirt up in his hand. 'No point in wearing layers of wet. I'm really sorry for soaking you, Becky.'

The use of her name made her head shoot up. She hadn't told him it.

As if reading her mind, he said. 'I heard your friend, Jess call you Becky, yesterday.' He headed towards the door. 'I thought you'd prefer me to call you that, although ...' he beamed at her and winked as he opened the front door, 'you'll always be Fifi in my eyes.'

He was gone before she could reply.

The phone rang as Max was driving away and Becky's tummy did a little flip. For some absurd reason, she wondered if it might be him – but how would he have her number and why would he call her anyway?

She was behaving like a schoolgirl with a crush – and she didn't even like him. In fact, she was furious with him. He'd just added a soaking to the list of abuses and she had been so cold and shocked that she'd forgotten to shout at him.

'Okay lady, you've got some explaining to do,' Jess said on the other end of the phone. 'Why was Max carrying you over the threshold and what the hell were you two doing in there for the last half an hour? And, why did he leave carrying what looked decidedly like an item of clothing? Give me details and don't leave anything out.'

Becky laughed despite herself. 'Good God! Is there no privacy in this village?'

'Of course there isn't. So...?'

'Well ... he came round last night after you and Susie left and one thing led to another. We got married in secret this morning and we've just consummated it. Needless to say, like most celebrity marriages, it didn't last. I'll be calling the Pope for an annulment as soon as my nosy friend gets off the line.'

'The Pope won't annul a consummated marriage.'

Becky roared with laughter. 'I tell you all that and that's the bit you pick up on! And you know I'm not a Catholic.'

'I know. Seriously, what's been going on? I didn't think you liked him.'

'I didn't. Don't. Nothing's going on. The twerp drove into a puddle and saturated me. Then, he did his macho man impression, manhandled me into his car and drove me home. He carried me because I was too cold to walk. I had a shower; he stayed in the kitchen and had coffee. He took his shirt off, simply because it was wet through. That's it. End of story.'

'Okay fine. I'll just make up my own story then.'

'Don't you dare Jess! And don't say anything to anyone else either. You know what this place is like. Mrs. Mary Nosy-Parkes has already started putting two and two together and making a thousand and one nights.'

'Too late, I'm afraid. I saw her peering out of the window just as Max was leaving. Not sure how good her eyesight is or how much she could see from that distance but it is a straight line of sight from the Stores to your door. I could see quite clearly, and I'm only a few doors closer.'

'Oh God.' Becky dropped onto the sofa. 'That's all I need.'

'Fancy lunch in the pub? My treat.'

'I'd love to Jess, but I've already got soaked once today; I don't fancy a second time. Besides, my coat is still saturated. For something that threadbare, it seems to be holding a lot of water. Have you been out? It's like a monsoon out there.'

'No. That's the beauty of living above my salon. I can get to work without getting soaked.'

'Why are you at work? It's Sunday.' Becky rose, strolled over to the window and glanced up the road to Jess' salon.

40

"Prime Cuts Too" was next door to the butchers, and although an alleyway separated them; Jess had thought the name was amusing.

'I was thinking about redecorating and I've been trying some of those tester pots we got last week. You're right by the way; Lime Fizz does look like vomit.'

'I hate to say, "I told you so" but, "I told you so". Any decisions?'

'Yeah. It looks fine the way it is. So, if a few hundred quid is any use to you, it's yours.'

'Aw Jess. That's really generous but you're not made of money. You paid for all the wine yesterday, too. At this rate, I'll owe you and Susie more than I do the banks.'

'You don't owe us anything. You'd do exactly the same if the shoe were on the other foot. I mean it Becky, it's yours – and don't use it to repay the banks, use it to get yourself something nice or something practical even. Like a coat that actually keeps out the cold and wet.'

Becky choked back a sob. 'That's a lovely idea Jess, and I really do appreciate the offer but –'

'But you won't accept handouts and you've got to sort it out yourself. I know. I've heard it a hundred times. For once in your life Becky Cooper, why don't you just let someone help you?'

'Don't get cross Jess. And I do let you help me – all the time. You and Susie are always paying for stuff for me and you're always buying Lily things.'

'Yeah, yeah. And look at everything you've done for us. You helped me get this place and you designed all my flyers and publicity stuff, not to mention my website. You saved me an absolute fortune and that's not including all the hours you helped out in here when I first started.'

'That's what friends do.'

'Exactly. So, let's not hear any more of this, "I owe you and Susie" nonsense. Susie's business wouldn't have survived without you either; your contacts and networking have kept "Beckleston Bridal Belles" in monetary wedded bliss. What time are you expecting the Coopers to bring Lily home?'

Becky glanced at the antique French ormolu clock on the mantelpiece; it was one of the few family heirlooms she had – so far – managed to keep. It had been an anniversary present from her father to her mother and it reminded Becky of happier times. 'About four, they said. They'll have a cup of tea and then head off home.'

'God, if they're staying for tea, you'll need a drink. I'll bring the big umbrella and pick you up in an hour. Don't argue. A Sunday roast and a bottle of wine is what we all need. I'll call Susie and get her to meet us there too. See you soon.' And with that, Jess rang off.

CHAPTER SIX

'I need to talk to you Max,' Margaret called out as he
dashed in from the rain.

He poked his saturated head around the door. 'Can it
wait until I've had a shower and put on some dry clothes?
It's like the sky's turned into an ocean out there. I'm sure it
doesn't rain like this in London.'

'Good heavens! You're soaked through! Of course it can
wait. Go and have a shower before you catch your death.
I'll pour you a whisky.'

'Thanks. See you in fifteen minutes.' He raced towards
the stairs, leaving little pools of water in his wake.

Exactly fifteen minutes later, Max trotted back down. He
entered the sitting room, a smaller room towards the back
of the house and collapsed onto a sumptuous sofa in front
of a large stone fireplace, containing a roaring fire.

'What a day,' he said, letting out a sigh and taking the
glass of whisky Margaret handed him. 'Thanks. Now, what
do you want to talk to me about?' He took a large swig and
smiled as the liquid warmed him.

Margaret ambled over to a wing-back chair diagonally
opposite him and sat down, nursing a glass of sherry. She
cleared her throat.

Max eyed her thoughtfully. 'Is something wrong?'

'What? Oh no. No ... nothing's wrong. In fact,
something rather good has happened.' Margaret gulped
down the contents of her glass.

'Really? So, are you knocking back the sherry in
celebration then? I'll get you another.' He got to his feet
and marched to the drinks cabinet. He poured them both
refills, passed the glass of sherry to his mother then
resumed his seat. After a few minutes of silence he said,
'Are you planning to tell me, or do you want me to guess?'

Margaret gave him a nervous-looking smile. 'I don't
want you to get cross and if you really don't like the idea,

then, of course, I'll call back and say no, but personally, I think it would be rather jolly and it would be lovely for our first one to be someone we know, especially someone so nice and ... and easy-going and ...' She gulped back the second glass.

'Mother! What's going on? Our first what?'

'Wedding darling. Our first wedding. I've just had a booking for August.'

Max blinked several times in surprise. 'Well. That's great – isn't it? Although, are you sure the place will be ready by then? There's still a lot to do. Is seven months enough time to get it all done – well six really. Beginning or end of August?'

'The end. The Bank Holiday weekend to be precise. She wants to arrive on Friday and have the wedding on the Sunday.'

'Okay, almost seven months then, so ... wait a minute. You said, "someone we know". Whose wedding is this – exactly? And why do I have a dreadful feeling that I'm not going to like the answer?'

'Lizzie's,' Margaret said, bowing her head slightly but fixing her eyes firmly on her son's face. 'But if you –'

'Oh shit! Sorry, Mum, but you must be joking.'

Margaret shook her head slowly from side to side but didn't speak.

'But why? I mean, why on earth, out of all the wedding venues in the world, would she choose to have her wedding here?'

Again, Margaret shook her head.

'You ... you didn't suggest it did you? God, Mum!'

'No! It was Lizzie's idea. She called me this morning, to confirm it but I told her that I'd have to check with you and that if you said no then –'

'Oh great. Thanks Mum. Now, if I say no, I'll look like a jealous ex. Brilliant.'

'No you won't. Lizzie herself said that if you felt in any way awkward – or if I did, then she would understand

44

perfectly and they'd look for somewhere else. She just thought it would be good, for all concerned. Jack is perfectly happy with the idea but, if you'd rather not, that's absolutely fine. You were going to be invited anyway, so, either way, you'd be at the wedding. At least if it's here, you can escape to your own room if it all gets too much.'

Max sneered. 'What am I, twelve? And, I could escape wherever it was held, so that doesn't work as an argument in its favour. I'm amazed Jack agreed to it – actually, no I'm not, I said he was far too easy-going for my liking. Oh God. I really don't have much choice do I?'

'Of course you do! Look Max, you said a few months ago that you were over her but if that's not the case then I'll call her and say that it's my decision. That I've thought about it and decided it's not appropriate and that I hadn't mentioned it to you. Or, I could say that I've checked with the builders and it won't be ready in time. I really don't mind. Truly I don't.'

Max sighed loudly and got up to pour himself another very large whisky. He held up the sherry decanter. 'You?' he asked.

Margaret nodded. 'Good God yes!'

She held out her half-full glass and Max filled it to the brim. He did likewise with his empty whisky glass then he flopped onto the sofa and stretched his long legs out in front of the fire.

'I am over her. That's not the problem. I think it might feel a little weird though, watching her marry someone else but you're right, I would be going to the wedding so I'll see that anyway.' He took a large swig from his glass and stared into the flames. 'No. I'm fine with it. Tell her it's okay with me. In fact, tell her it's my wedding present. I'll foot the bill for whatever it would cost to hire this place for the weekend. And that doesn't mean you can double the price, Mother.' He grinned at her over the rim of his glass.

'Double it! I'll treble it if you're paying,' she said grinning. 'Why don't we say it's from both of us? I'd like that.'

'Fine.'

'And what shall I say we're paying for? The venue hire, decorations, accommodation, food –'

'Whatever you were planning to provide as a "Wedding Package" is fine with me.'

Margaret giggled, a little tipsy from three glasses of sherry. 'Do you know, I haven't the faintest idea! I haven't thought that far ahead. I'd better find someone who knows about this sort of thing, I suppose and hire them to organise it.'

Max shook his head. 'You've taken a booking for a wedding despite the fact the place is still a wreck, you have hardly any staff and not the first idea of what needs to be done. Bravo, Mother! I think your new business is off to a flying start.'

'Don't worry about it dear, it'll all sort itself out. Actually, a more pressing problem is, I've totally forgotten to arrange anything for lunch! We may have to have bread and cheese.'

Max threw her a mock look of horror then smiled. 'Best adjourn to the pub then. They do Sunday roasts there and it's stopped raining so the walk will do us both good.'

The Beckleston Inn was a rambling fifteenth century building, too large for such a village but built in the days when Beckleston was on one of the main routes to London and when the village held a large market, attracting both vendors and purchasers, from miles around.

Those days were long gone; the railway had put paid to the market because better prices could be obtained by transporting goods to London and years later, the building of the motorway network meant that no one need ever pass through Beckleston, except by choice.

Terry and Trisha Walter inherited The Beckleston Inn from Trisha's parents in 2001 and, after winning several thousand pounds on the National Lottery, they were able, not only to keep the place going but also to renovate it and hire a chef to improve the restaurant menu from standard pub fare, to gourmet dining. They sectioned off part of the Inn as an á la carte restaurant whilst still serving traditional favourites like Ploughman's Lunch and sausage and chips in the newly renovated "Bistro and Carvery Bar". They also sold bar snacks such as crisps and sandwiches in the main public bar area as Trisha had decided, she would cater for all her patrons taste requirements.

Becky, Jess and Susie were seated at a table to one side of the large inglenook fireplace in the "Bistro and Carvery Bar" and were scanning the dessert menu when Max and Margaret Bedford strolled in.

Jess glanced up. 'Speaking of something tasty, Max Bedford's just walked in.'

Becky was facing towards the fire but she swivelled in her seat, blushed crimson then buried her head in the menu.

Susie let out a deep and meaningful sigh. 'I know I said you could have him Becky but I'm beginning to regret it. I think I can honestly say that he's the most gorgeous man I've ever seen.'

'I don't want him! You're welcome to him as far as I'm concerned,' Becky said trying to force her eyes to focus on the menu. Somehow though, she seemed to be looking in the direction of the bar – and Max Bedford.

Max scanned the crowded room for a vacant seat, after buying drinks. He spotted Becky, Jess and Susie – who all seemed to be staring in his direction – and a smile formed at the corner of his mouth as he saw them hastily turn away.

As luck would have it, the couple sitting at the table on the opposite side of the inglenook, were just putting their coats on to leave.

He strolled over to the, now vacant, table and put the drinks down then glanced over to his mother who was studying a poster about a Valentine's Day Dinner and Dance. It was pinned to the wall near the front door and

47

Max wondered why on earth she should be so mesmerised by it. He hoped she wasn't thinking of finding herself a new man in Beckleston to go with the new house and new business venture then he realised, with a feeling of some dread, she was more likely thinking of finding him a new woman.

'Good afternoon ladies,' he said, turning his attention towards the opposite table and looking directly at Becky.

'Hi,' Jess said, 'it's nice to see you again.'

Susie just grinned and Becky threw him a brief smile then buried her head in the menu again.

Margaret spotted Max and made her way towards him.

'May I introduce my mother to you,' he said, when she reached the table. 'Mum, I'd like you to meet Becky, Jess and Susie.'

Margaret beamed at them. 'How lovely to meet you all. I'm Margaret Bedford. Do you all live in the village?'

She glanced from one to another, quickly appraising them and wondering whether one of them might be the, "something interesting" her son had mentioned. If she had to guess, she would say the one with the long blond hair and the large bust; definitely Max's type – but the pink and blue-haired girl was rather stunning, in an outlandish sort of way and the brown-haired one was very pretty, even without any make-up. She prayed it wasn't all three of them. In London, Max could get away with seeing more than one woman at a time but in a village, especially a village like Beckleston, if it was still the Beckleston she remembered, it would be impossible, not to mention, unforgivable.

'It's lovely to meet you too,' Jess said, returning her smile. 'Yes, we all live – and work in Beckleston. I own "Prime Cuts Too", the hair salon and I live in the flat above, Susie owns "Beckleston Bridal Belles" and also lives above her shop and Becky lives in Rosemary Cottage – and she's Superwoman.'

48

Jess winked at Becky who raised her head from the menu and was clearly, about to object.

'Actually,' Jess continued, 'Becky is an Events Organiser, amongst other things. If you want something done, she's the one to ask. From children's parties to society weddings, she's your girl. She organised the Valentine's Day Dinner and Dance Derby – I noticed you reading the poster – Oh! Becky painted that too. I forgot, she's also an artist and –'

'And *she's* sitting next to you and getting more embarrassed by the second!' Becky said, 'Mrs. Bedford doesn't want a sales pitch Jess – but thanks for the vote of confidence.'

Margaret's eyes darted towards Max whom she noticed had his eyes firmly fixed in the direction of Becky then she glanced back towards the poster by the door then back to Becky.

'Well ... it just so happens that a sales pitch may be exactly what I do want and please, call me Margaret,' she said. 'The poster's awfully good; was the original a watercolour?'

She removed her coat and passed it to Max to hang on the hook, on the wall near their table then directed her full attention back to Becky.

'Um. Yes. I painted the watercolour then scanned it in to my computer and added the text.'

Margaret thought Becky seemed slightly taken aback by the remark and couldn't help but notice her flushed cheeks. She wondered whether that was from the wine, the fire or because she found compliments awkward to accept.

'And you've organised the Valentine's bash? Why the "Derby" part? Is it a race to find a partner? That sounds rather fun. You would enjoy that wouldn't you dear?'

She grinned at Max and he grinned back.

'Well, not exactly. It's actually a dance competition, in the church hall. Judges watch all the couples entered and each couple has a number; when a couples' number is called, they leave the floor. The dance continues until there's only one couple left and they're the winners. It's just a bit of fun really. It's been held for several years.'

'Oh I see. That does sound like fun. "Strictly" comes to Beckleston. I noticed there are various ticket options.'

'Yes. There are tickets for the dance at the hall or tickets for dinner here in the Bistro and Carvery, from a set menu, and the dance combined. It's really good value. You can buy them from Trisha, at the bar. The profits go to charity.'

'And, it's this Tuesday? Well, we'll certainly have to see if there are still tickets available for that, won't we Max?'

'We certainly will,' he said, meeting her eyes, 'I'll go and ask right now, and whilst I'm there, I think I'd better buy these lovely ladies something to drink.' He rose from his chair. 'Another bottle of wine?'

'Oh no! Thank you. We're just leaving,' Becky said.

'Are we?' Jess asked.

'Yes,' Becky said.

'That's a pity. Mum, would you like wine with lunch?'

Margaret raised her eyebrows.

'Silly question,' Max said, 'Of course you would.' And he headed to the bar.

'And, you've organised weddings too?' Margaret resumed her questioning.

'Yes. Quite a few. In fact, I just finished one a couple of weeks ago, as it happens.'

'Really? Well, that is interesting. Do you have a portfolio or some such thing? I'd love to discuss this further but I've interrupted your Sunday lunch for quite long enough already. Perhaps you could come and see me at the house, one day next week – would that be convenient? I'm at Beckleston Hall and I've got a few things that I'd like to chat with you about, including a wedding I need to arrange.'

CHAPTER SEVEN

'So, d'you think Max is getting married again?' Jess asked, as soon as they left the pub. 'And why did we have to run off? I thought we were having dessert.'

'We didn't "run off"; I just didn't want him buying us drinks and as to whether he's getting married again, I have no idea and couldn't care less. Possibly I suppose but the bride's parents would usually organise things, not the groom's so it could be for someone else in the family.'

'There is no one else in the family. It's just Max and his mum,' Jess said.

'Really? No cousins then or aunts and uncles or –'

'Oh. Well possibly. I must ask Connie Jessop, she's bound to know.'

'Yes do,' Susie said, linking arms with Becky in a gesture of support. 'I'll be *so* disappointed if it's Max. I really thought the two of you would be perfect together. He has so much to offer you.'

Becky tutted. 'To be honest, I'm more interested in what his mother may be thinking of offering me. It sounded as if she's looking for someone to arrange not only a wedding but some other things too. Wouldn't that be fantastic? Assuming she hires me, of course.'

'Of course she'll hire you!' Jess said, wrapping her scarf tightly about her neck. 'Bloody hell it's freezing. It wasn't this cold when we went into the pub was it?'

Susie shivered, visibly. 'No, it wasn't. Perhaps we'll get more snow.'

'Oh I hope not!' Becky stuffed her hands in her raincoat pockets. She could feel the icy wind biting right through to her skin. Her winter coat was still saturated from the soaking she'd received earlier and she'd had to resort to her summer raincoat, which was totally inadequate in this weather. Her teeth chattered and every bone in her body suddenly ached; she prayed she hadn't caught a chill.

They all quickened their pace and arrived at Becky's

moments later.

'Want to come in for a coffee and some cake? The Coopers won't be here for another couple of hours.'

'Definitely! I can hardly feel my hands,' Susie squealed.

Large flakes of snow began falling the moment they stepped inside and Becky poked at the banked-up fire to revive it, while Jess and Susie went to the kitchen and started making coffee.

The telephone rang as Becky threw some logs on the rekindled flames and seeing from the caller display that it was the Coopers, she grabbed the handset, unable to stop a sudden rush of fear running through her.

'Hello. Is everything okay?' She tried to control the panic gnawing at the pit of her stomach.

'Hello. Yes, everything's fine here – except for the snow.' Sarah Cooper said. 'It started an hour ago and there's at least a couple of inches on the roads already. We would have left immediately but we were having lunch and we thought it might just be a quick flurry. We didn't expect this. Harry's still happy to bring Lily home but we wondered what it's like there and we don't want to get stuck somewhere. What do you think? We'll do whatever you want us to.'

Becky could feel tears pricking at her eyes. She had really been looking forward to having Lily home. She missed her so much when she went to stay with Jeremy's parents. At least she would be safe there though. The thought of her being stuck in a car in a snowdrift or worse – being involved in an accident didn't bear thinking about. Becky forced painful memories to the back of her mind.

'I think you should stay home. It's literally only just started snowing here but the flakes are huge and it won't be long before it settles. It was pouring earlier too and now the temperature's dropped, the roads will turn to ice. Better to be safe than sorry.'

'That's what I thought you'd say. If it had been forecast, we'd have left this morning, but all they said was rain!'

'Same here. It's not your fault Sarah. May I speak to Lily?'

'Of course. Lily darling, Mummy's on the 'phone. I'll call you tomorrow and see what the weather's like then.'

'Mummy! Mummy! It's snowing! Can I make a snowman! Will you come, help me?'

Becky could feel her heart breaking from love and missing her child. 'I wish I could sweetheart but the snow has made the roads dangerous. Grandpa will help you. Don't stay out for too long though; it's very cold. I miss you darling.'

'Miss you, Mummy.'

'Have you had a good time?'

'Uh huh. We did lots and lots.'

'That's good. What did you do?'

Lily spent the next ten minutes telling Becky about the zoo, the cinema, the theme park and all the other places she'd been during her week with her grandparents. By the time she'd finished Becky was missing her so much, she had tears running down her cheeks; she wanted desperately to hug her daughter.

'She's not coming back today then?' Jess said, handing Becky a mug of coffee when she'd finally been able to bring herself to say goodbye.

Becky shook her head, too upset to speak.

'Was she upset?'

Becky wiped her eyes with her hand and sniffed, grabbing a tissue from the box beside her and blowing her nose. 'No. You know Lily. Nothing fazes her. She was a bit disappointed that I couldn't go and help her build a snowman but she got over it when Harry said he'd get the sledge out and pull her around the garden.'

'Which naturally, upset you even more,' Susie said.

'Naturally. I miss her so much. I could really use a hug right now.'

'I'll hug you.' Jess grabbed Becky in a bear hug. 'Is that better?'

53

'Apart from the fact that I can hardly breathe, yes. Thanks.'

Jess grinned and let her go. 'Why don't we open a bottle of wine and watch a DVD later?'

'Or we could build a snowman too,' Susie suggested. 'What? Why are you both looking at me like I'm a raving loon?'

'I suppose,' Jess said, 'it's because you are!'

The next morning, the snow was several inches deep and still falling and, as Becky had predicted, the reporters on the radio were warning of hazardous driving conditions and advising people not to attempt to drive unless absolutely necessary.

Becky stood in her kitchen, cradling a mug of coffee and watching the snow. She could picture Lily rushing out to check on the snowman she'd built yesterday. Harry had helped her send Becky a photo via his mobile phone and Lily had been thrilled when Becky had called her and told her how wonderful it was.

She shook herself mentally. She had got to stop getting so emotional about this. Lily was having a great time and would be home soon. In the meantime, she had to try and salvage Valentine's Day. There was no chance of the snow miraculously disappearing by tomorrow and none of the elderly residents would want to venture out in this weather. At this rate, the entire evening would be a disaster.

Becky made a few calls – to Trisha, the vicar, Jess and Susie, Doreen and some others and was absolutely astonished to hear that, by hook or by crook, they'd get to the Dance. She called everyone she could think of who owned a four wheel drive and before long, she'd arranged for almost everyone attending, to be picked up. Perhaps it wouldn't be a total disaster after all, she thought, and by lunchtime, she was beginning to feel rather optimistic.

She peered through the front window and saw that the snow had finally stopped. People were venturing out and she had to admit to herself that if Lily had been at home, they would have thought this was wonderful. Becky had always loved playing in the snow ever since she was a little girl and now she had a daughter to share that innocent pleasure with, she loved it even more. There was something about snow that made the world seem an especially magical place – provided that you didn't have to actually *go* anywhere.

She saw the Range Rover pull up outside and for a split second, panic seized her; she thought it might be someone from the banks – or worse. She felt oddly relieved when she recognised Max Bedford's athletic frame, almost sprint up the garden path. She opened the door before he reached it and surprised even herself, by smiling warmly at him.

'Good morning! What brings you here in this weather?'

Max stopped in his tracks as if she'd caught him by surprise. For a moment, he just stared at her and their eyes held then finally, he smiled. 'Good morning. You look ... very pretty today.'

Becky felt the colour flood her cheeks as she remembered what she was wearing and suddenly wished she'd made a better choice. Her dad's old blue cardigan over a faded T-shirt and leggings with a pair of thick wool socks, were fine for lolling about the house in, but not for entertaining visitors and she realised she hadn't got any make-up on and wasn't even sure she'd brushed her hair. He was being sarcastic, obviously.

'I wasn't expecting visitors,' she said as coolly as she could.

Max's brows creased then little gold lights twinkled in his green eyes as the corners of his mouth broke into a grin. 'I wasn't being sarcastic! I'm serious; you do look very pretty. May I come in? It's freezing out here.'

Becky felt flustered but opened the door wider and stepped aside to let him enter. Was he being genuine, she wondered, or was he just using a line?

'Why is it that you women want us men to pay you

compliments but when we do, you never believe us?'

'Perhaps it's because we women know when we look like a bag of old clothes – or maybe it's because we're just so used to your insincerity.'

She watched his eyes travel the length of her body and her skin began to tingle under his scrutiny. Her breathing quickened and her heart picked up speed. My God, she thought, I'm getting turned on just by his eyes.

'Believe me Becky, you look nothing like a bag of old clothes,' he said, stepping closer. 'In fact, I'm having a really hard time stopping myself from just grabbing you and kissing you right now.'

Becky couldn't hide her astonishment. She swallowed the lump in her throat and half opened her mouth to speak but she couldn't think of anything to say – which was just as well – she couldn't trust her voice at the moment. She tried to look away from him but her eyes wouldn't let her and they took in every inch of his body, remembering what he had looked like as he had stood, bare-chested in her kitchen only yesterday. It was as if she had X-ray vision and could see straight through his obviously expensive coat, to the tanned, firm body beneath. Her mouth felt suddenly dry and she licked her lips.

She didn't even realise he'd moved but she felt his arms encircle her and his mouth covered hers in a kiss as passionate as it was, unexpected. Her head swam and the tingling in her body turned to high voltage shockwaves. She felt as if she'd been hit by an avalanche and her arms reached out for him, desperate not to be swept away.

This was madness, utter madness. She didn't even like him, her brain tried to tell her but her heart told her to shut up and kiss him back. And for the first time, in more years than she could remember, she listened to her heart.

CHAPTER EIGHT

'OH MY GOD!' Jess was clearly stunned by Becky's revelation as they sat at their usual table in The Coffee Cake Café, an hour later.

Susie, on the other hand, wasn't so much surprised as she was eager to have details. 'So ... what was it like? Is he a really good kisser? Of course he is; what am I saying? Did he ... did you ... well, you know, did it get further than just kissing?'

'Susie!' Becky blushed furiously but she sounded disappointed when she answered. 'No ... But I think it could have. Just imagine how awful that would have been! Me, having sex at lunchtime on a Monday and with a complete stranger. And I don't even like him!'

Jess burst out laughing. 'Good God yes! The end of the world as we know it. Come on Becky, you having sex again at any time would be pretty bloody amazing!'

'Don't be mean!'

'I'm not! I'm being serious. It's been five years or more since you even kissed a man – let alone had hot, passionate sex with one. It's just ... well, so unlike you. And he's not a complete stranger, you've met at least three or four times now and as for not liking him – who are you trying to kid?' Jess winked.

'That's not fair,' Susie said in Becky's defence, 'before she met Jeremy she was always having hot sex with men.'

'Susie!' Becky almost dropped her cup of coffee and her eyes darted around the café, although, apart from the three of them, Doreen, and her friend, Violet Wren, the place was deserted. 'Thank heavens no one heard that. I wasn't always having hot sex, or any other kind of sex for that matter. I only dated two other men before I met Jeremy.'

Susie shrugged. 'Yeah well, it always seemed to me like you were. What I mean is, you were never without a boyfriend.'

'Okay. That's true but I can assure you, I wasn't having

sex! I didn't "do it" until my sixteenth birthday and that was only because I wasn't thinking straight, after Mum and Dad ...'

'Oh God! Me and my big mouth.' Susie squeezed Becky's shoulder. 'I'm so sorry. I didn't mean to bring back painful memories.'

'I know you didn't. It's okay.' Becky took a deep breath. The accident in which her parents died had happened just before her sixteenth birthday and yet sometimes, it felt like just days ago. 'They've been gone sixteen years now. I'm not saying I don't still miss them – I do, almost every day but let's face it, life can be very, bloody cruel – you just have to deal with it.'

'And it's certainly been cruel to you, more than once, first your real dad abandoning you then ... sorry! I'll shut up.' Susie cast her eyes down to her cup and stirred her coffee.

Becky leant towards her and gave her a playful shove with her shoulder. 'It's okay Susie. Honestly.'

'Let's get back to Max and that kiss,' Jess said. 'It was really good wasn't it? You just have to look at him to know that it would be.'

Becky blushed again but she nodded in agreement. 'I hate to admit it, but it was. Oh Hell, *it was*!'

'O-M-G the girl's in love! You've gone all starry-eyed,' Jess teased.

'I haven't! And I'm not in love, I can assure you. In lust, perhaps, but definitely not in love!'

'Lust is good. In fact, lust is even better,' Jess said, clearly considering the options. 'No messy emotions to complicate things. Just pure unadulterated sex! What could be better?'

'Winning the Lottery, at this point in my life.'

'Oh. Yes well that's true but you'd have to buy a ticket to do that – and we all know you don't.'

'I've got better things to spend my hard-earned money on. You know as well as I do that you stand more chance of getting run over than you do of winning that – and with my luck, we know I'd get run over ... by a bus ... and a lorry.' Becky smiled sardonically then her mind drifted back to her long-dead parents.

'So anyway, back to Max,' Susie said. 'Why did it stop at a kiss and what happened after? Are you going to see him again? Did he say anything? Tell me! I have to have details.'

Becky dragged her thoughts back from the past, remembering instead, what it had felt like to be in Max's arms. 'His mobile rang. Actually, it was almost erotic. It was in his pocket and set to vibrate!'

Both Jess and Susie sniggered simultaneously.

'So what happened? Did he answer it?'

'After a few seconds, yes. He ... he sort of pulled away and gave me a really odd look, like ... like he didn't know where he was or something. Then he said, "Sorry, I have to get this" and just answered the phone. It was his mum – I think – yes, it must have been because he said something along the lines of "I'm just asking her now. I'll call you back," and he hung up.'

'And?' Susie said.

'Um. I'm not really sure. The vicar turned up as Max answered his phone. I opened the door, thinking I could quickly get rid of him but Max said he had to dash; he'd come to ask if I'd go and see his mum later this afternoon – to discuss the wedding. He said he'd come back and pick me up at four. That was it.'

'What?' Susie slumped back against the chair. 'One minute he's sweeping you off your feet and the next it's all business! What did you say?'

'I said okay.'

'Okay! What do you mean you said okay?'

'I said okay, I'd be ready at four.'

'Dear God. You clearly are out of practise with men aren't you?' Jess said then glanced at her watch. 'Right, we've got a couple of hours. Come on.' She got up and headed for the door.

'Where are we going? A couple of hours for what? Don't you need to get back to work?'

'Fiona's there. We're hardly rushed off our feet today. We're going to yours to search through your wardrobe to find the sexiest dress you've got.'

'What do I need a sexy dress for?' Becky hadn't moved from her chair.

'That's obvious even to me,' Susie said, grabbing Becky's hand and pulling her to her feet, 'to make sure the next time Max sees you, he doesn't want to stop at just kissing.'

'I told you on the way here, you're wasting your time. I don't have a sexy dress,' Becky said as Jess and Susie rifled through her wardrobe.

'I thought you were just saying that,' Jess said patently disappointed. 'Everyone has at least one killer dress. You must have had one before you got married. And what about all the posh events you organise? We've been to some and you've definitely worn good stuff to those. Where are they?'

Becky dropped onto her bed and clasped her hands in her lap. 'I ... I've sold most of them ... on Ebay. I've just kept the business outfits. It looks more professional anyway.'

'You sold them? When?' Susie's voice held a note of incredulity.

'Just before Christmas. I wanted to buy Lily something nice and ... well, apart from that wedding in January and the New Year's Eve party just before that, business had been a bit slow. I needed to keep up the repayments on the agreement – although, that might all be a waste of time now and, what with everything else, that didn't leave much.'

'You haven't heard back from your solicitor about the letter then?' Jess said.

Becky shook her head. 'No. I'm kind of hoping no news

is good news. Anyway, I got quite a bit for the stuff I sold and it meant I could give Lily a nice present and have money to tide us over for a few months and some for her birthday in March. I thought things would start to pick up again in the spring. Of course, that was all before the letter arrived last Friday.'

Jess sank onto the bed beside her. 'I had no idea things were so tight Becky. I knew you didn't have cash to throw around but I thought you were managing.'

'I am managing. I ... I just had to sell a few things to do so. That's why it would be so great if Margaret Bedford gave me some business.'

'Right! That's it. You wouldn't take that money I offered you yesterday but you're having it and I'm not going to take no for an answer, unless you never want me to speak to you again. I'm serious Becky. This is shit. You shouldn't be selling your clothes to make ends meet. God, if Jeremy were here I'd wring his bloody neck myself! Sorry – but I would.'

'Me too! And I've got some savings you can have Becky. Don't argue. You can pay me back when you're Mrs. Bedford, if you must.'

Becky threw her arms around her friends and promptly dissolved into floods of tears.

'Hell! I look awful! There's absolutely no chance of Max wanting to be anywhere near me, looking like this, let alone kiss me! Not that I want him to, of course. Why do I always go red and blotchy when I cry? He'll be here in less than an hour! And ... what will Mrs. Bedford think, seeing me like this?' Becky peered at her reflection in the dressing-table mirror, pulling faces and opening and closing her eyes repeatedly.

'That's not going to improve things,' Jess said. 'Go and have your shower; I'll make some tea and then I'll do your hair and make-up. And stop pretending you don't want the man to kiss you again, we all know you do. There's nothing

61

wrong with lust Becky and sex is fun – even you must remember that.'

'Vaguely, although it's been so long, I'm not sure I'll remember how. Oh! I've just realised something.' She turned away from the mirror and looked at Jess and Susie. 'How can I think about getting involved with Max if I'm hoping to work with his mum? She'd be furious. What am I thinking?'

'I don't think you are thinking. That's what lust does to us,' Susie said, sighing loudly.

'Thank heavens it didn't go any further. Could you imagine it?' Becky jumped to her feet, almost knocking over the stool she'd been perched on. 'Right! That's it. Even if he is considering kissing me again – and I'm not sure he is – I'll have to tell him I can't mix business with pleasure.'

'Let me know how that goes,' Jess said, heading for the door.

'Maybe he thought the same,' Becky said pacing back and forth across the bedroom floor. 'Maybe, when his mum called, he realised what he was doing and that's why he left so abruptly.'

'Maybe. And maybe you'll have just a towel wrapped around you when he comes to pick you up – which you will – if you don't get a move on.' Jess grabbed Becky's hand and pulled her towards the bathroom.

'Okay, I'm going!'

'What I don't get,' Susie said, following them out of Becky's bedroom, 'and it's been bugging me ever since you told us – is why he came to see you in the first place. What I mean is, they have a phone; why didn't he just call and tell you or why didn't Margaret call and ask? Why send Max to tell you that he'd come back for you later? I think he just wanted to see you and was using it as an excuse – and his mum was obviously fine with that.'

'Why would he want to see me?'

Jess sighed. 'Sometimes Becky, I really think you know

nothing about men. You've just shared a passionate kiss and you're asking why he would want to see you. He clearly fancies you! Didn't you see him staring at you in the pub?'

'I ... he was looking at me, that's true, but I think he was just listening to what I was saying.'

'Yeah. Well, I think he was wondering how he could get you in his arms – again.'

'Again? What do you mean again? Have I missed something?' Susie asked in a concerned tone.

'Yesterday morning – he carried Becky in from his car, remember? We told you in the pub.'

Susie nodded, obviously relieved that she was up to date with events.

'Do you really think he's interested in me?'

'Yes Becky, I do,' Jess said. 'Although I'm not sure Susie's right about the phone call. Unless you gave him or his mum your number or your surname, why would he know either? Maybe that was exactly why he turned up here – because they don't have it. Anyway, that doesn't matter now.' Jess gave Becky a shove. 'Go and get showered.'

At five minutes to four, Becky, Jess and Susie watched as Max strode up the snow-covered path without the slightest hesitation; it had taken them ages to get to the café and back to Becky's again in the snow and they'd slid and slipped all over the place.

'How does he do it?' Susie said. 'The man is obviously a demigod.'

'Perhaps he just has good all-weather boots,' Becky said, practical as ever.

'Nope. He's a demigod. And doesn't he just ooze sex appeal? Why don't you just go for it and make sure his mum never finds out?'

'Because, as good as he might be and as tempted as I am – yes, don't say it – I agree, he's not bad but, he's not quite as lovely as having a roof over my head. I've been thinking about it. Men, you can always find, work, is harder to come by. Besides, just look at him. He can have any woman he wants – and has, if even half the gossip is true. I've got enough problems already. Do I really need to give myself more?'

'You need to have some fun,' Jess said, 'and I'm pretty certain Max is the man for that. You said yourself you were "in lust". Just let your hair down and enjoy it. You don't have to fall in love with the guy!'

'But what happens if I do? What then? I'm not sure I could handle losing someone else I love.'

Jess and Susie exchanged glances.

'Then walk away before you do,' Jess said. 'The minute you think it's more than just lust, more than just fun – end it. That way, you'll be in control. You'll be the one who does the leaving. You never know, that may actually do you some good; break the cycle or something.'

Becky considered this for a few seconds until she heard the doorbell ring. 'If only I could Jess. Wouldn't that be something?' She made her way towards the front door then looked back and smiled at them. 'Okay. Wish me luck. I'll see you two later.'

'Good luck!'

'Go get 'em, girl!' Jess said. She waited until Becky had closed the front door behind her then she turned to Susie. 'Right Susie, you and I have work to do. Monday may be your day off but I'm sorry to say, you're going to have to do some serious sewing!'

CHAPTER NINE

Max was feeling anxious. Kissing Becky hadn't been something he'd considered and it had taken him almost as much by surprise as it had obviously taken her.

He wasn't going to deny that he was interested in her. There was something about her that had struck a chord with him the moment he saved her from slipping into the drained pond on Saturday. He couldn't say exactly what it was, but he knew he wanted to see her again. When he'd bumped into her in the Stores, later that day, it had only confirmed it for him. She was so ... so argumentative.

He grinned to himself; perhaps that was the fascination. Most women he met seemed to fall at his feet the minute he smiled at them. Becky, on the other hand, clearly wanted to slap his face.

She hadn't slapped his face when he'd kissed her though. She'd kiss him back and, if his phone hadn't rung, he was pretty sure they would have ended up doing much more than just kissing. She'd looked so damned sexy in that old cardigan and those leggings. Some women were sensual without even trying and Becky Cooper was definitely one of those women, he thought.

'Hi,' he said when Becky opened the door.

'Hi.'

She looked completely different from the way she had just a few hours earlier. Now, she wore make-up, not too much but enough to see she'd made an effort and she'd done something with her hair. He hoped it wasn't for his benefit. She looked pretty, but not in the same, naturally sexy, way.

She stepped onto the path and he saw her immediately begin to lose her balance. Her heeled, leather boots slid on the snow and he grabbed her to stop her from falling. This time, he held her at a distance.

'Haven't you got anything more suitable than those boots?'

'More suitable for what?'

'The snow. You live in the country, surely you possess a pair of walking boots or something? Wellingtons even.' He could see she was flustered by his words.

'I'm meeting your mother for business, not a stroll in the woods. I can't arrive in wellingtons. Besides, we're going in your car.'

'Yes – but you've got to get to my car.' He sighed deeply. 'I suppose I could carry you again.' He saw the red flush, through the perfectly applied make-up.

'Don't trouble yourself. I am perfectly capable of getting to your car without your help.'

She stepped confidently forward but he could see it wouldn't be long before she fell on her very pretty little bottom.

'For heaven's sake.' He swept her up and marched to his Range Rover depositing her abruptly beside the passenger door. 'It's open.' He walked around to the driver's side and got in.

Becky got in and slammed the door.

'Are you sure that's shut?' He didn't try to hide the sarcasm in his tone.

'I'm not certain, let me check.' She opened the door and slammed it so hard, the vehicle actually shook.

Max grinned to himself. 'Okay Fifi, let's go.' He floored the accelerator and with a spray of snow and mud, they shot off towards Beckleston Hall.

Neither spoke but he could see she was gritting her teeth.

'Are we going to discuss what happened earlier?' he asked.

'You were your usual macho self and I had a little "female" tantrum; what is there to discuss?'

Max grinned again. 'I meant earlier than that, when you kissed me.'

She turned to face him. 'When I kissed you! When you kissed me you mean!'

'Okay, I'll agree I started it but you definitely joined in.

66

Are you going to deny it?'

For a moment she didn't reply then she turned away and looked out of the passenger window. 'It would have been rude not to.'

Max was surprised. He hadn't expected that. 'So, you were just going along with it in an attempt at good manners? I like your style. Tell me, where would you have drawn the line on courtesy? When I was undressing you? Making love to you? Giving you an –'

'Okay, thank you! Kissing. I draw the line at kissing.'

'Good to know. That's obviously something else we "incoming would-be gentry" need to learn; the limits of good manners. When someone kisses you in Beckleston, you kiss them back, to be polite, whether you want to or not. Anything else I should know?'

'Not at the moment.'

Minutes later, he pulled up outside the front door of the Hall and turned to face her. 'Would you like me to carry you in, or can you manage?' He smiled and leant towards her.

'I can manage perfectly, thank you.' She released her seatbelt and made a rapid exit.

'Don't slam the ... okay, too late.' He wondered what he'd done to upset her. As long as he lived, he would never understand women.

Becky waited by the front door and Max opened it for her.

'After you,' he said bowing his head slightly.

'How kind.' She strode into the hall.

'Becky,' Margaret called to her from a room towards the back of the house.

It was a room she knew well and she wondered if the Bedfords were using it as a sitting room too. She didn't have to wonder for long.

'We're in here. We're using this room as a sitting room because it's much smaller than the others and, in this weather, much warmer.'

67

She followed Margaret in and her tummy did a little flip, apart from the furnishings, the room hadn't changed one bit since the last time she'd sat in it, so many years ago.

'Do sit down Becky, over here, near the fire. You look frozen. Is that coat warm enough?'

'It's fine thanks,' she said, a little too defensively, she realised.

'Darling, take Becky's coat and get us all a drink would you. Becky, this is Victoria, my oldest and dearest friend. She's staying with us for a few days.'

'Not so much of the "oldest", if you don't mind. Hello Becky, it's lovely to meet you.' Victoria stretched out her hand and Becky shook it.

'Hello. It's lovely to meet you too. How long have you been friends, if you don't mind me asking?'

'I don't mind at all,' Victoria said, smiling warmly. 'We've known each other since our early school days.'

'Yes, more than sixty-five years ago but do you know, I can still remember those days as if they were just last year. What would you like to drink Becky?' Margaret said.

'Oh, um, nothing for me thank you.'

'Nonsense! You need something to keep out the cold, doesn't she Victoria?'

'Definitely. I'd recommend the Drambuie. Very warming. Have you ever tried it?'

Becky smiled. It had been her mother's favourite. 'Yes. My mother loved it. Oh! I don't mean she drank it a lot, I just meant it was her favourite drink.'

Both Margaret and Victoria grinned.

'We know what you mean dear,' Margaret said. 'It's one of our favourites too. Pour Becky a glass of Drambuie, please Max.'

Max brought the drinks over and winked at Becky as he handed hers to her. The glass was almost full. 'I'll make sure you get home safely, don't worry.'

'How comforting.' She saw the lights in his eyes dance with devilment but noticed he'd filled the other glasses almost to the brim too.

'I'll leave you to it,' he said. 'Just yell when you're ready to go. I'll be somewhere or other in this vast pile.' He smiled and left the room.

'I can't believe this weather. I wondered if the Valentine's bash would have to be cancelled but Max tells me you've organised lifts for everyone. You really are a superwoman, aren't you? Cheers,' Margaret said, raising her glass.

Becky wondered how Max knew that but she didn't want to ask. 'Cheers,' she said, raising her glass too. 'I'm far from being a superwoman, unfortunately. It's just that everyone enjoys the social events in Beckleston and they put so much effort into helping make them a success, it would be such a shame if some of them missed out just because of some bad weather. The village is a real community, as you'll soon find out and all I had to do was ask a few people for a few favours. I did nothing really; it's the locals who are the real stars.'

Margaret and Victoria exchanged what Becky thought was a rather odd look but they both smiled at her.

'And modest too. I like that, especially as it would have been so easy for you to tell me you went out of your way to organise rides for everyone, which you clearly did. That would have been an added sales pitch.'

'But not true. Really, I made a few phone calls, nothing more.'

'Well, nevertheless, I'm impressed. Let me tell you what I have planned for here and you can tell me whether it's something you'd be interested in taking on. Am I to understand from our conversation yesterday, that you run your own business?'

'Yes. I've been organising events for ... for about ten years, professionally but I used to help out with events even in my early teens, so I know a fair amount about it and have quite an extensive network of contacts, suppliers etc.'

'Splendid. I was originally looking to employ someone

on a permanent basis, possibly even to live-in but I think, if you feel you have the time, that employing you on a freelance or contract basis would work just as well. I could then employ an assistant or something to help with the day to day requirements. So, what I'm planning is this. I want to promote the place as a wedding venue, amongst other things, possibly some corporate events, stately home weekends for the American market, painting holidays, perhaps even creative writing courses.'

Becky took a large gulp of Drambuie, now thankful Max had filled it to the top, she felt she was going to need it. What Margaret was saying would be a full time job, even for someone with her experience, which would be wonderful, if she could make it work. It would mean financial security, depending on what sort of fees Margaret might be willing to pay.

'I can see I've taken you rather by surprise, dear. You thought you were coming here to discuss a wedding and you've ended up with a full time job!' Margaret smiled warmly. 'Don't panic. They're only ideas at this stage and I don't expect anything to be up and running until the end of the year at the earliest, apart from the wedding. That, of course, is already booked and it must be something really special. Naturally, the bride will have a large say in exactly what she does and doesn't want and it, effectively, is a relatively small and private family wedding. Not sure of exact numbers yet. Max may be able to throw some light on that but it's fixed for the last weekend of August, the Bank holiday, so we need to get our act together. Max and I are paying for everything this end. Lizzie will sort out her side of it.'

Becky's hands were starting to tingle. She thought she was about to hear that it was indeed Max who was getting married and the thought of that, bothered her far more than it should have.

'I'll need your contact details,' Margaret said. 'Is it okay for me to give Lizzie your phone number so that the two of you can discuss what she wants? I'll give you hers too. She lives in Scotland so it'll be a bit difficult for her to get down here very often but she is a bit of a perfectionist and I know, from experience, that she knows exactly what she wants as far as weddings are concerned. Max and I both love her dearly, so it's very important to us that she's completely happy with everything. No expense should be spared – although we'd both rather you didn't tell her that. She would hate to think we were spending a fortune on her big day. She's such a sweet girl. I'm sure you two will get on like a house on fire.'

'I'm sure we will,' Becky said, already feeling envious of this paragon of virtue Max and his mother both loved so dearly.

So it was true; Max was getting married. She remembered the kiss and how he'd seemed almost as surprised by it as she was. Then she remembered what he'd said to her in the car a short while ago. Was he flirting with her to have some fun? Or was he worried she might tell someone about it? Somehow, she couldn't see Max Bedford being worried about anything much at all.

Becky went into professional mode. 'Her name's Lizzie?'

'Yes, Lizzie Marshall. Once you've spoken to her and got an idea of what she wants, you can work out what it'll cost, a ball park figure obviously at this stage and a rough estimate of your fees, if that's possible and we'll get the funds organised. And Becky, I meant it when I said, no expense spared. That goes for your fees too. Don't try to under price yourself to get the job. That's really not necessary, you've got it. Let me know when you've spoken to her and we'll have a proper meeting to discuss things in more detail. So, that's it then. Our first wedding at Beckleston Hall.'

Becky wrote the date down in her notebook, together with the telephone number Margaret gave her. She handed Margaret her card. 'That's got all my details on, including my mobile and email.'

'I think that deserves a toast,' Victoria said. She held up her glass and Margaret and Becky did likewise. 'To Lizzie Marshall's wedding.'

'To Lizzie Marshall's wedding,' Becky said, 'and to Max of course.' She saw the odd look the women gave her.

'Why to Max, dear?' Victoria asked. 'For footing the bill you mean?'

'Well yes ... and ... because it's his wedding too.'

The roar of laughter took her completely by surprise.

'Isn't it?' she asked.

'Good heavens no! Whatever gave you that idea?' Margaret said.

'Max and Lizzie? That ship sailed long ago,' Victoria added. 'And it will take a very special woman to get Max down the aisle again, won't it Margaret?'

Margaret nodded. 'A very special woman indeed!'

Becky was utterly confused – and strangely, relieved. 'Sorry, I ... well I thought, when you said you were paying and that you both loved her dearly, well ...' She was lost for words.

'Oh, of course, dear. No wonder you misunderstood, you don't know about Lizzie and Max. We're paying for the wedding as our wedding present to her and the reason we both love her dearly is because, she is Max's ex-wife. They divorced two years ago but they're the best of friends. It's a long story and one that Max may tell you himself, one day, but suffice to say, this is Lizzie Marshall's wedding and the only part Max is playing in it, is signing the cheques.'

CHAPTER TEN

'So,' Max said, getting into the Range Rover to take Becky home, 'I hear you thought you were going to be organising my wedding. That must have felt a tad awkward.'

'No. Why should it have?' She avoided his eyes as she sat on the passenger seat and pulled the door closed.

'Okay. You're determined to pretend that nothing happened between us, I see. By the way, thanks for not slamming the door this time.'

She sneered at him. 'I'm not pretending. Nothing did happen between us. We kissed; big deal. People do it every day.'

'True.' He started the engine and headed down the drive. 'But people who kiss like that are usually dating, at the very least.'

Becky sucked in a breath. He clearly wasn't going to let this drop. 'Look Max,' she said staring straight ahead, 'I have no idea why you kissed me and even less idea why I let you, but the thing is, I'm going to be working with your mother now.'

'And that affects us how?'

She swivelled in her seat to look at him. 'Because I don't mix business with pleasure.'

'I'm hoping I'm the pleasure bit in that. And ... I think that's possibly the nicest thing you've said to me since we met.'

She saw his sideways glance and the hint of a smile on his lips and she swivelled back, peering out of the passenger window. 'Very funny,' she said.

'Mum wouldn't mind – you mixing business and pleasure, I mean.'

Becky tutted. 'This isn't just about your mother. This is also about me – and what I want.'

'Fair enough. Who are you going to the Valentine's thing with?'

'What?' Her head whipped round.

73

'It's a simple question Becky? Who are you going to the Valentine's Dance with?'

'I'm not telling you.'

'That's mature. I take it that means you don't have a date.'

'No it doesn't! It means it's none of your business.'

'I'm making it my business. Do you have a date?'

She fiddled with her seat belt 'I ... I'm the organiser so I have to be on hand in case something goes wrong.'

'It's organised. What can possibly go wrong at this late stage?'

'You'd be surprised.'

He pulled up outside her cottage, switched off the engine and turned to face her. 'You're right, I would. And even if something did, why would that stop you from having a date?'

'Because ... well, I might have to dash off and leave him.'

She released her seatbelt and was about to open the door but he leant his arm across her and stopped her.

'Do you want me to carry you up the path?'

She held her breath, wondering if he might kiss her again then quickly shoved the door open. 'No. I'll manage thank you.'

Ignoring her, he turned and got out. 'At least hang on to my arm, just in case.' He offered her his crooked elbow.

Reluctantly, she slipped her arm through his. She was glad she did. The path was becoming increasingly icy. They walked to her door in silence and he waited whilst she let herself in.

'Well. Goodbye – and thank you,' she said, giving him a half-hearted smile.

He beamed at her. 'My pleasure. I'll pick you up tomorrow at seven. I'll book a table at the Inn for seven fifteen and – I'll risk you having to dash off.' He turned and strode down the path.

'You'll never get a table at this short notice,' she called

after him, rather taken aback by his remark. 'And I haven't agreed to go with you anyway!'

'Yeah, yeah. See you tomorrow at seven,' he said, without looking back.

'Of all the arrogant, pig-headed ...'

Becky slammed her front door as Max jumped into his car and drove off.

'You'll never believe this Jess,' Becky said, holding the phone to her ear whilst she poured herself a large glass of wine. 'I'm organising a wedding at Beckleston Hall and guess who is getting married?'

'Don't tell me it's Max. I thought he was too good to be true.'

'It's not Max, although I thought it was at first, especially as he's paying for the wedding, jointly with his mother.'

'His mum?'

'No. She's in her seventies.'

'So, you can still get married in your seventies. There's no age limit, you know, which is just as well, for the three of us.'

'I've been married once. I'm not sure I want to do that again. Anyway, I'll tell you because you'll never guess, especially after what Connie Jessop told you. It's his ex-wife! Jess? Jess, are you still there?'

'I'm here. You mean ... Max's ex-wife?'

'The one and only. At least, I assume there's only one ex-wife. Actually, now I think of it, they didn't say. Perhaps he's been married more than once.' Becky took a gulp of wine; she felt she needed it after everything that had happened today.

'No,' Jess said. 'Connie said he was only married once.'

'But Connie said his wife ran off with someone and that he was heartbroken and was still trying to get over her. You don't pay for the wedding of someone you're trying to get over, do you?'

75

'No. I suppose you don't. How strange. So, hold on a minute. His ex-wife is getting married in his mum's house and he and his mum are paying for it?'

'Yep.' Becky flopped onto the sofa.

'Wow! Have you told Susie?'

'Not yet. I'm going to call her now.'

'Can we come round?'

'Of course you can, but it's getting very icy out there so you need to be very careful. Oh and I ... No. I'll save that bit of news until you get here. Give me half an hour will you? I want to call Lily before she has her bath and goes to bed.'

'Okay. You call Lily and I'll call Susie. See you soon.'

Jess and Susie arrived with two bottles of wine and a "Beckleston Bridal Belles", bag.

'Ooh! What's in the bag? Let me guess, you've found a dress for me to borrow. Actually, I really hope you have. The other bit of news, and one I'm not sure is good or bad, is ... Max has asked me to be his date for the Valentine's do and, he's taking me to dinner at the Inn. Well, to be honest, he didn't really ask me, he told me and I know we always go to the dance together so I can still tell him to get lost, if you'd rather.'

'Don't be an idiot,' Jess said. 'Of course you won't tell him to get lost.'

'No way! Do you think either of us would dump him to be with you?'

Becky smiled. 'Yes. Actually I do.'

'Okay, but you wouldn't let us so that's that. Here.' Susie handed her the bag. 'And it's not for you to borrow; it's for you to keep. I threw a few pieces of material together this afternoon. I think it'll fit but I've brought my pins in case it needs a bit of tweaking. Go and try it on.'

Becky opened the bag and peered inside. She pulled out a dress of the richest chocolate brown and creamiest ivory, she'd ever seen. It was made from several layers of chocolate brown, silk chiffon that billowed out from an empire-line, band of ivory taffeta just under the bust. From the centre of the bust area there was a clasp made up of tiny pearl-like beads which swept the low neckline down into a bra top effect. The chiffon straps were overlaid with more pearl beads at the shoulders. Its sheer beauty brought tears to Becky's eyes.

'Don't start bawling. You've got to look your best for tomorrow,' Susie said.

Becky hugged both her friends then dashed upstairs to try it on. When she looked in the mirror, she hardly recognised herself. She ran back downstairs and twirled around the sitting room with the fabric clinging to her hips then floating away.

'Oh Susie, this is magnificent. You're an absolute genius. You really should have been a designer. I've never worn a dress like this – in my entire life. It feels ... well, sort of like I'm wearing nothing, it's so light and yet, it feels as if I'm wearing fairy wings.'

'Okay, no more wine for you,' Jess said grabbing the half empty bottle and hugging it to her chest.

'I'm serious. It's as soft as gossamer. Is it really mine?'

'Yes Cinderella, and you shall go to the ball. Fairy wings; gossamer; what are you going on about?' Jess shook her head but smiled, nonetheless.

'I'm just so excited. This has been one of the best days of my life for ... well, since Lily was born. First Margaret offering me a job and now getting this exquisite dress, not to mention having two of the best friends in the entire world.'

'Um. Aren't you forgetting another couple of pretty spectacular events?' Susie said. 'Like, Max kissing you and then asking you to be his Valentine date. I'd say they both rank pretty highly.'

Becky smiled like a child locked in a sweet shop. 'I'm still not sure if that's good or bad, to be honest. He makes me so mad and yet ... that kiss was pretty sensational.'

'And wait till he sees you in that dress. I think tomorrow night may be the best night you've had in a great many years.' Jess winked at her.

'You'll need shoes too,' Susie said, reaching into her handbag. 'I brought these because they're what I'd suggest to wear with it but you're welcome to pop in to the shop tomorrow and see if there are any others you prefer.'

Susie handed her a pair of chocolate brown satin high heeled shoes that matched the dress to perfection. They were open toed court shoes with two little pearl beads in the centre of the scooped down front.

Becky slipped them on and her smile grew even wider. 'They're perfect Susie. Thank you. Thank you both so much. I-'

'Don't say it; we don't want you to repay us. They're a gift. Now go and take them off before we all turn into pumpkins,' Jess said.

She refilled their glasses as Becky ran up the stairs, two at a time.

CHAPTER ELEVEN

Jess and Susie arrived at Becky's at five p.m. with two bottles of sparkling wine, to help her to get ready for her big date. They gave her a manicure, pedicure, did her make-up and her hair, and even they were stunned by her appearance when she was dressed and ready to go.

'You look fabulous!' Jess said as Becky checked her make-up for the umpteenth time.

'I can't believe how nervous I am,' she said, knocking back another glass of wine. 'The only thing I've been able to eat all day is a slice of toast.'

'Then you'd better slow down on the wine!' Susie said, taking the glass out of Becky's shaking hand.

'It's been so long since I've had a date, that just the thought of it is making me light-headed. I needed the wine to steady my nerves.'

'Well, I think if you have any more, it'll have the opposite effect. Just breathe and try to keep calm.'

'That's easier said than done. The butterflies in my tummy are having a rave ... on crack ... and have clearly downed several gallons of alcohol! I really hope I can eat something at dinner otherwise Max will think I'm one of those women who obsesses about their weight, saying they're full after eating half a lettuce leaf. Oh God! Let me have just one more small glass of plonk. I really need it!'

'No!' Susie said, 'you'll be drinking at the restaurant. If you have any more on a practically empty stomach, it won't just be your butterflies who think they're at a rave.'

'Okay,' Jess said. 'He'll be here in about fifteen minutes so we'll head off.' She hugged Becky and grabbed the remaining wine. 'And I'm taking this, just to be sure. Have fun. We'll see you later, at the dance.'

Susie hugged her too. 'Calm down; you'll have a great time.'

'I'll grab my coat and wait outside,' Becky said. 'I could use the air.'

She put on her coat and waved her friends off then she waited by the door, holding her new shoes in her hands. She'd put on a pair of wellingtons as she didn't want to get them ruined in the snow.

She saw Max's Range Rover pull up and she considered dashing back inside, in case it made her look too eager but she thought he might have seen her so she started to make her way down the path.

He was clearly surprised to see her walking towards him when he got out.

'Am I late?'

'No. I just thought I'd save you the trouble of leading me up the garden path.'

The remark wasn't lost on him and he smiled. 'I'm not completely sure who's leading whom,' he said, strolling round the car to meet her. 'I'm glad to see you're wearing sensible boots. At least I won't have to carry you.'

She reached the passenger door and he opened it for her. Their faces were just inches apart as she stepped forward to get in.

'You look lovely,' he said and then, 'and you smell pretty good too.'

'Thanks. It's called "Seduction".' She held his eyes for a split second then lowered herself slowly onto the seat.

He sucked in a deep breath. 'It's working.'

They arrived at the Inn in a matter of minutes. Max had booked a table in the á la carte restaurant and Becky was surprised to find it wasn't just any table, it was the best table in the house; the secluded one in the corner beside the other inglenook.

Becky excused herself and headed to the Ladies to change her footwear, remove her coat and to check that she still looked okay whilst Max headed towards the table. A few minutes later she was walking towards him.

He was studying the wine list and talking to Trisha, who was laughing with him as though they had known one another for years.

'We'll have a bottle of ...' he stopped mid sentence and his mouth fell open, his eyes full of admiration – and something more. He slowly rose from his seat, in a trancelike state and watched her approach.

Becky felt herself blushing under the intensity of his gaze.

Even Trisha looked stunned.

'Hi Trisha, how are you?' Becky avoided Max's eyes.

'I ... I'm fine thanks Becky. I hardly recognised you love. You look amazing!'

The flush in her cheeks deepened. 'Thanks. You look good too.'

Trisha smiled then turned her eyes back to Max, who was still staring at Becky. 'Sorry Max, what did you say you wanted?'

He didn't answer.

Becky walked around Trisha and slid onto the padded velvet covered bench-seat. Max had taken the seat with its back to the restaurant leaving her the seat facing outwards.

Trisha coughed. 'Would you like me to come back in a few minutes?'

Becky smiled at Max, glanced at Trisha then back to Max. 'Whatever you want is fine with me,' she said.

She saw a look of what she thought was desire flash across his eyes and then he seemed to pull himself together.

'A bottle of Bollinger, please Trisha.' He handed her back the wine list, sat back down and resumed his appreciative appraisal of Becky. 'Are you sure about that?'

Becky was confused. 'Am I sure about what?'

'That whatever I want is fine with you – because, right now, all I want *is* you.'

She didn't know what to say. She cast her eyes down and fiddled with her fork. He was good at this, but then he should be. If any of the rumours about him were true, he had a lot of experience with women, she, on the other hand, hadn't been with a man for five years.

'I meant the wine,' she said, glancing up at him from

81

under her lashes. 'How do you do it? You seem to have everyone eating out of your hands and you've only been in the village for a few days. This table, for example. How did you manage to get this at such short notice?'

He shrugged. 'I told Trisha I wanted the best table in the house, why?'

Becky shook her head. 'It doesn't matter.'

'Is something wrong?'

'No. No, everything's fine.'

She could tell by his eyes that he thought she looked good and yet, he'd said nothing. When Trisha had complimented her, he could have agreed but he hadn't, he'd simply ordered Trisha's most expensive champagne as casually as one would order a glass of house wine. He'd said he wanted her – and even she could see that he was serious but he hadn't said she looked pretty and for some absurd reason, she wanted him to say that more than she had wanted anything for a very long time. She saw the troubled look in his expressive, green eyes.

'So, I'm going to be arranging your ex-wife's wedding,' she said, as coolly as she could.

Trisha returned with the champagne before Max had a chance to answer. She opened the bottle and poured a little into his glass.

He tasted it, nodded and smiled up at Trisha. 'Thanks Trisha, it's fine.'

She filled Becky's glass then topped up Max's. 'I'll give you a few minutes and then I'll take your order. Enjoy.' She winked at Becky, put the bottle in a wine cooler and headed back towards the kitchen.

Max raised his glass. 'Happy Valentine's Day, Becky.'

She raised hers. 'Happy Valentine's Day to you.' She took a sip of champagne, then another and another. A tear began to prick at the corner of her eye. She remembered the last time she'd sat in this very seat with a glass of champagne on a Valentine's Day many years ago; the day Jeremy had proposed.

She shook her head and cleared her throat. What on earth was wrong with her?

'Are you sure you're okay? You seem a little ... distracted.'

'I'm sorry. I ... I just remembered the last time I sat here, a long time ago. This is where my husband proposed. God knows why I thought of that. It ... it must have been the champagne and ... and Valentine's.' She glanced at him briefly then looked away.

'He proposed here – on Valentine's Day?' Max's brows knit together. 'I'm sorry. I had no idea.'

'Why should you? Anyway, as I said, it was a long time ago. Water under the bridge and all ... Oh God! I can't believe I just said that. What the hell is wrong with me?'

'Okay.' Max put his glass on the table and reached out for Becky's free hand. He squeezed it and gave it a gentle shake. 'Look at me Becky. I'm getting worried now. Are you feeling okay? Do you want to go? Just say. I don't mind honestly. Whatever you want is fine with me.'

She took a deep breath and looked into his eyes. She could see his concern and she could see he meant every word. She smiled shyly. 'Is this where I say – all I want is you? Sorry Max, I'm being ridiculous, I know. The truth is; I think I'm a little tipsy already and I'm really nervous. It's been a very long time since I've been on a date and I haven't eaten hardly a thing all day. I was so looking forward to it and Jess and Susie made me this exquisite dress and I thought, for the first time in years, I actually looked quite good and you ... you haven't even said I look nice!'

His mouth fell open in surprise. 'I ... I said you looked lovely when you got in the car!'

'Yes! When I was wearing an old coat. You haven't said anything since ... well, about my dress.'

'Is that what's bothering you? Good God, Becky. Don't you possess a mirror? I honestly didn't think you'd need to hear me say it. Wasn't it obvious? I couldn't even finish my sentence once I saw you. You look ... sensational, unbelievably beautiful, stunning. There are no words sufficient to describe the way you look. You must know that, surely?'

Becky raised tearful eyes to his but she smiled at him. 'Now you're being ridiculous. I just wanted you to say I looked pretty, that's all. You said it when I looked like a bag of old clothes!'

He smiled and his eyes were full of warmth. 'Oh Fifi. I'm sorry. To tell you the truth, I really couldn't think of anything to describe how gorgeous I think you look – how lovely I think you are, so I didn't say anything. I suppose, in a way, I'm nervous too. Don't look at me like that. It's true.'

'I don't believe that. From what I've heard you've got women falling at your feet. You've had hundreds of them. I can't imagine you could ever be nervous.'

His smile faded and he let go of her hand. 'Well, I don't know who told you that and it really doesn't matter. Yes, I've been out with a great many women – although not hundreds, I assure you – and yes, I can throw a line as good as the next man but that's all they are – lines. They don't mean anything. It's a different matter when I'm being sincere; when I think my own feelings may be involved – and it's been a very long time since that's happened to me, so believe me, I'm nervous too.' He knocked back the contents of his glass.

'I'm sorry Max I didn't mean to offend you.'

He smiled again. 'I'm not offended. Whether you believe me or not is up to you but I can assure you of one thing; I'll never lie to you. I haven't lied to any of the women I've dated since my divorce. I lied to someone once and it cost me a very high price. I'll never do that again, especially not to someone I care about – even a little.'

Becky tried to understand what he was saying. 'Are ... are you saying you care about me – a little?'

He took her fingers in his, stroking them with his thumb

and his eyes held hers. 'The truth? I don't know what I feel but I know I feel something. From the moment I first met you, I couldn't stop thinking about you and I wanted to see you again. I even asked Martin Parkes about you but he wouldn't give away any secrets, he just said you were a lovely young woman – which I already knew. The morning I drove through that puddle – that was because I didn't see it, I was preoccupied peering out of the window to see if it was you walking down the street. So yes, I care about you. I'm not making any promises and I'm not looking for a serious relationship so I don't know where this may lead but I know I want to see you again.'

'Have you decided what you want?' Trisha had returned to take their order.

'Sorry Trisha, will you give us another few minutes, please?'

'No problem Max,' Trisha said, smiling then she walked across to another couple to take their order instead.

'Wow!' Becky said, slightly taken aback. 'And I just wanted you to say you thought I look pretty.'

Max winked at her. 'I hope we've established that you do – very much so.'

'I ... I don't know what to say.'

'Just say, you'll see me again, assuming you enjoy yourself tonight, that is. If you don't, just say no. I can take it, and one thing I will promise, no matter what happens, it won't affect your business relationship with Mum.'

'My life is really complicated Max, I – '

'Let's not worry about that. Let's just see how tonight goes and take it from there, okay? Now, we'd better get some food inside you, or you might get drunk and start dancing on the table.' He let go of her hand and started reading the menu.

Becky beamed at him. 'I can assure you, that is one thing I'll never do.'

CHAPTER TWELVE

'Have you spoken to Lizzie yet?' Max asked when they'd ordered.

'No. I was going to call her today but as it's Valentine's, I thought I'd leave it until tomorrow. What's she like?'

'She's lovely. I think you two will get on very well.'

'That's what your mum said. She's very fond of her too isn't she? How long were you married, if it's okay to ask?'

Max leant back in his chair and rested his hands on the edge of the table. 'It's fine. We dated for about a year, were married for four, sort of separated for just over two and we divorced, amicably, about two years ago. It was my fault we split up. I did the old cliché of having an affair with my secretary. Lizzie found out and she left. I spent the next two years trying to get her to come back but, well, things had changed, for her anyway. Then she met Jack – and that's an unbelievable story that I'll tell you some day, she may even tell you herself. Anyway, she met Jack, fell head over heels in love and that, as they say, was that. I knew I'd lost her – for good, so we divorced, and now she's marrying Jack.'

'Wow!' Becky twisted her glass back and forth on the table. 'So ... it was you ... I mean, so you had an affair?'

He nodded 'Are you shocked?'

'A little, yes, to be honest.'

'I did say I'd tell you the truth.'

'Yes you did. But ... if you loved her so much why ...? ' She put her hands in her lap and studied them, avoiding his eyes. 'Sorry, it's none of my business.' She could feel him watching her.

'Why did I have an affair? I've asked myself that question a hundred times.'

She raised her eyes to his. 'Any answers?'

He shrugged and smirked. 'Not really. I suppose the truth is, because I could. No, I don't mean, because I thought I could get away with it. I mean, because I clearly didn't love my wife enough not to. It sounds trite but, if I'd really loved Lizzie as much as I thought I did, I wouldn't have done it. I wouldn't have risked losing her. I really do believe, if you love someone, truly love them, you wouldn't do anything to hurt them. I knew Lizzie would be hurt but I did it anyway. That's not real love.'

'But ... you said you tried to get her back so you must have loved her.'

'I did. I still do, in a way, but not enough. Never enough.'

'How ... how do you feel about her getting married – and getting married at your mum's house too? Are you really okay with it?'

He topped up their glasses as he said, 'Six months ago, I'd have said I wasn't, not completely. Now, yes, yes I'm fine with it. The venue did take me a little by surprise but, somehow, it seems right. She deserves to be happy. I want her to be and Jack really is great. They're a perfect couple.'

'That's good.' She wasn't sure she totally believed him, in spite of the fact that he'd told her he wouldn't lie.

'So, what about you? I'm assuming you're divorced too. You don't wear a ring and I didn't notice any wedding photos in your house but you said your husband proposed in here – was it an unpleasant end?'

Becky hung her head.

'You don't have to talk about it if you don't want to. Just tell me that you're free to see me and that I'm not going to get a visit from an irate husband – that's all I need to know.'

She lifted her head and smiled weakly. 'I'm a widow. My husband ... died ... five years ago last Saturday, to be precise.'

'Oh God, Becky. I'm so sorry. How awful for you.'

She nodded. Max seemed genuinely shocked and she wondered if she should tell him? He'd been open with her, even admitting he'd had an affair. She took a deep breath and a large gulp of champagne.

'I met Jeremy at university, we lived in the same house-share. It wasn't love at first sight, in fact, I'm not really sure when we went from being friends to being in love, it just sort of happened. Anyway, we married on my twenty-fifth birthday and I thought we were happy, then, he seemed to change. I actually thought he was having an affair because he became rather secretive and, little things kept happening. Then I fell pregnant with Lily and –'

'You've got a child?' Max looked stunned.

'Yes! I ... I thought you knew. Surely someone in the village mentioned it?'

Max shook his head but didn't speak.

'Well, she's five next month. She's with her grandparents at the moment and I'm missing her terribly. I ... Oh! I see. If you didn't know then ... I ... I suppose this changes things, as far as you and I are concerned doesn't it? You don't want to date a woman with a child in tow do you?'

At that moment their meals arrived and, for what seemed like hours but was only a matter of minutes, Max studied her face.

'So that's who all the pictures are of, in your house?' he said when they were alone again. 'I thought they were your niece or something. It didn't even occur to me for some reason. Wow!' He emptied his glass in one gulp then he cut into the pan-fried turbot he'd ordered.

Becky had ordered the same but now that it was in front of her, she wasn't sure she was hungry. She took a few mouthfuls and had to admit, it was delicious.

'I take it things have changed,' she said, after several minutes of silence. 'I understand. Don't worry.' Tears began to prick at her eyes and she couldn't look at him. 'We'll call it quits after dinner. You don't have to take me to the dance, Jess and Susie will be there so –'

'Hold on a minute,' he said, putting down his knife and fork. 'What makes you think things have changed? Because you've got a daughter you mean? Do you think that changes me wanting to see you again?'

She raised her eyes to his. 'Well doesn't it? Lily is the most important person in my life and my life revolves around her, if I'm going to be honest. You hadn't bargained on having a five year old around had you? Even if our relationship was just a bit of fun, a child in the picture puts a bit of a dampener on it doesn't it? It's okay, I truly understand.'

'Whoa! I'll admit I didn't know and I'll also admit it is a bit of a shock. I've never dated anyone with a child before so I have no idea what's involved but it doesn't stop me from wanting to see you. I'm not looking for a serious relationship, as I told you, but your daughter doesn't change things from my perspective.' He picked up his cutlery. 'This turbot is excellent.'

Becky didn't know what to think. The last thing she had thought she wanted, just a few days ago, was a man in her life, especially a man like Max Bedford. Now, as she sat across the table from him, listening to him telling her that he wanted to see her again and that he wasn't going to run away at the mention of her daughter, she realised that she didn't want a man – she wanted Max Bedford.

She knew she was taking a risk. He'd made it clear that a long term relationship was out of the question and he'd admitted to cheating on his wife. If anyone should be running away, it should be her but she knew she wouldn't – not yet anyway. It had been a very long time since she'd felt like this about a man, any man, and perhaps her friends were right. Perhaps it was time she had some fun and lived a little.

'So, when will Lily be home?' he asked between mouthfuls.

'She was due home on Sunday but because of the weather, she's stayed on a few extra days. They live over an hour's drive away and, whilst that's not far, I'd rather Harry didn't drive in bad conditions – just in case. He's in his late seventies and he's definitely a fair weather driver. As soon as the roads clear, they'll bring her home.'

89

'Why don't you go and get her?'

'I ... I don't have a car. I had to sell it a few years ago. Things were ... tight after Jeremy ... died.' She didn't want to tell him that, effectively the car had been repossessed.

'I'm sorry. You were telling me about him. You thought he was having an affair. Was he?'

'Oh. No ... he ... he had ... a gambling problem.' Becky cast her eyes down and toyed with the napkin on her lap.

'What?'

She nodded. 'I actually didn't find out until ... oh, I may as well just say it.' She raised her eyes to his. 'Shortly after I told him I was pregnant he disappeared. No note, no phone call, nothing. I thought he'd had an accident but there was no trace of him. Then, I discovered he'd emptied our joint bank account and ... and an account handled by his firm – he was a solicitor – which held a large inheritance from my parents, even though, that was in my sole name. He'd forged my signature.'

'Shit! And run off with the money?' Max was clearly stunned.

Becky nodded.

'You said he died. How? Sorry, if this is too painful, just say.'

'It was five years ago, the pain has subsided – a bit. Apparently, he lost it all, rather quickly and, having nowhere else to go, he came back here a few months later ... and ... well, the police said he threw himself in Beckleston River – or fell. They found his body in the January, a few days after my birthday; Lily was born that March. His parents were devastated. They couldn't believe their only son could do such a thing. I was just numb. If it hadn't been for Jess and Susie, I don't know how I would have got through the first couple of years.' She realised she was rambling. She licked her lips and gulped down the contents of her glass as if her revelation had parched her.

Max leant back against his chair. 'Bloody Hell! And your parents? You said one of the accounts held an inheritance from them. Was it a trust fund they'd set up or are they ...?'

Becky sucked in a deep breath and nodded. 'They ... they died in a car crash just before my sixteenth birthday.'

'Shit Becky!' Max leant forward and took one of her hands in his. 'You've had it really tough. I'm so, so sorry.'

She shrugged, trying not to show her pain. 'That's life, as they say. Well, that's taken a bit of the fun out of this evening hasn't it?' She forced a smile. 'Perhaps we could change the subject. I'm not sure I can handle much more of this doom and gloom. I ... I'm astonished all that came out actually. I don't usually tell anyone. Oh ... and Jeremy's ... financial problems ... are not common knowledge so ...'

'I won't say a word, don't worry. I'm glad you told me though.' He squeezed her hand in his and smiled.

'I don't know why I did, to be honest. I hardly know you after all.'

'Sometimes, we need to share things Becky and sometimes, it helps if it's with someone we hardly know. You can trust me not to repeat anything you've told me. Would you like a dessert or coffee or something?'

Becky shook her head. 'No thanks.'

'Perhaps, we should head to the dance, then, if you're feeling up to it. I'll get the bill.'

'Thanks Max. I could do with letting my hair down a bit.'

She studied his face and somehow, she knew he was telling the truth. Her secrets were safe with him. Her heart, on the other hand, might be a different matter.

CHAPTER THIRTEEN

Becky was enjoying herself, despite the painful memories that had flooded back in the restaurant earlier. Everyone was paying her compliments and Max was being so attentive and thoughtful that for one night, she thought she could forget her past and all her present worries; even forget she was a mother and instead, be a sexy, vibrant young woman, dancing in the arms of the most incredible man she was ever likely to meet.

She couldn't believe she'd gone from thinking that he was an arrogant twerp – and a lot worse, to thinking that he was someone rather special, in a matter of a few days. Of course, she had no illusions, in spite of the wonderful things he'd said. Men like Max Bedford didn't fall for women like her, especially when they had a child to consider, she knew that. She was just different, that must have been it. He was used to women falling at his feet at first glance. She hadn't, and he had found that intriguing, possibly even a challenge. But even if she only had this one night with him, she was beginning to believe, it would be worth it.

He'd said he wanted to see her again but that could have been a line. She'd have to wait and see. If she did see him again, she'd have to make sure that Lily didn't get attached to him – but she didn't really think there was any risk of that. Max was hardly the type of man who would want to take the family out. She'd probably only see him in the evening, once Lily was in bed. Or maybe only at the weekend. He'd told her that he lived in London.

It had been years since she'd thrown caution to the wind and she'd been so busy trying to juggle money, pay off Jeremy's debts, be a mother and maintain her business, that she'd forgotten how to be a woman and, she'd forgotten that she actually used to enjoy having sex.

She spent the evening dancing, laughing and having fun. And she spent most of it in Max's arms, desperately wanting to kiss him but knowing that was one thing she couldn't do in public, and desperately wanting to make love with him – and that was obviously, another.

'Did you have a good time tonight?' Max asked when he pulled up outside her cottage, shortly after midnight.

'The best. Thank you so much Max. I honestly can't remember when I last enjoyed myself this much. I'm sorry I spoiled dinner by telling you all that stuff. I can't believe I did. I never tell anyone.'

'I'm glad you did and you didn't spoil dinner one bit.'

She wondered what to do next. Max was sitting at a slight angle, watching her and she suddenly realised that he didn't seem to have any intention of getting out. Had he had second thoughts already? Something very cold wrapped itself around her heart and started squeezing.

'D ... did you have a good time?' she asked, half afraid to hear his answer.

He brushed a stray hair from her cheek with his hand and something flashed across his eyes. He smiled and his voice was soft when he spoke.

'Even better than I expected.' He turned her face to his with his fingers and leant across and kissed her.

It wasn't like his previous kiss. It was soft and gentle, tentative almost and he pulled away after just a moment.

'Shall I walk you to the door?' he asked, his seatbelt still fixed in place.

Becky was confused. Had this all been a game after all? Had he indeed "led her up the garden path" as she'd first suspected he might? Now that he knew he could have her, he no longer wanted her, was that it? She thought she might burst into tears any minute. Should she ask him in? Would he say no? She shook her head, afraid her voice would betray her.

'I'll call you,' he said but he didn't ask for her number.

She took a deep breath, gave him a quick, false smile and pushed open the door. 'Of course you will,' she said, her voice full of emotion. She got out and stumbled up the path, completely forgetting that she hadn't changed her footwear.

She opened the door and almost jumped out of her skin. Max was beside her and was spinning her around to face him.

'Don't get upset,' he said, his troubled eyes searching hers. 'I will call you; tomorrow, first thing.'

'You don't have my number.' She couldn't look at him and cast her eyes down.

'Yes I do. Apart from the fact that you gave it to Mum yesterday, I looked up your address and phone number the minute I found out your surname – which was on Saturday after I saw you in the Stores. Mary Parkes told me and she would have told me a lot more besides if Martin hadn't come out and sent her off to make him tea.'

Becky was astonished. 'On Saturday! But ... when you took me home on Sunday, you asked for my address.'

'Beckleston's a small village and there's only one R. Cooper – for Rebecca obviously – but I didn't know exactly where Rosemary Cottage was, although ... I was actually looking for it that morning, when I soaked you. Martin Parkes wouldn't tell me anything else about you – but I did at least, have your name, address and phone number.'

She couldn't believe what he was saying. 'Look Max. I'm not sure what's going on here. One minute you say that all you want is me and that you got my name, address and phone number within hours of meeting me, and the next, you're giving me a peck on the cheek and saying you'll call! I'm not expecting a serious relationship – you've made it perfectly clear you don't want that – and I'm not asking you to make me any promises or commitments; I know this won't last, but a bit of consistency would be nice. You either want me or you don't, which is it?'

Max blinked several times in surprise. 'I thought I'd made that abundantly clear and I kissed you on the lips, not the cheek. I want you and you don't know quite how much, believe me –'

'Then why wouldn't you get out of the car?'

He let out a deep sigh. His hands were resting on her shoulders and he let them slide down the length of her arms then took her hands in his. 'Because I knew if I did, I wouldn't want to get back in, at least, not until the morning – if then. I didn't want to put you under that pressure. If I kiss you properly tonight, I'm not going to want to stop, and I don't trust myself. I wouldn't force you, obviously, but – and I say this not out of conceit but out of honesty – if I want to get someone to go to bed with me, I can, believe me.'

She did believe him. She raised her eyes to his. 'You wouldn't need to stop.'

He gazed into her eyes. 'Are you saying ... Becky, are you sure? Are you really sure you want to do this? There's no rush. After everything you've told me tonight about your life, I completely understand why you'd want to take things slowly; get to know me. I can wait until you're ready. Honestly, I can wait.'

'I can't. I'm ready now.' She stood on her tiptoes, grabbed his coat collar pulling him towards her, and kissed him on the lips.

He wrapped his arms tightly around her in response, kissing her deeply then he swept her up in his arms, carried her inside and kicked the door closed behind him.

It was everything she knew it would be – and a lot more besides. To say Max was a good lover would be a gross understatement. He was sensational. Becky had only had three lovers before him so she wasn't widely experienced in this field but even she knew, any man who could give a woman that many orgasms in just one night and so much pleasure that, at one point, she honestly thought she would pass out from sheer bliss, was something special.

Even when she finally fell asleep, he gave her pleasure – she dreamed of him – and when she opened her eyes and found him staring at her, with a heated look of passion in his eyes, a tidal wave of excitement swept through her.

'Good morning gorgeous,' he said, when he finally pulled away from kissing her.

'It certainly is. That's the best wake-up call I've ever had.'

'That's just the slumber setting, wait till the bells really start ringing.'

He kissed her again and she wriggled herself closer to him, needing to feel every inch of his firm body against hers. He kissed her mouth, her neck and eyes, then back to her mouth again. His strong, smooth hands caressed her breasts and then his mouth replaced them. His hands slid down, gently stroking her stomach, her hips and then inside her thighs. His mouth followed.

When he slid his finger inside her, stroking her with his thumb she gave a gasp of sheer pleasure; almost surprised pleasure. Every time he'd done this last night it had felt different, better than before and this morning was no exception. New waves of excitement built within her; new yearnings took hold. She didn't want it to stop and yet, she wasn't sure how much of this her heart could take; it felt ready to burst from her chest, like the jet engine of a seven-four-seven, revving up, racing as momentum increased then roaring as it lifted off the ground and into the heavens.

Her blood grew red hot in her veins; her head pounded in time with the drum-beat of her heart; every nerve in her body sang out in operatic proportions then finally, deep inside, the climax, taking her completely by surprise even though she had felt it building and should have been expecting it.

His mouth found hers and she kissed him hungrily.

'More?' he said, passion still burning in his eyes.

'Hell yes!' She pushed him on to his back and kissed him then her mouth followed on his body, the exact path he'd taken on hers. She climbed on top of him and slid him into her, closing her eyes as she felt him inside her. She knew she gave him as much pleasure as he gave her and she revelled in it. Moving faster, rolling her hips to increase the depths he reached.

She had never felt this sensual or sexy or abandoned and she savoured every minute, every glorious second until he too, reached the point of climax and she slowed the pace down, drawing out the final moment until neither of them could hold back.

'You're incredible!' he said after a few minutes. 'And that's not a line. I really mean it. I think I can honestly say, I've never wanted a woman as much as I want you or as many times in one night.' He kissed her to prove his point.

'It's that perfume,' she joked. 'I told you it was called "Seduction"; it obviously works. Jess bought it for me for Christmas. The gift that goes on giving.'

'Are you sure it's not called "Viagra"? I've never taken it and thank God, I've never needed to but even I didn't think it was physically possible to get so many erections without chemicals.'

She wriggled her hips so that she could slowly kiss his neck, then his eyes, then his ear lobes, then his nipples.

'You're insatiable,' he moaned softly. 'I'm not sure I've got any energy left.'

She lifted her head and her brown curls fell across her flushed cheeks. Her eyes filled with passion. 'Well,' she said 'I'll see if there's something I can do about that.' And she knew exactly what that was.

'I needed that,' Max said leaning back against the headboard and pulling Becky into his arms. 'I hadn't realised how hungry I was – for anything other than you, that is, until I smelt that toast.'

Becky had made toast and coffee, whilst Max had dozed off for a few minutes and she'd brought them up on a tray. When they finished eating, she moved the tray onto the bedside cabinet.

Resting her head against his chest, she revelled in the feeling of his skin against hers. His arms made her feel secure and she hadn't felt like that in a very long time. As she listened to the rhythmic beating of his heart, she realised she didn't want this moment to end; she didn't want to let him go. She raised her face to his and looked into his eyes.

He smiled down at her 'I could get used to this,' he said, gently stroking her hair with one hand and holding her close with the other.

'Me too.' She kissed him softly on the lips then moved down to his neck.

'Hold on,' he said, pulling away from her. 'Sorry to be unromantic but, I need to go to the loo; blame the coffee.'

She smiled and watched him get out of bed and head to the bathroom. The sight of his naked body made her hope he wouldn't be long.

He wasn't. 'I hate to tell you this,' he said, climbing back into bed beside her, 'but it's snowing again.'

Her mood changed instantly. 'Really?' Her eyes filled with tears.

'What's wrong Becky? Oh, it's Lily isn't it? More snow means she won't be back today doesn't it?'

She nodded. 'Or anytime soon, at this rate. It took over a week for the roads to clear when we had that last lot of snow in January. Country roads aren't high on the Council's list of priorities.'

'Why don't you go and get her?'

'I told you, I haven't got a car.'

'No – but I have. And I'm used to driving in the snow. I drive to France every year for skiing so this is no problem for me, I can assure you. Of course, I can't account for others but I'm a good driver and I've never been involved in an accident. Sorry – that was tactless of me after what you told me about your parents. What I meant was ... well, Range Rovers are pretty safe to be in anyway. Just say the word and we'll go.'

Becky's eyes shot to his face. 'Do you mean it? Really? You'd do that – for me?'

His brows knit together. 'Of course I would. It's not a big deal.' He looked her straight in the eye. 'I'd fight dragons for you Becky. No! Actually, that's not true. I rather like dragons. Never bumped into one of course and I'm not sure I'd feel the same if one breathed fire on me but I'd like to think we could be friends. I'd fight monsters for you though, so going to pick up Lily's a cinch.'

Becky laughed. 'You're mad.'

He studied her face for a moment then said, 'About you, I think I am. Now give them a call and say we'll be down in about an hour or so.'

'Oh Max. I don't know what to say. Thank you, thank you!' She kissed him frantically.

He reached over and grabbed the phone from the bedside cabinet. 'Call now, before I change my mind and decide not to let you move from this bed.'

She took the phone and dialled the Coopers. She told Sarah that a friend had offered to drive her and that she'd be picking Lily up. They were obviously surprised but Becky didn't give them a chance to discuss it. 'We'll be there by eleven-thirty,' she said. It was nine-forty-five when she hung up.

'How can I ever thank you for this Max?'

'You said they're about an hour away, maybe a bit longer in this weather but we still have about twenty minutes. I know exactly how you can thank me. Come here Fifi.'

CHAPTER FOURTEEN

The snow had started to settle on top of the layer still remaining from the previous snowfall, and by the time they were nearing the Cooper's, there was at least another inch on the pavements. Some of the main roads had been cleared and gritted but the new snow was covering the layer of grit and Becky knew she wouldn't be happy until she, Lily and Max were safe and warm in Rosemary Cottage.

She was grateful to Max for doing this, and the journey down had been almost a breeze. There weren't many other vehicles on the roads and they'd made good time, despite starting out a little later than planned. She never felt totally at ease in a car though, after losing her parents in a motorway pile-up and, although it was a freak accident, motorways made her anxious.

Max seemed to sense this and he told her funny stories about his childhood and the strange and wonderful Christmas presents his father had made him, like the money tree, where he'd got a branch and taped pound coins on every twig shooting off it, just to prove that money can grow on trees. To a six year old boy, that was magical.

'Dad used to say we should believe in magic and that anything is possible if we want it enough. He died ten years ago – actually, just before I met Lizzie, and it really knocked me for six. I still miss him.'

'He sounds like a wonderful father.'

'He was the best.'

'That's one thing I feel torn about. In one way, I wish Jeremy had seen Lily but part of me is glad he didn't. It was bad enough him abandoning me when I was pregnant but if it had been after Lily was born, it would have been worse somehow.'

'I don't know anything about it, apart from what you've told me and he obviously had a serious problem but I don't know how any man could abandon his wife and child. I don't think I ever could. I don't know, of course, never having been in that position but, some things you just believe aren't in your character.'

'It happens more than you think,' she said, glancing out of the passenger window and casting her mind back, to yet more painful memories.'

'Is this the road?' Max asked a few minutes later. The Sat Nav says it is, although she has been known to lie to me before.' He grinned and slowed down until a woman's voice said, 'You've reached your destination.'

'Sorry, I was miles away. Yes, this is it. Do you want to meet the Coopers?'

'I'd better say hello. It would be rude not to.'

They got out of the car and walked up the path. At the door, Max gave her a quick kiss.

'Might be the last chance for a while,' he said, smiling longingly at her.

Sarah Cooper opened the door before she had chance to reply and a mini version of Becky, all brown curls and deep brown eyes, threw herself into her mother's waiting arms.

'Mummy, Mummy! I love you!' Lily squealed as Becky lifted her up and hugged her tightly to her.

'I love you too sweetheart,' Becky said, covering her daughter's face in kisses.

'Hi, I'm Becky's friend Max.' He held out his hand to Sarah Cooper and to her husband Harry who had joined the commotion at the door.

Sarah took Max's hand and shook it gingerly, eyeing him up and down and clearly wondering what sort of "friend" he was to Becky.

'Won't you come in?'

'Actually Sarah, Harry, if you don't mind, we'd like to get straight back on the road. It's still snowing and I won't be happy till we're home. Thanks so much for taking care of Lily. I'll call you soon. Say 'Goodbye' to nanna and grandpa, darling.'

'Bye. Are we going in that big car Mummy?' Lily had already moved on to the next bit of excitement.

'Yes darling, we are. This is Max and he is driving us. Say Hello, and say thank you to nanna and grandpa, Lily.'

Lily turned a beaming cherubic face towards Max 'Hello.' Then to her grandparents, 'Thank you.' Then, clinging to her mother, she turned her eyes back to the Range Rover, eager to get inside and see what new things she could find.

Harry handed Max Lily's case and Max said goodbye to them as Becky thanked them and promised she'd call. She didn't hug them and a slight tension was evident to all parties, except Lily.

Lily climbed onto the back seat and Becky strapped her in.

'May I have my music please?' Lily asked.

'Of course you may.' Becky reached into her daughter's bag and pulled out her iPod.

'Would you like me to sit next to you?'

'No thank you, Mummy, you can sit with the nice man.' Lily switched on her music and beamed at Becky and then at Max. 'This is a big car,' she yelled above her music, 'and it's very nice.'

Max smiled at Becky. 'She's obviously got good taste – and five going on fifteen by the sound of her.'

Becky nodded and smiled at Lily who was now happily singing along to her favourite tunes and investigating her surroundings.

'She's very grown up for her age and so independent, it worries me sometimes.'

'Never worry about that,' Max said as they both got in and he pulled away from the Cooper's house. 'Independence is a good thing. Tell me to mind my own business if you want but, is there some tension between you and Jeremy's parents?'

Becky's eyes shot to his face. 'Was it that obvious?'

'Yes.'

'Well, yes, there is. They were so shocked about what happened and, to be honest, we had some really bad arguments, in the beginning. They even said they were going to see if they could get a custody order for Lily.'

'What?'

Becky nodded. 'It was partly because they didn't believe Jeremy would have done what he did; stolen the money and forged my signature on my inheritance fund and then, when he turned up in the river, Sarah almost accused me of taking the money myself and pushing Jeremy in!'

'Shit! She didn't! Sorry.' He glanced in the rear-view mirror at Lily but she was still singing happily and making her teddy bear dance on her lap.

Becky glanced round too, smiled at her daughter then turned back to Max. 'It was a truly awful time. I don't really blame her. I couldn't believe he'd done it myself so imagine how hard it was for them – and, he was their only son so they idolised him. I think people lose their sanity when someone dies, especially so suddenly and horribly and we all said things we wouldn't have under normal circumstances. We didn't speak for several months though, from just after Lily was born in the March, to her first Christmas. Harry sent a card and a present for her and I wrote and thanked them and said they could come and see her on Boxing Day for tea. It was not a fun day, I have to say but since then, things have got a lot better and last year, I let her stay with them for a few days every few months and that has increased now to a week or in this case, ten days. She's their only grandchild so it's important for them to spend time with her.'

'I would have told them to Fu ... get lost. You're nothing short of a saint Becky.'

'I'm far from that. Actually, I did some horrible things. I boxed up all his things, the stuff he'd left; he only took a few things when he left.'

'Apart from all the money you mean?'

'Apart from that, and I drove over to their place, dumped it all on their doorstep, rang the bell and left. Even the wedding photos, in fact, every photo I ever had of him.

That was mean.'

'No it wasn't. What happened about the money? Sorry, I'm not prying but did you sue his firm for negligence, fraud and embezzlement or something?'

'No. I hired a solicitor but they argued that I couldn't prove it wasn't my signature, that Jeremy was my husband and therefore I had full knowledge, and that he'd taken the money from me after the funds had left their control. That part was true. He transferred the money to our joint account then out again to one in his own name. He did it over a period of several months and not in a lump sum, so no one ever questioned it, me included. I had a separate business account, thank God and I was so involved with my business and that account that Jeremy handled all our personal stuff. He did ask me to sign a couple of things regarding the inheritance fund and told me they were for investment and such like. I didn't check properly. I trusted him, completely and utterly.'

'And he took every penny?'

'Two hundred and fifty thousand pounds and change.'

'Two ...!' Max almost swerved the car. 'Sorry but sh..God. Did he leave you with anything?'

'He left me Lily and she's worth more to me than all the money in the world.'

Max didn't respond.

'I know it's unbelievable that I had no idea and it was my fault because I never checked our bank account, but Jeremy always asked me if I needed any cash and he drew it out and gave it to me. I actually thought he was being considerate and saving me the effort. It was only during that last week that I started to worry because I got a call from the bank holding my business account. They were checking my request to transfer all the money into my joint account at another bank. The business account was in my sole name, fortunately. I said I'd made no such request so they stopped the transaction. I had to go and see them and they showed me a form with my signature on. It was only then I started to panic and check the other accounts. They were empty. I honestly thought we'd been hacked or something, you know, that someone had stolen our identities. I couldn't get hold of Jeremy, he wasn't answering his phone and when I called his firm, to ask about my inheritance fund they said they no longer dealt with it as I'd instructed another firm – which I hadn't. One of the partners spoke to me and suggested I needed to speak to my husband, urgently, and said that they had fired him two days before, on suspicion of attempting to embezzle client funds. They had contacted the police.'

'Bloody Hell! And every penny of yours had gone?'

'All of it and a lot more besides.'

Max glanced across at her. 'What does that mean?'

'It means, not only did he waste all of our money, apart from the money in my business account but he also borrowed a further forty thousand pounds from various banks, credit cards and loan companies, all in joint names. I managed to reach an agreement with them all, or I thought I had, to stop the interest accruing, repay reduced amounts and in monthly instalments. I've spent the last five years trying to do that but it may all be to no avail.'

'Jesus Christ Becky!'

'I'm sorry. I don't know why I'm telling you all this. No one knows the full details apart from Jess and Susie, my solicitor, Jeremy's parents and all the creditors of course. His firm managed to keep it out of the press and obviously, there was no prosecution.'

'I'm glad you've told me. Why did you say to no avail?'

'I got a letter on Friday saying that one of the creditors hadn't agreed to the reduced repayment scheme. This creditor has been taken over and they are going for the full amount owed and all the interest, so they're all saying the agreement's void and going for the lot. With actual interest, the debts come to something in the region of sixty or seventy thousand or more and I've only paid off about fifteen. I've got about another ten to pay assuming the original agreement still stands. If it doesn't, well, I'll lose everything.'

'Good God, Becky!'

They travelled for a while in silence until Max pulled up outside Rosemary Cottage.

'Listen. I know now isn't the time because you want to be with your daughter but this is rubbish. Your solicitor is clearly useless. I'll come back later, when Lily's in bed and you're going to give me all the paperwork on this and I'm going to get it sorted. We'll make an appointment to see my solicitor. Don't argue. I was a banker remember? Oh sh.. I mean, no wonder you took an instant dislike to me. You must really hate the banks. I remember you called me "an arrogant London banker".'

'I did and I'm so sorry about that. I had no right to take it out on you. And, I shouldn't really hate the banks, it isn't really their fault. They didn't know Jeremy was a lying, cheating, thief. But I can't ask you to get involved in this, it's a real nightmare, I can assure you. You've got better things to occupy your time.'

'Not until I can see you again I haven't and you didn't ask, I offered. I can help Becky, trust me, I know how the banks work and I will sort this out for you. What I don't know or can't sort, my solicitor will. He's one of the best in the City.'

'But ... I can't afford –'

'Oh for heaven's sake Becky, forget about that. I know this is difficult for you and I know you may feel you hardly know me, although, after last night, I think you know me a lot better than most people.' He smiled. 'Now, come on, the sooner we do this the sooner you can stop worrying about it and it must have been one hell of a worry if you've been struggling to pay all that money back over the last five years with the prospect of another few years to go.'

He turned round to see Lily. She was fast asleep and her head was lolling to one side, her bear clutched firmly in her little hand.

Becky turned round too and their eyes met.

'The carefree innocence of childhood,' he said. 'You open the door and I'll bring her in and her bag.'

He got out and gently lifted Lily into his right arm, then grabbed her bag with his left hand. She let out a little sigh and nuzzled up against him. He realised he couldn't remember ever picking up a child before, although he thought he must have, at some stage. Some of his friends had kids.

She smelt of soap and he had the most bizarre and overwhelming urge to protect this little girl from any and all harm. Stupid, he knew and yet he couldn't deny he felt it, just like he couldn't deny that, the more he got to know about Becky, the more he realised, he would find it very hard to leave.

'Can you put her on the sofa please? I don't want to take her to her room. Having been away for so long I don't want her to wake up and feel disorientated.'

Max put her down gently and covered her with the throw resting on the sofa back.

Becky watched him, surprised and yet not, by his thoughtfulness. She realised she had totally misjudged him when she'd met him on Saturday morning and it struck her that people are so often not what we think. But she also knew how easy it was for people to deceive.

She had thought Jeremy was considerate and caring, although his mood swings had troubled her from early on; she just chose to ignore them. When he proposed, she had doubts but she'd come to depend on him and, apart from Jess and Susie, she had no one to turn to. She thought she loved him but, more importantly, she thought he loved her. He promised to protect her and take care of her and at the time, she had really needed someone to do that.

Almost as soon as they married, he changed. His moods got worse and she had wondered, more often than she cared to admit, whether Jeremy had, in fact just married her for her inheritance. He knew about it because he worked for the firm handling her parents' estate; he also knew it became hers on her twenty-fifth birthday, the year they married.

Max could turn out to be the same, she realised. He wasn't after her money – she didn't have any now – but he wanted her and he could, if it suited him, she thought, lie and cheat to get what he wanted. Yet there was something about him that made her feel safe. She'd told him more about herself in the last twenty-four hours than she'd told most people who'd known her all her life and he hadn't judged her or belittled her but he had taken control, and that did remind her of Jeremy. The similarity ended there, as Max's next words proved.

'Okay, as she's asleep, do you want to dig out the papers now? I can take them with me or read them here, whichever you'd prefer. Naturally, I won't do anything without asking you first but I would like to see if I know anyone at the banks involved and to chat it over with my solicitor, if that's okay with you. I'll tell you exactly what he says – or we can phone him together, if you'd prefer. He'll be in the office now.'

'No ... in case Lily wakes up, I'd rather she doesn't hear it. I know she's young and wouldn't understand but children pick up much more than we think. I'll get them and you can read them here or take them, I don't mind either way.'

Max nodded. 'Shall I make some tea?'

'Oh, sorry. Yes please, if you don't mind.'

'Don't be sorry Becky. It's not a problem. Come here.' He walked towards her and she met him halfway. He wrapped his arms tightly around her and kissed the top of her head then he let her go, smiled at her and went to the kitchen to make the tea.

Becky found the papers with ease; she kept them all together in a large box. She picked it up and carried it to the kitchen, placing it on the counter. 'Are you sure you don't want to reconsider? There are a lot of papers.'

He turned and glanced at the box, raising his eyebrows in mock surprise. 'I needed something to read.'

She went to him and put her arms around his waist, tilting her face up to his. 'Lily's clearly a better judge of character than I am. You really are a nice man, aren't you? How will I ever be able to thank you for all this?'

A wicked smile spread across his lips and he pulled her tighter to him. 'The same way you did this morning, only, not right now, of course. I'll accept delayed thanks.'

'And, will you take instalments?'

'I'll take anything I can get.'

He kissed her tenderly, a long, slow, gentle kiss that seemed to touch her heart and soothe her soul.

When they finally stopped, Becky saw Lily standing by the kitchen door, watching them. She had one finger in her mouth and was holding her bear in her other hand. 'Lily!' Becky pulled herself away from Max. She hadn't wanted her daughter to see this.

'Was the nice man kissing you, Mummy? Like they do on the telly?'

'Um!'

'Yes,' Max said in a gentle tone, before Becky could think of anything to say. 'Your Mummy and I like one another. Do you mind me kissing her?'

Becky looked horrified but Lily tilted her head to one side then shook her abundant curls and smiled. 'No. It's nice of you to kiss Mummy. Nobody kisses her 'cept me. Do you like it?'

'Yes, I like it very much.'

'Do you like it, Mummy?'

Becky was stunned. Max had handled Lily's question truthfully and simply, whereas she would have made up some silly excuse, effectively lying to her child. 'Yes, Lily, I like it very much.'

Lily nodded several times as if she agreed. 'May I go and play with my dolls?'

'Of course you may darling. Would you like something

to drink?'

'No thank you.' She smiled at Max. 'You may kiss Mummy again, if you like.'

'Thank you Lily, I will.'

Lily turned and skipped off to her room, humming a tune.

'Definitely five going on fifteen,' Max said. 'Now, as I have your daughter's permission, where were we?'

CHAPTER FIFTEEN

Max left fifteen minutes later, taking the box of papers with him and saying he'd call. When the phone rang an hour later, Becky thought it might be him. She saw the number on caller display and recognised it as the number Margaret had given her, for Lizzie.

'Hi, Becky, this is Lizzie Marshall, is this a convenient time to have a quick chat?'

She sounded nice, Becky thought. 'Hi Lizzie, yes, it's fine. I'm looking forward to working with you on your wedding.'

'Me too. Margaret says you are very experienced so I'm open to your suggestions but I just want a small wedding, nothing too fancy, despite the fact that Max and Margaret are footing the bill and have no doubt told you, to spare no expense.' She giggled.

'Um, actually yes, they have.'

'I knew it. They are such lovely, generous people. Have you known them long?'

This question took her a little by surprise. 'Um. No. In fact, I only met Mrs ... I mean, Margaret on Monday and Max on Saturday but they both seem very nice.'

'Oh, they are. Now, Margaret also says your two best friends own a hairdressers and a Bridal shop, is that true?'

'Yes, Jess owns "Prime Cuts Too" and Susie owns "Beckleston Bridal Belles". I can highly recommend them both, not just because they're my friends but because they are true professionals and both very talented. Susie designs and makes many of the brides and bridesmaid dresses herself. The men's formal wear is standard, either for sale or hire. She sells everything you could want and has an online store as well as a website, showing her designs. If you give me your email, I can send you their details if you like?'

'That would be great. Is there a local florist too?'

'Yes, "Stephanie's Stems", I'll send you Stephanie's

111

details as well.'

'Excellent. I'm hoping to get down in a month or so, when the weather improves so we can all meet up then, if that's convenient but in the meantime, shall I just email you my thoughts and you can let me know what you think and any ideas you may have.'

'That would be great.'

They exchanged details and said their goodbyes and Becky rejoined her daughter. She'd been playing with her dolls and interestingly, the male doll with the blond hair had been renamed Max and the female doll with the brown hair, Mummy. Becky wasn't totally convinced she wanted to play this game but as it seemed to involve lots of drinking tea and kissing, it wasn't too bad.

The phone rang and she saw it was Jess. She left Lily playing and went downstairs, knowing Jess would want details of last night which she didn't want Lily to hear.

'We couldn't wait any longer,' Jess said, 'I'm at Susie's shop and we've got you on speaker. What happened last night? I saw his car was there this morning until about ten forty-five so it's obviously very good news. Did I see him carrying Lily today? Is she home?'

'Yes, to both. He stayed, we had the best sex EVER and I do mean EVER and this morning, he took me to get Lily and what's more, I've told him everything, I'm not really sure how, he just seems to be so easy to talk to. He says he may be able to help me with the banks and he's taken the papers to read. Wouldn't that be great? Hello? Are you still there?'

'We're here,' they said in unison.

'That's amazing. I told you he was perfect for you didn't I?' Susie said.

'And we both told you, you needed a man. I haven't heard you sound this happy since ... well, since Lily was born.'

'I know. I must admit you were both right and I was wrong. Of course, it'll all end in tears but even so, I won't regret it. These have been the best two days of my life so far, apart from Lily, of course.'

'So, he knows about Jeremy, the debts, the suicide?'

'Everything. He even knows about my rift with the Coopers and my mum and dad's accident. I can't believe how much I've told him. Oh and Jess, he told me the reason for his divorce. Connie got the wrong end of the stick. It was Max who had the affair, although he did regret it and spent two years trying to get his wife back – but, that's not for general consumption so if anyone asks, please say you don't know.'

'We will. So, he had an affair? Does that worry you?'

'Why should it? It was a long time ago and he clearly realises it was a very big mistake. Anyway, it won't affect me. We're not likely to last very long.'

'Why do you say that? He must like you a lot to go and get Lily with you and to take on the banks, this could be it Becky, your new start and a chance for real happiness.'

'It could be, but I doubt it. Max Bedford can have – and admits he has had – a great many women, can you honestly see him wanting to stick around here for very long with a woman who has a child? I'm just a novelty. He's rich, he's gorgeous, he's great company, caring, thoughtful and, you're so right about him Susie; he is a demigod. I can't even begin to describe the things he did to me last night and this morning and ... let's just say ... I've had sex more times in the last twenty four hours than I had on my two week honeymoon! And not just sex but heart stopping, head pounding, thinking you might just die from pleasure sex!'

The line went dead.

A few minutes later, they called back. 'Um, you know we had you on speaker, well, because we were listening we didn't notice but the vicar came in and, we hate to tell you this but, he heard the whole of the last few minutes conversation. I don't know who was more shocked, him or us.'

'OH MY GOD! Did he know it was me on the line?'

113

'Possibly.'

'What do you mean possibly?'

'When he left he said, "Tell Becky my lips are sealed but my confessional is always open."'

Max called fifteen minutes later to ask if he could pop in that evening and Becky told him Lily went to bed at about seven-thirty so anytime after eight would be fine. At five minutes past eight, he pulled up outside.

He had a bottle of wine in one hand and an iPad in the other and as soon as she had closed the door, he put them on the table and pulled her into his arms.

'I can't believe how slowly time goes when you're waiting to go somewhere,' he said after kissing her. 'I checked my watch hadn't stopped, every few minutes, for the last hour.'

'Do Rolex watches often stop?' she asked, raising her eyebrows and tilting her head back to look at him.

He grinned, 'Anything's possible, as my dad used to say. Oh, by the way, I popped into the Stores on the way here and the vicar said to give you his regards when I saw you next.'

Becky flushed crimson and buried her head in his chest. 'Dear God.'

'Is something wrong?'

'Um. I know I shouldn't have and please don't be cross but Jess and Susie called to ask about last night and they had me on speaker. I didn't tell them everything honestly but I ... I mentioned that I had sex last night and ... as everyone saw us together ... it was obviously with you. The vicar dropped into Susie's and heard me say it.' She finally looked up at him. 'I'm so sorry Max. Are you cross?'

He burst out laughing. 'Did you just say sex or did you say good sex?'

'Um. I actually said heart stopping, head pounding, thinking you might just die from pleasure, sex.'

His eyes held hers and his smile lingered. 'And the vicar

heard that?'

She nodded. 'Every word.'

'Well, that's okay then. If you'd said it was dire, I would have been a little put out but heart stopping etc is good, so I don't mind in the least.' He tilted her head back with his fingers. 'Did you really think you might die from pleasure?' His eyes were like green sparklers.

'Several times.'

'Me too,' he said, his voice crackling with desire and he kissed her so passionately that they both forgot they were in her sitting room and her daughter was asleep upstairs.

They tore off their clothes as if they were on fire and fell in a naked tangle of arms and legs onto the sofa, desperate to join their bodies, both giving and taking pleasure at the same time and both reaching climax simultaneously.

'It's a good thing the vicar didn't see or hear that,' Max said after a few minutes, 'he'd excommunicate us both.'

'It's a good thing Lily didn't see it,' Becky said, hastily remembering her sleeping child and grabbing her clothes. 'Even you would have trouble explaining that.'

Max threw on his clothes. 'I'm sure I'd think of something.'

'I'm sure you would. Does anything bother you?'

He thought for a minute 'Not much and certainly not what people think of me, unless it's someone I care about of course.'

'I wish I could be more like you. I seem to worry about everything. I've been worried about you finding out what the vicar heard ever since he told Jess and Susie that I could go to confession.'

Max sniggered. 'I'd like to be a fly on the wall at that. I didn't know you were Catholic.'

'I'm not. Actually, I'm not really religious at all but that doesn't stop him trying. He's not Catholic either, by the way. Are you – religious I mean?'

'No. Did you really think I'd be cross? I knew you'd tell Jess and Susie – I just hoped you'd say something nice.'

'Jeremy would have gone mad if the vicar had heard about our sex life – not that there was much to hear on that score. He was more interested in gambling than he was in me, I realise that now.'

Max lifted her chin with his fingers and kissed her on the nose. 'I know it isn't going to be easy for you Becky and I understand completely why you would but I'm not Jeremy and I think you should try not to compare us.'

'I know and I'm sorry. Believe me; you are absolutely nothing like him.'

'No need to be sorry and I'll take that as a compliment but I'm not perfect by any means. I have faults, all I'm saying is, you've spent the last couple of hours worrying about something unnecessarily. Anyway, talking of worrying, I may have some good news for you on the financial front. Let's open this wine and I'll tell you what I've done so far.'

He opened the bottle and they sat down then he turned on his iPad and showed her a list of her creditors with the full amounts; the reduced amounts; the amounts she'd paid off so far, and what was left to pay, if the agreement remained valid, listed next to each one.

'I managed to speak to the creditor disputing the agreement; as it happens, I know the Managing Director personally. Obviously they can't discuss your finances with me unless they have your written permission but I've explained the situation, told them I'm now involved and we're instructing solicitors to contest your liability. There are problems with this for several reasons, some of the loans you are jointly and severally liable for, some of them have a forged signature but you know you did sign some things so proving that's a problem and, you've accepted liability, but we could try to argue duress on some. The best thing is to try to renegotiate and, if you are happy for my solicitor to do this, we can get the ball rolling tomorrow. The ones I know personally, will accept, including the main one I spoke to today; my solicitor can get the rest. I'm fairly confident they'll all agree.'

Becky couldn't believe what he was saying. 'Are you saying that I can get the agreement re-instated or perhaps, just pay a little bit more?'

'No. I'm saying we should be able to get it reduced so that you have to pay less. Banks are always prepared to negotiate. They don't want to drag a widow and her young child through the courts, especially not for the relatively small sums involved. I know they don't seem small to you but the debts are distributed between a lot of banks and institutions and you've been paying them regularly for the last five years. I don't know how you managed it.'

'So, I may not lose everything then? Oh Max, thank you so much! Is ... is your solicitor very expensive?'

'Not very – and don't worry about his bill, I said I'll take care of that.'

'No Max. I couldn't let you do that.'

'Oh couldn't you? You didn't ask me to get involved, I offered and I offered my solicitor. I'm paying his bill and I'm not going to have an argument about it so you may as well forget it and just let us do what we can. We may not succeed but I'm pretty sure we will.'

And although she didn't know why, Becky thought so too and she couldn't stop the tears of sheer relief from rolling down her cheeks.

Max put his arm around her and pulled her close, tenderly kissing her head and stroking her hair. She hadn't realised how tired she was and ten minutes later, she was asleep in his arms.

Becky awoke and for a moment, she wondered where she was. She'd been having a wonderful dream about Max and she stretched her legs and arms, like a contented cat that had most definitely, got the cream.

Then she remembered and sat bolt upright. She was in bed, under the duvet, fully clothed. The last thing she remembered was falling asleep on the sofa in Max's arms.

It was still dark and she peered at the clock. It was ten fifteen. She switched on the light and saw a note, in Max's hand writing. It read, "Goodnight and pleasant dreams. I'll call you tomorrow. Max xx. P.S. Here's my phone number if you want to call me. xx"

She grabbed the phone and dialled; he answered after the second ring.

'Hello sleepyhead,' he said.

'Oh Max I'm so sorry, I didn't mean to fall asleep. Thank you for carrying me upstairs.'

He laughed. 'Don't apologise Becky, neither of us got much sleep last night. I'm going to bed soon too. And it's no wonder you are shattered, what with everything else going on in your life at the moment. I didn't mind, honestly.'

'But you read all those papers, made those calls, came round to tell me about it and I'm asleep within half an hour!'

'Not quite half an hour – and you did make me very welcome – and very happy.'

Becky blushed just thinking about it. 'You made me very happy too. You ... you could have stayed. As long as you left before Lily woke up.'

'I did consider staying but you know as well as I do, neither of us would have got any sleep if I had and I'm heading up to town first thing, so I need some. I won't be back until Saturday. I've got some things to do. Now, get some sleep and I'll call you in the morning.'

'Oh!' She couldn't hide the disappointment or the surprise, in her voice.

'Any chance you're free on Saturday evening? Perhaps the three of us could go out for an early dinner or something?'

'The three of us?' She couldn't think clearly. 'Oh! You mean you, me and Lily?'

'No. I meant you, me and the vicar. Of course, you, me and Lily. Nothing fancy. I've no idea what five year olds like to eat so I'll let you choose the venue. Unless ... you'd rather Lily didn't spend time with me until we know whether this is headed somewhere.'

'Um.'

'That's okay. I completely understand. Children can get attached and you don't want her to get used to having me around and then, one day, find I've gone. How about I come round later then? After she's gone to bed, around eightish? I can bring a take-away, if you want.'

'Max I ... may I think about it and let you know tomorrow? You're right in thinking I'm worried about her getting attached. She's already renamed two of her dolls, Max and Mummy and I don't want her to get hurt. Do you really understand?'

'Of course I do. Is my doll good-looking?'

Becky smiled. He didn't sound annoyed and that was a relief. She didn't want to upset either of them. 'Yes. In a plastic, sort of way. He drinks a lot of tea and spends a lot of time kissing Mummy doll.'

'Ah! A life-like model then. That's good. Goodnight sweetheart. I'll call you tomorrow.'

'Goodnight Max.' She hung up and collapsed back onto her bed. All she could think of was the fact that he'd just called her sweetheart.

CHAPTER SIXTEEN

Max did better than call; he arranged for "Stephanie's Stems" to deliver a huge bouquet of flowers at eight-thirty on Thursday morning, which was pretty amazing for two reasons: first, because the shop didn't open until nine and second, because Stephanie delivered it personally.

'Wow! When did he order these?' Becky asked, truly stunned but knowing immediately, they were from Max.

Stephanie smiled. She was in her fifties and had known Becky for over twenty years. 'This morning. I'd been to a flower market and was unloading the pickup; he was on his way to the station. He stopped and helped me; even though he was wearing the most expensive suit I've ever seen then asked if I would deliver these to you first thing. He chose the blooms himself. I'm so pleased for you Becky. He's such a nice man and he seems really smitten. I saw you at the Valentine's Dance; he couldn't take his eyes off you.'

Becky blushed crimson. 'Thanks Stephanie but it's early days and I'm not expecting it to last. Thanks so much for this. I know you don't open until nine or do your own deliveries, I hope it wasn't a nuisance.'

'Of course it wasn't! I'm delighted to do it Becky, both for you and for Max. It's a pleasure, but I must get back now. Have a lovely day dear.'

'And you Stephanie. Thanks again.'

'Don't thank me dear, thank Max.' She beamed at Becky then trotted off down the road towards her shop.

Becky took the flowers inside and opened the card. It was in his handwriting, in ink, clearly written by fountain pen and it read, "Fifi, Think of me, counting the hours until Saturday, With Love, Max. xx"

She held the card to her chest and her eyes filled with love. Last night he'd called her sweetheart, now he'd sent her the biggest bouquet of flowers she'd ever had in her life, with a note sent with his "Love". Was there just the smallest chance that he really was falling for her? She still found it hard to believe. Then she remembered what Max had said his father used to say, "Anything is possible" and her heart soared. 'Anything is possible,' she repeated to herself and she really hoped it was because, whilst she wasn't sure whether Max was falling for her or not, she was sure that she was falling for him – in a very big way.

The doorbell rang and Jess and Susie pushed Becky playfully aside when she answered.

'We've come to see the flowers,' Jess said. 'Susie saw them being delivered and called me. Bloody hell! They must have cost a small fortune!'

Susie spotted the card Becky was still holding. 'What does it say?'

Becky handed it to her and she read the words out loud then said, 'Wow! With Love. Things really are heading in the right direction aren't they? Tell me, have you started calling him darling yet? Only I seem to remember someone assuring me that, whatever else they may call him, they'll never call him that.'

'Very funny. And no, I haven't. But he is, you know, a darling, I mean. He's so thoughtful and clearly generous and – I can't say for an absolute certainty of course, because we never really know anyone, even if we think we do, but, I don't think he would knowingly hurt me, not if he could help it. He's gone to London until Saturday but he asked to take me and Lily out to dinner on Saturday night.'

'He's not a demigod,' Susie said, 'he's a God. Hold on to him my girl and don't let anyone take him from you.'

Becky shook her head. 'If he wants to leave, I can't stop him and if he wants to be with someone else, I can't stop that either. You can't force people to love you.'

'No, but you can tie them to the bed and lock them in!'

Jess grinned. 'That may be what you have to do to keep a man Susie, although, now you come to mention it, tying Max to the bed, locking him in and having your way with him, might not be such a bad idea Becky!'

'Don't give me ideas!' Becky said, still laughing, 'and

don't get me thinking about him and sex, it's hard enough trying to concentrate on anything else as it is. I keep grinning to myself, for no reason, and I keep remembering something he said or a look he gave me or something and my entire body feels warm and tingly. I think I could actually have an orgasm just thinking about the man!'

'I think we all could!' Susie said. 'Where are you going for dinner on Saturday?'

'Oh. I haven't said yes yet. I don't want Lily to get attached to him and then get hurt when he leaves.'

'Bloody hell Becky! Why must you persist in thinking he's going to leave?'

'Because everyone I love seems to, whether they plan to or not.'

'Oh! Okay, that's a bit "Freudian" or some other such psycho-babble. I know your mum and dad died and that was shitty and I know Jeremy left you and that was just as bad but we're still here – unless you're saying you don't love us – which you'd better not be or I'll give you a good slap, and Lily's not going to leave you, so why the hell should Max?'

Becky shook her head. 'I know, it's stupid but it doesn't stop me thinking it. And you've forgotten someone, my real dad left me too, when I was Lily's age.'

'Yeah. I had forgotten that, you're right. But not everyone does – or will, so stop being so bloody maudlin will you and just enjoy the moment. I've never seen you this happy. Say yes to dinner on Saturday. Lily needs to spend some time with him sooner rather than later; if she doesn't like him, you wouldn't take it any further anyway.'

'True but she likes him already, she's named one of her dolls, Max.'

'Just say yes Becky,' Susie said. 'Take the risk. You're more than half in love with him already, in my opinion. You need to see how he is with Lily. You don't want to find out he's the kind of guy who would make her sit in a corner or something when she's naughty. Not that I think he is for one minute.'

'Neither do I. Oh God! I haven't called him and thanked him for these flowers yet. Go and make some coffee whilst I do that you two. I don't want you hearing what I say. Hey, shouldn't you both be at work now anyway?'

'Ten minutes – just enough time for coffee.'

They headed to the kitchen and Becky dialled Max's number.

'Hi Fifi. How are you this morning? Did you sleep well?'

She giggled. She was getting to like him calling her Fifi – even if it was because of a poodle. 'I slept very well thanks and this morning, I got your beautiful flowers. Thank you so much Max. They are truly spectacular.'

'I'm glad you liked them. I thought they'd remind you of me. I didn't want you to forget me while I'm away.'

'I can assure you, there's no chance of me forgetting you Max, and you'll only be away for two days – won't you?'

'Yes, back on Saturday but two days is a long time.'

'I'm counting the hours too – and speaking of Saturday, if your offer to take Lily and me to dinner is still on, the answer's yes please.'

'Of course it is. That's great. Shall I pick you up around five?'

'That's perfect. And Max – bring your toothbrush, I want to show you just how much I appreciate these flowers. I'm not into kinky sex at all, I'm afraid, so I hope you won't be disappointed but I might just tie you to the bed and have my wicked way with you. I want to kiss every single inch of your body.'

He didn't respond and she wondered if she'd said the wrong thing. She heard him clear his throat.

'Thanks for giving me such a clear idea of what to expect and I'm not in the least bit disappointed. That's not an area I'm interested in either. I'm on a rather packed commuter train so it's a bit difficult for me to respond appropriately but your suggestion sounds very interesting and I won't rest easy until we've tackled that from every angle. I may even have one or two ideas of my own. I'll call you this evening, when I've had a chance to give it the consideration it deserves and, believe me when I say, I'll be thinking of little else all day.'

Becky giggled excitedly. 'I'm so sorry Max. I forgot you would still be on a train. I'll speak to you later. Thanks again for the exquisite flowers.'

'Don't worry, I think I handled the situation.' He chuckled. 'And, as you said, you can thank me on Saturday. I'll call you later. Enjoy your day.'

Max hung up and caught the eye of a young man sitting opposite, grinning at him.

'Phone sex?' the man said.

Max raised his eyebrows then grinned broadly. 'Yep.'

Six men, all wearing suits and looking very professional, nodded knowingly.

CHAPTER SEVENTEEN

Becky and Lizzie exchanged emails, bouncing ideas around for the wedding and by Friday, Becky had arranged to meet Margaret at the Hall, to give her a ball park figure on the cost, as well as her fees.

Not having a car, she walked to the house, through the fields, still covered with slowly melting snow and she remembered all the happy times she'd spent playing there; feeding lambs, in the days when the fields were full of sheep and feeding the ducks on the pond near the copse.

When her parents had died, just before her sixteenth birthday, Beckleston Hall had passed to Edward Beckleston, her father's younger brother, under the terms of an ancient entailment dating from the day Beckleston Hall was built. He allowed her to remain at the Hall until he sold it, two years later to pay death duties and to enable him to move to South Africa. He was the last of the Beckleston line and was unable to sire children so the entailment ended with him, the final living son, once he had inherited.

In any event, Becky had no legal title to the estate; she thought of Horace Beckleston as her father but he was not – not by blood.

Margaret, Victoria and Becky settled in the small sitting room at the back of the house, drinking tea and eating homemade cake in front of a roaring fire, which immediately banished Becky's sad memories.

'Lizzie wants a fairly simple wedding, with just family and close friends,' Becky said. 'They'll need between fifteen and twenty of the bedrooms and were hoping to make a weekend of it, arriving on the Friday and having a quiet dinner, spending Saturday preparing, having a celebratory dinner and dance on the Saturday evening then the ceremony on Sunday with a wedding brunch to follow around twelve and everyone leaving around two. She wants something thrown in for entertainment on the Sunday morning, pre-ceremony.'

Victoria raised her eyebrows. 'The party before the ceremony? That's a recipe for hangovers and disasters.'

'But so Lizzie,' Margaret nodded. 'She had something similar when she and Max married, remember?'

Becky felt her stomach lurch. It was ludicrous but the thought of Max preparing to marry the woman he loved sent an arrow of jealousy into Becky's heart.

Victoria smirked. 'Good heavens, I'd forgotten that! Didn't Max's best man vomit over the vicar and another friend was found in the vestry fornicating with someone else's wife. A fight broke out I seem to recall.' She gurgled with laughter remembering the scene.

'Yes. Max of course was unfazed by the whole thing, Becky. He sent the vicar off to get changed, broke up the fight, temporarily reunited the wife and her husband and by the time Lizzie arrived ten minutes later, she never suspected a thing. She nearly had an apoplexy when someone told her afterwards.'

'You can always rely on Max in a crisis,' Victoria said.

'True,' Margaret said, 'but let's hope this one goes off smoothly.'

'Well, I have suggested she might want to rethink that schedule, precisely because someone will get drunk; it is a wedding after all, it seems to go with the territory. She's getting back to me after she speaks with Jack tomorrow.'

'Do you have an alternative?'

'Um. I've suggested Friday as per her schedule, the ceremony on Saturday, early evening, outside if the weather's good – the sunsets can be glorious at that time of year – followed by the celebratory dinner and shorter dance, a firework display around nine to nine-thirty – everyone loves fireworks and then back to the dance until midnight. Brunch the next day from ten finishing at just before twelve; people will be starving if it's later. They're leaving for their honeymoon sometime around one to one thirty so I've suggested saving the cake cutting until twelve and serving cake and champagne, tea and coffee, then. People will head off after that.'

'I like the fireworks idea. Start the wedding off with a bang, so to speak,' Victoria grinned.

'I agree. Everyone loves fireworks. Let's hope she goes with your schedule. Will you organise a marquee for outside, in case it rains?' Margaret asked.

'No. No point in being outside unless there's a good sunset. We would set up a pergola for the bride and groom and have festive poles lining the aisle. Chairs can be brought out in the afternoon, if the weather's good, if not, we'll have the ceremony in the ballroom with an outdoor bar on the covered terrace and an indoor one just inside the French windows.'

'Oh! You seem to know this house well. I suppose, living in the village you came here on occasion,' Margaret said.

'No. I was brought up here. I lived here until I was eighteen, when the house was sold.'

Margaret's tea cup dropped to the floor, smashing into tiny shards on the oak floor just as Max walked through the door.

'Good God! You're a Beckleston!' The colour drained from Margaret's face and she followed her tea cup to the floor, collapsing in a heap.

Max was by her side in seconds gently lifting her onto the sofa. Victoria flapped around her and Becky dashed to the drinks table and poured her a large brandy handing it to Max who passed the liquid beneath his mother's nose. She came to and Max held the glass to her lips as she gulped down the contents.

She seemed disoriented and then her eyes landed on Becky and a look of hatred flicked across them. 'I would like you to leave,' she said.

'Mum are you okay? What on earth happened?' Max's eyes shot from his mum to Becky and back again. 'It's Becky, Mum, remember. Why would you want her to leave?'

'Because she's a Beckleston, Max. And I will not have a Beckleston in my house! Get her out of here.'

She spoke the words quietly but with such venom that Becky turned on her heels and fled, not waiting to explain that she wasn't a true Beckleston – not by blood at least.

Tears of shock were coursing down her cheeks as she ran. She had no idea what had happened. One minute everything was fine, the next, Margaret was looking at her as if she were the devil incarnate. She'd said that she wouldn't have a Beckleston in her house and Becky didn't understand; the Hall was the Beckleston's ancestral home, if Margaret hated them that much, why would she buy it?

She ran blindly, not really knowing where she was going, not really caring. She'd seen the look of horror on Max's face. Max! What was he doing there? He'd said he was away until Saturday but it was early Friday afternoon – and, he hadn't come after her. Could she expect him to? His mother had just collapsed.

Thoughts were whirling around her head as she ran then she felt the ground disappear beneath her and that was the last thing she remembered.

Becky's head was pounding. Someone was shining a light in her eyes and she wanted them to stop. She lifted her right arm and a searing pain shot through it.

'She's coming round,' a voice said.

'Thank God.'

Becky recognised Max's voice and slowly opened her eyes. She was in bed in the Yellow Room at Beckleston Hall. For a moment she thought she'd travelled back in time. This had been her bedroom when she'd lived here, but she saw Max leaning over her, concern evident in his eyes. Dr. White had just stepped back from examining her and Margaret and Victoria were holding one another as if for support, standing across the room, near the window – and she saw that it was dark outside.

'Lily!' she shrieked in panic. 'I must get Lily!'

'Shush Becky, Lily's fine,' Max said softly, then, 'Jess, she's awake, you can bring Lily in,' in a slightly raised voice. 'She's okay isn't she?' he asked Dr. White.

The doctor nodded. 'It'll take a lot more than that to keep our Becky down. Her arm's badly bruised but I don't think it's broken. I'd like to get it X-rayed if it still hurts her tomorrow.'

Jess and Susie appeared at the door and Lily raced from them and tried to scramble onto the bed. Max lifted her up and placed her in Becky's outstretched arms and Becky hugged her, in spite of the searing pain. Tears rolled down her cheeks, half from the pain and half from relief at holding her daughter.

'What happened?' she asked when she finally felt able.

'You fell into the empty pond,' Max said brushing what looked like a tear from his eye.

Her memory returned and she glared at Margaret. 'Then, why am I here?'

'I brought you here,' Max said.

'I think I should leave.' She tried to sit up but Max gently restrained her.

'You've had a nasty fall and you need to rest. We'll see how you are in the morning.'

'I don't think your mother wants me here.'

'I do.' Margaret approached the bed. 'I'm sorry Becky. It ... it was such a shock, that's all. I ... I was taking out my bitterness and hatred for someone, on you and that was wrong of me. When you're feeling better, I'll explain but for now, please get some rest.'

'I ... I don't understand.'

'Mum will explain it all later Becky. I'm in the dark myself, so I'd quite like an explanation as to why my normally sane, kind and loving parent turned into a harbinger of Hell. Would you like something to drink?'

Becky was still confused but Lily was singing her a lullaby and she turned her attention to her child, momentarily ignoring Max. 'Are you okay sweetheart? Mummy was very silly and she slipped into an empty pond but there's nothing for you to worry about.'

Lily nodded. 'I know, Mummy. Are we staying here?'

Becky glanced at Max, who was nodding, then at Margaret, then at Jess and Susie. 'For tonight, I think we are. This used to be my room Lily. I came here when I was your age.' She saw Max and his mum exchange looks but she ignored them.

'It's very big and it's very pretty. I like yellow.'

'I do too. It's called The Yellow Room. All the rooms in this house have names.'

'Why?'

'So that you don't get lost. There are lots and lots of rooms here and you need to know which one you're in so that other people can find you and so that they don't get confused.'

'All pretty colours?'

'No, only some of them. There's a room called "The Oak Room" because it has oak panelled walls and there's "The Queen's Room" because Queen Elizabeth the First stayed there and –'

'The Queen!'

'Yes darling. Not this Queen but one with the same name a long time ago. This house is very old. Oh. There's a secret passage too.'

Lily sat upright and her eyes opened wide. 'Can we go and see it?'

Becky realised what she'd said. 'I ... I don't know if the new owners would want us to.'

'A secret passage? The new owners would love you to.' Max said casting his mother a decisive look. 'I'd like to see that too but not tonight.'

Jess and Susie came and stood beside the bed. 'How are you feeling?' Jess asked. 'You gave us quite a scare.'

'Fine, I think, although my arm hurts and my head feels like someone's been using it as a drum. How did you know where I was?'

'Max called us,' Susie said. 'We went and collected Lily from playgroup and came here. It's a good thing he saw you fall. You might have been there for hours otherwise. Why did you go towards the pond and not home?'

'Instinct I guess. I –'

'Always go to the pond when you're upset.' Jess finished her sentence.

Max hovered in the background.

'You saw me fall?'

He nodded. 'I came after you. I thought you'd go home so I headed down the drive but I heard you scream and I just saw you disappear into the empty pond. It's a good thing I got to you when I did. It's like a quagmire in there. God knows what would ...' he looked at Lily and stopped then said, 'You would have been very muddy.'

'Thank you,' she said, not fully comprehending that he had actually saved her life.

'Well, we'll leave you to rest,' Margaret said. 'Again Becky, I am sorry. Jess and Susie, you're welcome to stay, for as long as you like.' She smiled apologetically at Becky then she and Victoria left.

'Do you want me to leave too?' Max asked.

'Yes,' she said, 'but you two stay, please,' to Jess and Susie.

Max left without another word.

'What the hell is going on?' Jess whispered over Lily's head.

Becky shook her head. 'No idea. Could you try and help me sit up please?'

They helped her, and Lily jumped off the bed and danced around the room with her Teddy bear.

Becky smiled lovingly at her daughter. 'One minute everything is fine and the next Margaret is going mad. I said I grew up here. She yelled about me being a Beckleston and said she never wants a Beckleston in her house. Max walked in just as she collapsed on the floor. I...

I ran off in tears. If you'd seen the look she gave me. Pure hatred. And, that's another thing; Max said he'd be away until tomorrow. Clearly, he's not quite as honest as he claims to be.'

'I thought I detected a distinct cooling off on your part,' Jess said, 'but you must stop jumping to conclusions Becky. He came back earlier than he'd expected to – and he went to your house before he came here. He said so. And what's more, the bottom of that pond is like quicksand.' Jess lowered her voice so that Lily couldn't hear. 'You could very easily have died; seriously Becky. Think about that.'

'So, you really shouldn't be angry with him. His mum, yes, she's clearly a loon but him, no,' Susie said, 'The good thing is, you can blame it on concussion or something; pretend you didn't know what you were doing and just say sorry.'

Becky screwed up her eyes. 'Why do I do that? Jump to conclusions I mean? Could it really have been that serious?'

'Yes, it could but let's not dwell on that. I suppose, the reason you do it is because you trusted Jeremy so completely and never doubted him until he let you down so totally; now, you doubt first and trust later. It's only natural, but you need to stop and think a bit. Max looked really worried, didn't he Susie? I think I actually saw tears in his eyes before you came to. He was terrified you were badly hurt. This time, I think you do need to apologise.'

'Okay. I will. What's the time?'

'Seven-thirty.'

'Really? God. I must have been out cold. It's time for Lily's bed.'

'Do you want her to stay here with you? Personally, I think you'd be better off getting some rest. I could take her back and stay at yours, if you like,' Jess offered. 'I'll bring her back first thing tomorrow if you're going to be staying here for a while. She'll be fine. You know she will.'

Becky smiled weakly, 'I'm more worried about how I'll be without her. Lily darling. I've got to stay here just for tonight. Aunt Jess will take you home and stay the night then bring you back tomorrow or you can stay here with me. Which would you prefer?'

'Stay with you, Mummy.'

'Okay, shall I get her nightie and stuff and bring it back?'

Becky shook her head. 'She'll be okay for one night.'

As if on cue, Max knocked on the door. 'Sorry to interrupt but I remembered Lily goes to bed about now. Shall I take Jess to get some overnight things for her? She can sleep in here with you or there's one of those fold up beds I can bring in for her.'

Becky caught Jess' eye and Jess nodded.

'Thanks Max that would be great if you don't mind – taking Jess, I mean. Lily can sleep in this bed. It's big enough for both of us.'

'See you in a mo,' Jess said as she headed off with Max.

CHAPTER EIGHTEEN

Becky slept fitfully. She dreamed she was falling and screaming Max's name but he wasn't there to catch her. She woke with a start and almost jumped out of her skin to find him leaning over her.

'Bad dream?' he asked. 'You were screaming something.'

She turned to look at Lily but she was still curled up fast asleep. She let out a long sigh. 'Very bad dream, you weren't there to catch me.'

He screwed up his eyes in a look of contrition. 'I'm so sorry Becky. I –'

'I meant in my dream; you weren't there to catch me in my dream. You weren't to know I'd gone to the pond, earlier.'

'Jess knew.'

'Jess has known me most of my life. I owe you an apology. I ... I was angry and stupid and I took it out on you. I'm sorry. You said you weren't back until Saturday and when I saw you this afternoon, I thought you'd lied. My only excuse – and it's a poor one, is something Jess said. I trusted Jeremy completely and he utterly deceived me. Now, I assume people have deceived me and I don't wait for explanations. Can you forgive me?'

Max's eyes scanned her face. 'Of course I can – and do. And it's not a stupid excuse. It's perfectly understandable. I did say you need to try not to compare me with him, but it'll take a long time, I understand that. May I just ask you to do one thing? If you're having doubts about me or you think I'm not telling you the truth, ask me. I promised I won't lie to you and I won't.'

Becky smiled. 'I will. And you saved my life – again. I hear I could have died in the bottom of that pond.'

Max nodded. 'You could have. That's my fault. I should have asked Paul to put a fence around it. I just wasn't thinking. Now I'll tell you something. I came back early because I managed to get everything done a lot sooner than I'd anticipated. I was going to meet some of the guys for a beer but all I could think about was getting back and seeing you. I thought I'd surprise you. Do you believe in fate?'

Becky shrugged. 'I don't really know.'

'Well, I didn't – until today. If I had stayed in town, I wouldn't have seen you fall. Mum has just told me a story about when she was young. I'll let her tell you tomorrow; she owes you an explanation and I think you'll be able to forgive the way she behaved when you've heard it – or at least, understand why she reacted the way she did – and she is truly sorry about it, by the way. Anyway, it's about fate and people being in the right place at the right time. Fate put me in the right place at the right time today.'

'To save me, you mean.'

'To see you fall. I thought I'd lost you Becky and I never want to experience that feeling again.' He leant forward and kissed her softly on the lips. 'Now, try to go back to sleep and don't worry about me not being there to catch you; I'll be right here.'

She saw the blanket thrown across the armchair that had been pulled near the bed. 'How long have you been sitting there?'

'It doesn't matter; I won't leave you.'

'Max I'll be fine. Please, go to bed and get some sleep. You can't sit there all night.'

'I think you'll find I can. It's actually a very comfortable chair.'

She glanced at Lily then shifted her position so that there was space on the bed. 'If you are determined to stay with me at least come and sleep on the bed. It'll be a little more comfortable and ... I could really use a hug right now.'

His eyes searched her face then he grabbed the blanket and got onto the bed beside her, lifting her head so that he could wrap his arm around her.

She raised her face to his and looked him straight in the eye. 'I really am sorry Max. You've been so good to me

135

and I've behaved like a fool.'

He kissed on her nose. 'Stop apologising Becky, you have nothing to be sorry for. And please don't look at me like that or I'll forget you're hurt and that Lily's here and show you just how glad I am that I came back early. Now go to sleep.' He gently coaxed her head back down onto his chest and stroked her hair until, minutes later, she was asleep.

Becky woke to the sound of her daughter's dulcet tones. She was singing a very old song about robins and when Becky raised herself up on to her elbow, her heart did a pirouette. Max was holding Lily in his arms and they were peering out of the window down towards the lawn.

'Shall we go down and see if we can find something for him to eat?' Max said 'and we can make Mummy some breakfast for when she wakes up.'

'Yes please!' Lily said, one tiny hand resting on his back, the other one resting on his arm.

'Mummy's already awake.'

Max and Lily both turned surprised eyes to Becky and smiled simultaneously.

'Mummy! Mummy! There's a robin! We're going to find him some food.'

'That's a good idea.' She smiled at her daughter then at Max and her heart did another little dance. There was something in his eyes, a mixture of relief and contentment and it spoke to her of safety and security and total happiness; something she'd believed, until he had come into her life, she may never find again other than with Lily.

'How are you feeling?' he said carrying Lily over to the bed and sitting down with her on his lap.

It was such a simple gesture but it brought a tear to Becky's eye. 'Wonderful,' she said, truthfully. 'Even the pain in my arm has disappeared.'

He smiled, leant forward and kissed her forehead then stood up taking Lily with him. 'Come along little princess.

136

Let's go and get the robin and Mummy some breakfast.' He strode out of the room telling Lily why it was important to help feed the birds in winter.

Becky gingerly, got out of bed. She did feel wonderful but even she knew not to take any chances. She walked to the bathroom and it was only when she saw her reflection in the mirror that she realised she was wearing what was clearly, one of Max's shirts – and only that. She dashed back into the bedroom and saw on the ottoman at the foot of the bed, her clothes lain out, washed and dried and ready for her to wear.

Despite the fact that Max had seen her completely naked more than once, she blushed at the thought of him undressing her and also at the thought of his mother knowing he had. Unless, of course, it had been Margaret, which Becky somehow doubted.

She dressed and made her way down to the kitchen where she found Lily sitting at the table, on Max's lap, buttering toast. Margaret was sitting next to them and Victoria was making a pot of tea.

'Good morning,' Margaret said, smiling apologetically at Becky 'How are you feeling?'

'Very well thank you.' Becky hadn't forgiven her yet but she had no intention of being rude.

'Morning. You gave us quite a scare last night, my dear. Poor Max was beside himself with worry. It's good to see you looking so perky. Did I hear correctly? That used to be your room when you lived here,' Victoria said.

'Yes. Yes it did. Good morning.'

'Come and sit down and have a cup of coffee, or tea, if you prefer. Victoria's just made a fresh pot. Max and Lily are making you breakfast; aren't you dears?' Margaret pulled out a chair next to her.

Max grinned up at Becky. 'So far, you seem to be having a lot of butter and a little bit of toast.'

Becky smiled then walked towards the chair Margaret had offered her, and sat down.

'I know I owe you an explanation and I will tell you but I think it's best to save that until ...' Margaret glanced towards Lily.

Becky nodded and took the mug of coffee Max passed her.

'Won't you tell us about your life here and how you came to leave?' Victoria said, 'We'd all like to hear about it. I remember hearing that there were some magnificent parties and I actually came to one of the summer fetes, oh, it must have been over twenty years ago. It was quite something.'

Becky nodded. 'Yes. They were. Are you sure you want to hear about it?'

She glanced towards Margaret, who stretched out her hand and squeezed Becky's free one.

'Yes dear, we are.'

Becky gave a deep sigh. 'Well ... Firstly, I'm not actually a Beckleston; not by blood anyway.' She saw the looks passing between Margaret, Victoria and Max, just as they had last night but ignored them and continued. 'I can't remember my real father; he abandoned my mother and me, so my mother brought us to live in the village when I was about Lily's age. She met Horace Beckleston and they fell in love, despite their considerable age difference – she was twenty-four, he was fifty-nine – and they married within about a month of meeting. It seems he had led a rather reclusive life but he changed completely when they met.'

'Yes. I remember that. He had almost locked himself up like a hermit. Perhaps he had a guilty conscience,' Victoria said waspishly.

Again the looks. This time Becky didn't ignore them. 'Look, I don't know what's going on here and maybe when you say what you have to, I'll understand Margaret, but I can't help feeling you know something unpleasant about my father – Horace, I mean and I find that really hard to accept. He was one of the nicest, kindest men I have ever met. He loved both my mother and me completely and showed us nothing but love, devotion and gentleness from the first day we met until the day he ... died.'

'I'm sorry dear. You're right though, my story does involve Horace but we'll try to keep our opinions to ourselves. Please continue.'

'Okay.' Becky licked her lips. Talking about her life was stirring old memories and not all of them were happy. 'Well, suffice to say, I led a charmed life from the day they married. There were parties and dances, summer fetes and Christmas Eve balls, picnics and outings. It was every child's dream childhood. My father – Horace that is – changed my surname to his; he had planned to legally adopt me but for some reason, that never happened and he died when I was sixteen, with my mother, in a car crash.'

'Oh! How dreadful,' Margaret said.

Victoria added, 'That must have been awful.'

'It was,' Becky said glancing in Max's direction. She could feel him watching her.

He smiled comfortingly. Lily was playing with his long, agile fingers, making them into the shape of the church, then the steeple then opening them to show all the people. 'The vicar's there too,' he said and winked at Becky.

She smiled. She remembered playing the same game with Horace.

'That's it really. This house had been a magical place for me but once they were gone, it ... it lost most of its sparkle. I still go to the pond though, whenever I'm upset or need to think. It was a special place for all three of us. We had picnics there and swam in it and it holds such memories of wonderfully happy times. I'm sorry.' Tears were rolling down her cheeks and she brushed them away with her hands.

Max passed her his handkerchief. 'And now I understand why you were so angry with me that first day I met you, at the pond. You thought I was stopping you from being somewhere that meant so much to you. I'm sorry Becky. I had no idea.'

She shrugged. 'How could you?'

'So, what happened then?' Victoria coaxed. 'I remember the house passing to Edward, Horace's younger brother. He was a nasty piece of work, that one. He sold it didn't he? Did he throw you out?'

'No. Actually, he treated me rather well, in a detached and business-like way. He said he would have to sell the house but that I could remain until it was sold and he hired Connie Jessop as housekeeper to look after both the house and me. I was sixteen, devastated from losing my parents and not a happy person, so it was not a match made in heaven but we rubbed along. I spent most of my time with Jess and Susie when I wasn't at school; Edward sent me to Roedean as a boarder a few months after my parents' deaths but I spent all my holidays here. The house was sold when I was eighteen. I went to university and moved back here when I got my degree. I had always loved helping to organise the events here so I set up my business and, here we are today.'

'I thought there was some entailment or other which stopped the house from being sold. How did Edward get around that?' Margaret asked.

'He didn't need to. The entailment was binding on sons only. Neither Horace nor Edward had sons – or any children of their own come to that, otherwise the house could have gone to a daughter, after Edward, although not with the entailment. He was the last son and the entailment ended as soon as the last son inherited. He sold it to an American family but they never moved in for some reason and it started to deteriorate, although they retained Connie Jessop and Bill Jenkins, to make sure it didn't go to rack and ruin. The Americans sold it, obviously, to you.'

'Didn't Edward go to South Africa?' Victoria said.

'Yes. We used to exchange Christmas cards but that stopped after a few years. He hasn't been back and I haven't seen him since the day I moved out. It was odd last night, being in my room because it's almost exactly as it was the day I left. I've been back of course. Connie often used to let me pop in, when the Americans owned it, even though, strictly speaking, she shouldn't have but the last time I slept in that room, I was eighteen and heading off to university. Edward sold the house fully furnished; he just took a few pieces of value, himself and he allowed me to take a few mementoes and all of father's ... Horace's, diaries.'

'Hor ... Horace kept diaries?' Margaret said, an odd inflection in her voice and her eyes met Victoria's and held them. 'For how long?'

Becky saw the look passing between Margaret and Victoria,

'From about the age of twelve upwards – until the very day he died. I often re-read them, to remind myself of the happy days we spent here. I read them all when I first got them but now, I only read the ones mentioning my mother and me.' A thought suddenly dawned on her, a memory really, of something she had read. 'Oh my God! You ... you aren't THE Margaret are you? The one Horace fell in love with when he was nineteen?'

'May I go and see if the robin is still there, Mummy?' Lily asked, taking her chance to speak when everyone in the room fell silent.

'Oh Lily, I'm sorry darling. Of course you may,' Becky said dragging her eyes and her attention away from Margaret's startled face. 'You've been a very good girl sitting there so quietly and patiently. I'll get my coat and we can go and look.'

'I'll go with you,' Max said. 'Are you okay Mum?' He gave Margaret a concerned look. She had turned very pale.

'What? Oh. Yes I'm fine.' Her eyes were fixed on Becky.

'I ... I'm sorry I blurted that out,' Becky said. 'I hope I haven't made things worse. I –'

'No.' Margaret stopped her. 'It was just a shock to hear ... to know ... that Horace kept a diary. Although, he wasn't in love with me, I can assure you of that. I need to explain why I behaved the way I did yesterday; I need to tell you about my past.'

'Yes, and I really want to hear it. I have to say though, if you are the Margaret in his diaries, whilst I can fully understand you being upset, I can't understand why you would ... feel such loathing towards him. And he was most definitely in love with you. Until he met my mother, he had never loved anyone other than you – and he was fifty-nine when they met, as I believe I said. He had loved you and you alone, for all those years and he never stopped regretting the day he let you go.'

'What?' Margaret was clearly stunned. 'That's not possible. I ... I still have the letter he wrote me when he said ...' she caught sight of Lily jumping in the air and stopped. 'Now isn't the time but I'll show it to you and then you'll understand.' Her eyes filled with tears.

'And I'll show you his diaries – and so will you.' Becky turned to face Max. 'You can stay here, if you like; we won't be long.'

'No way. I've got to make sure you don't fall in the pond again.' He smiled and stood up, taking Lily by the hand.

'Don't worry, I've learned my lesson. I won't go near the pond until it's repaired and refilled. After that, I can't make any promises. Trespassing or not, it will always be a special place for me.' She smiled back at him.

'You're welcome to visit the pond whenever you want to Becky,' Margaret said, a hint of colour finally returning to her cheeks.

'Thank you Margaret.'

Max glanced from Becky to his mother, then Becky took Lily's other hand and they went to find their coats – and the robin.

'Are we still on for dinner tonight?' Max said when they got outside. 'I'll completely understand if you'd rather stay home and rest.'

Becky was miles away. She was thinking about the diaries and how unbelievably strange life can be. So many people with so many secrets. She was eager to hear Margaret's version of events; they were clearly very different to that of her father's.

'Sorry Max. I'm still trying to get my head around everything. Life is very strange isn't it?'

He nodded in agreement. 'Tell me about it. I feel as if my whole world has been turned upside down in a matter of days. I'm thirty-seven years old and until last night, I had never heard of Horace Beckleston or of my mother's involvement with him. I'll let her tell you about it but it strikes me that people shouldn't keep secrets. Nothing good ever comes of them.'

'I was thinking exactly the same. I can't wait to hear your mother's side of the story. I've a feeling it must be very different from my father's. About tonight though; I'm happy to do whatever you'd like. I'm fine, honestly.'

Max stopped walking and pulled Becky towards him as

143

Lily ran ahead to find the robin she'd seen fly into the holly tree.

'Whatever I'd like! Are you sure about that Fifi? I seem to remember having a rather erotic conversation with you about you planning to tie me to a bed and have your wicked way with me. I don't think you're quite up to that tonight are you?'

The look in his eyes made her go weak at the knees. How could he have such an effect on her? Just because little flecks of gold seemed to light up his eyes like miniature fireworks exploding around his dark pupils and because strands of unruly thick blond hair fell across his forehead and his generous mouth curved up at one side when he said something intentionally provocative. She watched his lips curve into a full smile and it gave her goose-bumps.

'I don't know about tying you to a bed,' she said. 'I'm seriously considering pulling you to the ground and making love to you right now. God, Max, everything about you turns me on. I want you so badly this minute that I don't even care if the vicar sees.'

She slipped her hands inside his coat and around his waist and started tugging at his shirt. She raised her face to his and saw his lips part and his eyes grow dark with passion then he seemed to pull himself together.

'You might not mind the vicar seeing but you would mind your daughter.' He nodded in Lily's direction.

Becky spun round in horror, saw her daughter standing at the foot of the holly tree then turned back to Max yanking her hands out from his coat. 'You see! You drive me so mad with longing that I even forget my own daughter! What on earth is wrong with me?'

'I think,' he said, taking her hand in his then heading towards Lily, 'we are both suffering from the same thing.'

'Becky dear. Lizzie is on the phone for you. Shall I tell her you'll call her back?' Margaret was standing on the terrace, waving the hands-free phone in the air.

Becky glanced towards Margaret then across to Lily.

144

'Go,' Max said, 'I'll look after Lily.'

'Good heavens, Becky!' Lizzie said, 'Margaret has just told me what happened to you! Are you okay? Don't worry about me. I can speak to you next week. It's not urgent. I should have told her not to bother you.'

'No, Lizzie. It's fine. How can I help you?'

'Are you sure? Margaret told me that you had a nasty fall. I hope Max is taking good care of you. He's the best person to have around in these situations, believe me. Always knows exactly what to do in a crisis.'

The mention of his name made Becky's heart do a little flip and she suddenly knew exactly what was wrong with her – she had fallen in love with Max Bedford.

The realisation was both thrilling and terrifying. She'd only known him for a few days and in that time, she'd gone from disliking him immensely to loving him – and that was a problem. He'd made it perfectly clear that he didn't want a serious relationship ... and yet ... the way he looked at her; the things he said ... was it possible that he felt the same? Of course not. She was being ridiculous.

And how could she fall in love with someone she'd known so briefly? It was just lust; just infatuation. It wasn't love. It wasn't.

But even as she told herself that – she knew it was.

'Becky? Are you okay?'

'Sorry Lizzie. I don't know where my head is at the moment,' she said, dropping sideways onto a chair and holding the back of it with her free hand, as if for support. 'Yes, Max is taking very good care of me, thanks. How are things with you?'

'Good thanks. I was really just calling to say that I've spoken to Jack and we both agree that your schedule is perfect so we're going with that. Jack came up earlier than expected yesterday so I called you in the afternoon and left a message. I was just a little worried that I hadn't heard back. Silly I know but actually, maybe not so silly. I was worried that something may have happened to you and it had! Good heavens, isn't life strange?'

'Max and I were just saying the exact same thing,' Becky said a little hazily.

There was a short silence then Lizzie said, 'This is absolutely none of my business Becky and you are perfectly at liberty to tell me so but ... are you and Max dating?'

The question took her by surprise. She considered denying it but if Lizzie asked Max and he confirmed it, that would cause problems. And what had she and Max just been saying about secrets?

'Yes. It's early days of course; we only met a week ago.'

'Oh. I see.'

There was something in Lizzie's tone that unnerved her. 'I hope it doesn't seem weird. Max being your ex-husband and me helping to arrange your wedding but, I can assure you, whatever happens between us, it will not affect your wedding one iota.'

'Oh no Becky. I wasn't worried about me.'

That clearly meant she was worried about Becky – or Max. Becky didn't like where this conversation was going.

She gave herself a shake, mentally and in her cheeriest voice said, 'Well, there's no need to worry about anything, Lizzie. I'll email you some menu samples on Monday, when I've had a chance to speak with some caterers and I'll send you details of the pyrotechnic company I would recommend for the firework display. Have you organised the cake or do you want me to do that here? There's an excellent cake shop in the village. Actually, come to think of it, Beckleston should be called the Bridal village. Everything one could possibly need for a wedding can be found either in the village or just outside of it, including a photographer. Shall I just email you everything and you can tell me how to proceed from there?'

'That would be perfect Becky, thanks. It seems my wedding is in very good hands – and so is my ex-husband, if you don't mind me saying that. Take care and I'll speak to you soon.'

'Mummy! Mummy! It's snowing!' Lily came running in, red cheeked with excitement, dragging Max along with her.

'Sorry. She wanted to tell you. Have you finished talking to Lizzie?'

Becky nodded. 'Is it darling? That's exciting. Shall we go and make snow angels later if it settles again?'

Lily nodded frenetically then ran to the window to peer out.

'How is she? Getting wildly excited I expect. Mum told me of your scheme for the wedding. I hope Lizzie goes with yours. Having the celebration before the ceremony is not a good idea – and I can speak from experience.'

Becky felt uncomfortable and she fidgeted on the chair but her discomfort had nothing to do with the padded seat. 'So I've heard. Max, please don't take this the wrong way but ... is there still something between you and your ex-wife?'

Max's brows knit together. 'In what way?'

'In the way that ... you still have feelings for one another. I know you said you're over her but is that really the case?'

'Yes! I told you. Six months ago I wasn't sure. Now, I am. I still care a great deal about her; I always will. And I think I can say that she feels the same about me but I no longer love her, in that way, or want to be with her. Why?'

Becky stood up and glanced out of the window, avoiding his eyes. 'I don't know. It's just a niggling feeling I get when I talk to her. She ... she just asked me if we were dating and when I said yes – which I hope you didn't mind, because we are, aren't we, dating I mean?' She shot him a worried look from under her lashes.

'I hope so,' Max grinned. 'And no, I don't mind you telling Lizzie.'

Becky gave a little sigh of relief but said, 'Well, she ... she seemed a bit concerned. I thought she was worried that if we broke up it might affect her wedding but when I assured her it wouldn't she said she wasn't worried about that. She doesn't know me so my feelings wouldn't concern her so that means she's either worried about you or ... or she's jealous and wants you back.'

Max burst out laughing.

'What's funny about that?'

'Oh Fifi.' He let out a huge sigh and shook his head. 'What am I going to do with you? I can assure you, she is not in the least bit jealous. And, if I'm honest, she's probably worried about you. You know that I cheated on her, I told you that, and that since then, I've been out with a lot of women. I'm sorry if this upsets you but you've got to face it, she has known me a lot longer than you have and she knows that, other than her, I haven't been serious about any of the women I've dated. She probably feels she should warn you but that it's not her place to do so. I'll speak to her and –'

'No! That would be really embarrassing, please don't. It's just that ... well I ... I know this is just a bit of fun to you and that you don't want a serious relationship and I – '

'Are you having doubts about me? It may have escaped your notice but I think I may be falling a little in love with you. I told you I'll be honest and I will. I haven't said that to anyone in a very long time – not since Lizzie in fact, and it would be really nice if, for just one moment, you'd give me the benefit of the doubt. I know what with everything that's happened to you, it's very difficult for you to trust people and now I know your real father abandoned you too, I can see why you have security issues but for heaven's sake Becky, give me just a little break and believe what I say.'

For the first time since she'd met him, he seemed cross, and she couldn't understand why. And, had he really just said that he thought he might be falling in love with her – a little?

'I'm sorry. I didn't mean to make you angry.'

'I'm not angry; believe me, you'll really know it if you ever see me angry and will you stop apologising. There's really no need.'

'I'm sorry,' she said, rather heatedly 'but you've had hundreds of women and know exactly what to do and say. This is fairly new to me and I'm scared. I've got Lily to think about too and she already thinks you're the answer to her prayers and the closest thing she's ever had to a father, can't you see that?'

Max opened his mouth to speak but she stopped him.

'No! Let me finish. Everyone I've ever loved or trusted has either left me, deceived me or died, so forgive me for wondering which one of those you may do. And as for thinking you may be falling a little in love with me, well, I really hope you are Max because I'm way past falling, I'm there. I've jumped without a parachute and that's a truly novel and terrifying thing for me. I just hope you'll be there to catch me, but excuse me for finding it difficult to believe that someone who's as gorgeous and who's as experienced and who's ... well who's nothing short of a demigod would actually want to be with me! Especially as you've made it abundantly clear that you don't want a serious relationship!'

Max looked stunned. And for the first time since they'd met, it seemed he had nothing to say.

Lily dashed out into the garden, chasing another robin and after a final glance at Max, Becky raced after her, tears streaming down her face.

'Are you crying Mummy?' Lily asked, turning to see her mother behind her.

Becky swept her into her arms and hugged her. It was several minutes before she could bring herself to speak. 'No darling. I just got a snowflake in my eye, that's all.' She kissed Lily's rosy cheek. 'I think it's time we went home.'

'And you haven't seen or heard from him since?' Jess asked, stunned by the latest instalment in Becky's love life.

'Nope!'

'Well, he'll call. You know he will. It's only been a couple of hours since you left. Maybe he's just giving you a bit of time to think things over. He said he's falling in love with you so he's not going to let you slip away that easily.'

'He said he thought he *may* be falling *a little* in love with me, that's not the same as saying he is.'

'You could call him and say sorry for storming off, I suppose,' Susie said, carrying three mugs of tea into the sitting room, from Becky's kitchen.

'That would go down well. He told me to stop apologising so I don't think calling to say sorry would actually put me into his good books again.'

'That's true. You do seem to apologise an awful lot lately Becky,' Susie agreed.

'I know, I'm sor ... Oh my God! It's like it's become an addiction. Can you be addicted to apologising?'

'You can be addicted to anything I suppose. Remind me again, why did you storm off?' Jess asked.

'Because I knew I was going to start crying my eyes out and I already felt like a silly little girl; besides, if you'd seen the expression on his face. First when I said he was the nearest thing to a father to Lily, that was a real surprise to him – and not a pleasant one by his expression and then, when I told him that I was head over heels in love with him well, it was as if I'd slapped him in the face! He looked ... horrified, terrified. I don't know. He certainly didn't look pleased. And he didn't say a word; he just stared at me with that look on his face.'

'I don't get it. It's okay for him to say he's in love with you but not for you to say you're in love with him? Explain that to me someone,' Susie said, dropping onto the sofa.

'I told you, he didn't say he was in love with me, he said

he thought he was on his way to falling *a little* in love with me, which, as far as I can tell, doesn't actually mean much at all – except that he likes me.'

'He likes you a lot,' Susie corrected.

'And you didn't see his face when you were sparko,' Jess added. 'Honestly Becky, if that guy's not in love with you then I don't know a thing about love.'

'You must stop running off though Becky. No one likes a drama queen.'

'I know. I really don't know what's the matter with me. Since I met him, I seem to go from being deliriously happy one minute to a blubbering idiot the next and then a teenager having a temper tantrum. God knows where the rational, reasonable although, somewhat paranoid, woman went.'

Three pairs of eyes shot to the ringing phone. 'It's him!' Susie said.

Becky stared at the caller display. 'Oh God! It is him.'

'Well then answer it!' Jess shrieked. 'And whatever he says – don't say you're sorry!'

'Or slam the phone down,' Susie added.

'Hello.' Becky tried to sound as calm as she could.

'Can you get Jess or Susie to babysit tonight? We need to talk. I'll pick you up at seven.'

'I –'

He'd already hung up, without waiting for her answer.

Becky had been rehearsing all day, at least, once she'd been able to stop crying and feeling sorry for herself she had. He was clearly going to give her the, "this isn't working" speech and end things before they got any worse. It was obviously too late for her, she was already head over heels in love but he had clearly realised he needed to get out now, before any more harm was done. She could still see the look of surprise and horror when she'd called him Lily's father figure and the even bigger look of abject terror when she'd told him she loved him.

She heard him pull up and she summoned her courage. She had faced the death of her parents, the loss of all her money, the deceit and suicide of her husband and been a single, working mother to her daughter; she could cope with Max Bedford dumping her. Surely? Whatever happened and whatever he said, she was determined that, at no time this evening, would she say she was sorry – or storm off.

She said her goodbyes to Jess and Susie and marched assuredly down the path towards him, in spite of the new layer of snow. She had no idea where they were going so she wore a plain red, wool dress and cardigan beneath her coat. She had her father's diaries in a bag in one hand – no matter what, Margaret deserved to read them – and a huge box of tissues in her handbag in the other. She would try not to cry but even she knew that was a foregone conclusion, so she may as well be prepared. It would be bad enough being dumped, to be dumped and have a runny nose, was unthinkable.

'You're late,' she said when he got out and came to the passenger door to greet her.

He was obviously so surprised by her comment that he didn't reply but merely held the door open whilst she got in.

'You look very pretty,' he said sliding into the driver's seat.

'Thank you.' She stared straight ahead. 'I've brought my father's diaries for you to give to Margaret. She should read them. She can give them back to me when she's finished.'

He started the car and drove off without a word.

'Oh,' she said as he turned into the drive of Beckleston Hall. 'I didn't mean you had to give them to her now.'

'I know, that isn't why we're here.'

'Oh. Why then? Is ... is Margaret going to tell me her side of the story?'

'I have no idea. Probably I suppose.'

'I ... I don't understand,' she said after a few minutes of silence. 'If we're not here because of the diaries and we're not here because Margaret wants to tell me her side of the story, why are we here?'

He pulled up outside the house, got out, and opened the passenger door.

'Well,' he said, shutting the car door behind her. 'To be totally honest, I was very tempted to throw you in the empty pond and save us both a lot of trouble but I thought better of it and instead, decided it's time you met my mother.' He grabbed her arm and shoved it through his, marching her towards the house.

'What are you talking about? I already know your mother ... unless ... are you –?'

'No I'm not adopted or Victoria's secret love child; Margaret is my mother.' He opened the door, helped her off with her coat and led her towards the sitting room. 'You've met her as Becky, the Events Organiser and someone her son knows. Now you're going to meet her as Becky, her son's girlfriend – and the woman he's in love with.'

He ushered her in before she could fully digest his words and she found herself standing with her mouth wide open in front of Margaret, Victoria and an elderly gentleman of a similar age to them.

'This is my girlfriend Becky everyone, Becky, you've met my mother Margaret, and her friend Victoria, I'd like you to meet Gerald a family friend of long standing and one of the best solicitors you're likely to come across.'

Gerald held out his hand, took Becky's in his, raised it to his lips and gently kissed it.

'Honoured to meet you,' he said, grinning at her 'and I mean that most sincerely.'

Becky tried to make her brain work but it was still stuck on Max's "and the woman he's in love with" so she simply smiled, and blushed profusely. She had to think of something to say in response.

'I'm sor ...' she began then quickly changed it to, 'so pleased to meet you. Do you live locally?' She couldn't think of anything else, on the spur of the moment.

'No. I live in town. Margaret and Max have kindly invited me down for the weekend. I arrived this afternoon. You live in the village, I hear. I drove through it; it looks a very pretty little place.'

'It is. I've lived here most of my life and the people are lovely; it's a real community.'

'Fifi, sweetheart, would you like some champagne? Gerald's brought us some rather good news so we're having a little celebration.'

Becky didn't think it was possible for her face to get any redder but she felt she was giving her red dress and cardigan a run for their money. "Fifi" and "sweetheart", in front of everyone. She smiled and nodded, her eyes searching his face.

He winked at her and handed her a glass of champagne. 'Come and sit down,' he took her hand and led her to the sofa, gently lowering her onto the seat beside him. Still holding her hand, he said, 'Becky had a rather nasty fall yesterday Gerald and, although she says she is, I'm not convinced she's fully recovered. I need to take good care of her.'

'Quite right too,' Gerald said, then as he remembered something, 'Fifi. Wasn't that the name of that gorgeous but rather temperamental poodle of yours Margaret? The one Max followed everywhere as though he were attached to her by a cord – and she wouldn't let anyone near her except him. Oh! I'm so sorry my dear. That was rather tactless of me. That sounded as though I am comparing you to a poodle, how incredibly rude.'

A huge grin spread across Max's face. 'That's precisely what Becky said when I first called her Fifi, well Madame Fifi to give her, her correct name.' He wrapped his arm around her and pulled her to him. 'She was furious, weren't you?' he looked her straight in the eye, 'but I think she realises now that I mean it as a sign of my affection.'

Margaret and Victoria both gurgled with laughter. 'You are incorrigible Max!' Victoria said, shaking her head.

'You should box his ears Becky,' Margaret added.

'But he did truly love that dog,' Gerald said. 'I've heard better reasons for giving someone a name as a term of endearment, but I wouldn't hang him for it. It's rather sweet.'

'Thank you!' Max said.

Becky looked into his eyes. 'I rather like it now, actually. I just need to think of something suitable to call him, in return.' Although the only word that sprang into her head was, "darling".

'You could always call me "Darling",' he teased.

He clearly was a demigod – he could read minds too.

'Becky,' Margaret said fifteen minutes later, 'would you give me a hand in the kitchen please? Dinner will be ready in about half an hour so if you two men want to go and sort out your business, Becky, Victoria and I will finish dinner.'

Becky's eyes shot to Max's face in a look akin to panic but he gave her a reassuring smile and a kiss on her nose. 'I won't be long Fifi and Mum won't bite, I promise,' he whispered.

She got up and followed Margaret and Victoria to the kitchen then Victoria said she was popping up to her room and would join them in a few minutes.

'I wanted to apologise,' Margaret said when they were alone, 'and to show you this. It doesn't forgive my appalling behaviour of yesterday I know but it may, in some small way, explain it.'

She handed Becky a worn and crumpled piece of paper; it was a letter dated December 31st, 1944. The ink was smudged and faded with age but it bore the Beckleston crest.

Becky read it aloud.

"Miss Pollard, it pains me to write these words but I feel I must. It appears you have formed an inappropriate attachment to me and for this I am sorry. I have given you no cause to feel thus and believe it is in both our interests to cease all and any contact. Your employment at the Hall has been terminated with immediate effect and I shall not see you again. I offered you friendship, you hoped for more and this I could never give. Our stations are far removed and you must surely know that I could never return your affections. Please do not attempt to contact me. It would not give me pleasure to humiliate you. Horace Beckleston."

Becky stared at Margaret in disbelief.

'It was 1944 when he wrote that. Times were changing rapidly. Most of the stately homes were being sold off. My parents were both killed in the war; I had no other family. I was working at the Hall as a housemaid having left school at twelve with little education. My prospects were limited but I always believed I was destined for better things. Horace was sent home that June, after being injured, you might know that, you said he kept diaries.'

'Yes. I read that it took him several months to fully recover.'

'It did. He was nineteen, I was fifteen – and very pretty, even if I say so myself. We met and fell in love; at least, I thought we had. We saw each other whenever we could and then, in November I discovered I was pregnant. I know that means nothing now but these were different times Becky. But people were dying in the war every day; there was a "live for today" mindset. He was surprised, of course, but he said he would find a way for us to be together. The old order was being swept away. The First World War had changed things greatly, the Second, more so. Perhaps people like us could marry. When you are fifteen and naive, you believe anything is possible. Then on New Year's Eve Edward came to find me, and said Horace wanted to meet me in the stables at eleven that night and that I should pack a bag. I thought it meant we were eloping or something. Instead, I found Edward waiting. He gave me that letter.'

Becky waited for her to continue but she didn't 'And that was it? You believed Edward!'

'It's in Horace's hand, I recognised it but no. I said there must be some mistake, that I would find Horace and ask him. Edward ... stopped me. I knew he was attracted to me but ... well. He was sixteen and a cruel, vain boy but he was as strong as an ox. I ... I couldn't ...'

'Oh my God! Are you saying Edward forced himself on you?'

Margaret gulped down the contents of the glass she had been holding and nodded. 'And he beat me. He told me to get out and never to return or that would seem mild compared to what he would do, he added, with Horace's blessing. I stumbled from there and ran. I didn't know where I was going. I had no money, no family, and no job, nothing in fact except the child I carried. A child unwanted by the father. A father who could have given it everything. A Beckleston of Beckleston Hall,' she said, dramatically.

'But, it's not true Margaret! He did want it; well, when he thought it was his, he did. You must read the diaries. I've brought them with me. He didn't know. Edward deceived you both. He told Horace a completely different story.'

'What? What do you mean Edward told him a different story?' Victoria had been standing in the doorway. She strode across the room and placed a comforting arm around Margaret's shoulder. 'It's okay. I know the whole thing. Well at least Margaret's side of things. What do the diaries say?'

Becky shook her head in disbelief. This was like something from a television drama and she was having trouble comprehending it.

'Edward told Horace that you and he were planning to elope, that you had been having a love affair for several months before Horace had returned, that you had tried to keep it a secret even from Horace but that Edward was trusting Horace to help you both run away. He said you were pregnant with his child. He ... he made Horace believe that you were, effectively, playing one off against the other. That you had made a play for Edward but when the elder brother and heir had returned you'd transferred your "affections" to him. Edward didn't say that of course, but he made it perfectly clear.'

'So Horace wrote the note cutting Margaret off?' Victoria said in stunned comprehension.

'No! Horace wrote no such note. The words don't even sound like his, not if you read his diaries. Edward wrote that note, forging his brother's hand! It's the only explanation. Horace says that you packed a bag and left without a word that night. He thought you knew what Edward had told him and rather than face them, you fled.'

Margaret dropped onto a chair. 'All these years,' she said, her eyes filling with tears. 'All these years I've hated him, thought he had used me then tossed me aside and all the time, he believed that I had lied to him and used him.' She shook her head in disbelief and sorrow.

'And the child? What ...?' Becky's voice trailed off. This was none of her business.

'I lost it. When I ran from here I had no idea where I was going. It was a dreadful night with torrential rain and no moon. I could hardly see a thing but I kept running, blindly running. I fled across the fields; trying to get as far away from Beckleston as I could. I remember reaching the brow of a hill and I thought I could see a road below so I started to make my way down but I slipped and fell, hitting my head on a rock. Then Fate intervened. Royston, Max's father was on his way home and had seen me fall. He took me to a hospital nearby and when I eventually recovered, he found someone to take me in. I told him the whole story a few months later. He wanted to kill both of them but then I would have lost him too. He got me a job in a shop and we married a year later. I was seventeen. He was twenty-one. He told me that he knew he was going to marry me the moment he saw me. Perfect man, perfect timing. We were very happy and very much in love until the day he died.' She sighed deeply. 'Max is the spitting image of him.'

Becky thought for a moment. 'Margaret, if you hated the

Becklestons so much why ... why did you buy Beckleston Hall? Surely this place holds terrible memories for you? Why would you want to come back here? Especially after living such a happy life with Royston.'

'Because of Edward's final words to me. He said that I was nothing and that I would never be the Lady of Beckleston or anywhere else for that matter. And, oddly enough, I had always loved this house; I still do. Royston passed away ten years ago and when the house came back on the market, last year, I saw it. I was actually at the dentist at the time. It was in one of those Country House type magazines and it was Fate. I am now the owner of Beckleston Hall, albeit it, more than sixty years later.'

'Everything comes around that goes around,' Victoria said. 'To discover, after all these years, that Horace did love you, though. That is truly incredible.'

'But he would have hated me if he believed what Edward told him, and if he didn't why wouldn't he have tried to find me? What ... what do the diaries say?'

'You need to read them Margaret. Basically, he didn't know whether to believe Edward or not. He loved you, so he didn't want to but – this is rather personal – you have a birth mark that ... well Edward told Horace about it and Horace knew that ... '

'That only someone I had been intimate with could possibly have seen it! Oh Good God! When Edward ... '

Becky nodded. 'I must admit, when I read the diaries I believed Edward. Of course, I didn't know you then but that sort of clinched it for me. It seemed to for Horace too. Although he didn't stop loving you, even then. He was sent back to the front, for the final few months of the war and when he returned, he sort of shut himself off – and he remained that way until the day he met my mother.'

Margaret squeezed Becky's hand. 'Thank you so much for telling me this. Of course, I want to read the diaries but until tonight, I thought ...well, that he felt nothing for me. So many years of hatred and all because of one cruel and evil boy. Becky, this makes me feel even worse about my treatment of you yesterday. Can you forgive a foolish old woman?'

Becky smiled warmly, 'Of course I can, if you can forgive a foolish young one.'

'There's nothing for me to forgive.'

'I ran away and fell in the pond! I must have caused all sorts of mayhem yesterday.'

'Oh. That wasn't your fault. Actually, I think, in the strangest way, that may actually have been a good thing. Not you falling of course, I don't mean that. Fate intervening; Max rescuing you.'

Becky blushed. 'Speaking of Max. Do ... do you mind about us. I know it's only been a few days and I know it may not last but –'

'Good heavens no! I couldn't be happier. It's none of my business so I won't interfere but I will just say one thing. Max has just introduced you as his girlfriend to Victoria, to Gerald and to me and I can say without even the slightest doubt, we are the only three people living whose opinions matter to him, other than yours, of course. Think about that Becky. And remember what I said, Max is the spitting image of his father.'

'Thank you so much for tonight Max,' Becky said when she got into the car and Max headed down the drive. 'I had a wonderful time.'

He smiled at her. 'I get the feeling it wasn't quite what you'd expected.'

She shook her head and smiled back. 'The complete opposite. I thought you were going to tell me it was over.'

He stopped the car abruptly and turned to her. 'What in God's name gave you that idea?'

She swivelled round to look him full in the face. 'Well, because when I said you were almost a father figure to Lily you looked horrified and when I said I loved you, you looked even more so. Terrified in fact. And you didn't say a word; didn't come after me when I left ... '

He shook his head and sighed. 'Oh, Becky. What am I going to do with you? I'll admit I was surprised when you said the father figure bit. Half the time I'm not totally convinced I'm an adult myself, let alone being a father figure to someone else and yes, I was astonished when you said you love me. After everything that's happened to you I knew you would find it difficult to trust me, it didn't occur to me that you could fall in love with me regardless. I knew you liked me – a lot, even though I'm not sure you really wanted to, that much was obvious but I thought I was the only one of us really in danger of getting a broken heart at this stage. Honestly, I thought you were holding back, especially as you said, more than once, that you didn't expect it to last.' He reached out a hand and stroked her cheek.

'But you let me go – when I said I loved you. I went back in to get our things and you were nowhere to be seen. I thought you'd had second thoughts, to be honest, after all, you were the one who said you didn't want a serious relationship and, well, you seemed to be angry with me.'

'I was angry with myself – and I needed to think. I wasn't expecting to meet someone and fall in love, let alone someone with a child. I knew I was falling for you but after you said those things, I realised it wasn't just my heart at stake; it was yours and Lily's too. And I had to consider the implications of that. The thought of being a father terrifies me, I'll admit that but the first time I picked Lily up, I wanted to protect her. Does that make sense?'

'Yes, it does.'

'But we've only known one another for a few days and I wanted to take things slowly, especially after everything you've told me about your past. And I'm not really sure what's happening half the time; it's all happened so quickly. And when you ran off again I – '

'I shouldn't have run off,' Becky interrupted, 'but you must understand, I meant it when I said I'm frightened,

161

you're so much more experienced at relationships and you seem to take everything in your stride, nothing seems to bother you. I worry about everything. I want so much to believe you and I do but then a little flicker of doubt sets in and I panic.'

'I understand that and I understand why, but I said I wouldn't lie and I won't. There are no guarantees Becky. I thought I was in love with Lizzie and it would last a lifetime; it didn't. I hurt her very badly and myself too. I don't ever want to do that again. But things are different. I met her shortly after Dad died and I don't think I was really ready, not for marriage and the whole settling down bit, but I thought I was. I really did love her but ... obviously, not enough. I've changed a lot since then but I want to be sure, especially as it involves Lily too.'

'But ... what are you saying Max? That ... that you think we might have a future together ... the three of us?' She couldn't believe her ears.

He smiled almost wickedly, 'And at least twenty others, if my mother has anything to say in the matter. Apparently, Beckleston Hall has twenty five bedrooms; I still haven't actually found them all.'

'It does, but –'

'Mum wants to fill the place with grandchildren.' He met her eyes and held them.

Becky let out an excited little giggle. 'Well then, we'd better go home and start practising,' she said, leaning across to kiss him on the lips then pulling away.

He reached out and pulled her back. 'I did mention I'm an only child didn't I?'

'Well,' she said, in the sexiest voice she could muster, 'in that case, we'd better start practising right away.'

Two days after Becky officially became Max's girlfriend he insisted on taking her to London to buy her a winter coat that would actually keep out the cold.

'It's because you don't want your *girlfriend* looking like a bag of old clothes isn't it?' she teased.

'Not in the least. It's fine with me if you want to wear old clothes – although I would draw the line at a bag – providing they keep you warm and dry. Your coat does neither. We can go to a vintage clothes shop, and buy you a coat there, if you like.'

'No. It's fine,' she said acknowledging that he was right. 'But I will repay you; I can't allow you to spend such a lot of money on me.'

'Oh can't you? It's my money Becky, and I'll spend it on whatever I want,' he said, childishly, pulling a face at her to give added effect. 'And I want to spend it on a new coat for my gorgeous girlfriend – oh, and a pair of good walking boots too.'

'No Max! That's definitely too much.'

'The boots aren't for your benefit, they're for mine,' he said, adopting a serious tone. 'I can't keep carrying you every time the weather's bad. If I'm going to sire twenty children, I need to look after my back.'

Becky gurgled with laughter. The children were a joke but each time he mentioned it, Becky felt something stir inside her and the thought of having a child with him, was one she found more appealing by the minute.

'And talking of children,' he said, 'I want to buy Lily a few things while we're in town. No. Don't argue.' He pulled her into his arms and kissed her before she had a chance to.

'I know you're seeing Jess and Susie this evening so I'm only popping in for a few minutes,' Max said one evening, handing her a letter addressed to Mrs. Rebecca Cooper,

'Gerald asked me to give you this. It's to do with Jeremy's debts.'

It was exactly two weeks after the Wednesday on which Max had taken the box of papers.

Becky took it from him and stared at the envelope.

'I know you're a very special young woman,' he said, 'but even you don't have X-ray vision. It might help if you open it.' He sauntered into the kitchen and took two glasses from the cupboard.

'I'm nervous. Is it good news or bad?'

'According to you, I'm a demigod, not Superman. I don't have X-ray vision either. Open it.'

Becky tore at the envelope. She knew Gerald had been dealing with it; she'd had a rather curt letter from her solicitor confirming he'd transferred the files to Gerald Merriton and confirming his fees had been paid in full – something else Max had paid for and dismissed as having done for his own benefit. He liked the way she thanked him, he said.

'Well?' Max said.

Becky read and re-read the letter and the attachments at least five times then raised disbelieving eyes to his. He was holding two glasses of champagne.

'You knew!' she said, her eyes filling with tears. 'Is this true?'

'Gerald never lies. And yes, I knew and yes, it's true – oh that rhymes! Here drink this.' He handed her a glass. 'Here's to a debt free future.' He clinked glasses and took a sip. 'I've brought another two bottles so that you can celebrate with your friends.'

'But how?' She still couldn't believe it. 'It took me over six months to get them all to agree to the original scheme and I had at least another three or four years of repayments to go!'

'Yes, and I told you that was rubbish. You had just lost your husband, your inheritance, and most of your money, you were hardly in a fit state to deal with these people and –

as I've said, your solicitor was useless. He should have contested the debts immediately. Some you still would have been liable for but some of them, in our opinions, you should never have agreed to repay although it would have been a complex issue to prove. We just said that, as they were now saying the original agreement was void, we would agree but we intended to contest the loans, basically, on the grounds I've just outlined, but that we were prepared to settle on the basis that they accepted what you'd already paid in full and final settlement. A couple of them got bolshie; we stood our ground and gave them twenty-four hours to agree. They did. Anyway, I just wanted you to know as soon as possible so that you can stop worrying.'

He kissed her on the nose and was about to head towards the door when she managed to shake herself out of her stupefied state and grab his arm to stop him.

'Max wait! Are you sure you haven't paid them or ... or something?'

He looked a little offended. 'I'm sure. I told you Becky, I won't lie to you.'

'I'm sorry. But how? I really don't understand. Why would they agree when they knew I was willing to pay them more? Why would they settle for less?'

'I've told you. They didn't want the hassle. When we said we would contest them, they weren't sure whether we would or not. We may have been on slightly dodgy ground but they didn't want it to drag out and let's face it, you have already repaid quite a bit of the money. Better to keep what they've got than waste more time and money trying to get more. There's always room for negotiation – if you know how to negotiate and believe me, Gerald does. I'll dash off; Jess and Susie will be here soon.'

'But I haven't even thanked you. How can I ever repay you for everything you've done for me? I must seem really ungrateful but the truth is, I'm in a state of shock; I can't really take this in. Does this truly mean that I won't have to repay anyone another penny?'

'Yep. That's what all the attachments are. We've checked and made sure that this time, they've all agreed. There's a letter from each saying the monies you've paid are in full and final settlement of any and all claims. They're all pretty similar. Gerald drafted the letters. That's it.'

'That's unbelievable. I've been paying this for five years and in just two weeks, you've wiped the slate clean!'

'Gerald did most of it. I just had a chat or two with some people I know. I told you, he is the best solicitor you are likely to meet. And the slate's not clean. You are indebted to me for one thank you; I did bring the letter here after all. You can pay me tomorrow.' He kissed her on her mouth but it wasn't his usual passionate kiss.

'Not so fast. Why are you dashing off?'

'Because Jess and Susie will think I can't leave you alone for five minutes.'

'They won't be here for another hour; it's Jess' late night and Susie had some meeting or other with the vicar – don't make any jokes. Lily's already fast asleep.' She wrapped her arms around his waist. 'I can't let you leave knowing I owe you a thank you, after all, having just got out of debt with one lot of bankers I don't want to start getting into arrears with another.'

'I'm not a banker now, remember – or anything similar sounding.'

She grinned up at him. 'One day, you must explain to me exactly what it is you are now, apart from a demigod of course. You did say, but I'll be damned if I can remember.'

'That's because every time I start telling you, you start seducing me, just like you are now.'

'I just want to thank you.'

'Okay. An hour you said; that should be sufficient time to thank me – at least twice.'

'So that's it? In two weeks you've gone from thinking you may lose everything to being debt free! That's unbelievable!' Jess said an hour later, curled up on Becky's sofa.

'And three bottles of champagne too! I seriously regret saying you could have Max Bedford,' Susie said.

'Like you had any say in the matter,' Jess teased.

'It is unbelievable though, isn't it? And you know what? I'm going to start believing in Fate.' Susie said.

'I think I'm a believer. What with Margaret's story, my parents' too for that matter, Lizzie and Jack – ooh! I haven't told you that one yet have I? About how Lizzie and Jack got together I mean. Margaret told me the other day. Not the whole story of course, just snippets but it's truly weird.'

'Don't waffle then. Tell us.'

'Well, when Lizzie left Max she went to stay with a friend in Scotland, bought a run-down farm, and converted it into a bed and breakfast. Jack and several of his friends went to stay for the weekend, for Jack's stag party – he was getting married two weeks later – and he and Lizzie fell head over heels in love. Margaret doesn't know all the details and it's actually quite complicated but apparently Jack then discovered his fiancée was sleeping with his best friend! Anyway, after lots of other things happening and lots of misunderstandings, Jack ended up with Lizzie and his friend ended up with Jack's fiancée.'

'Bloody hell! That's not fate, that's a French Farce!' Jess said, 'and we thought our lives were complicated. I'd like someone to fall head over heels in love with me.' She sighed.

'Perhaps if you didn't have pink and blue hair, someone might!'

'Thank you Susie! There is nothing wrong with pink and blue hair, besides, if you love someone, you don't care what colour their hair is, isn't that right Becky?'

Becky nodded and refilled their glasses, raising hers in the air. 'That's right. Here's to us all finding true love.'

'You've already found it, but here's to me and Susie

finding it.'

'True love,' said Susie. Then, after taking a couple of gulps of her champagne, 'I know you're going to laugh at me for saying this but ... I've fallen for the vicar ... teeth and all.'

They didn't laugh; they were too astonished to.

'Susie and the vicar? Yeah, I thought there was something between those two,' Max said when Becky told him the following evening.

'Well, so far nothing's happened but why did you think that? Jess and I had no idea.'

'Because he always seems to be popping in to see her. I've only been around for about three weeks but every time I see him he seems to be either going in or coming out of her shop. I know it's a Bridal shop and it's possible they have a common interest but really – every day?'

'Now that you say that, he does. I've seen it myself.'

'Catholic priests can't marry though can they?'

'I don't think so but he's not Catholic, he's Church of England. I told you, remember? The confessional thing was a joke. That's something I suppose, he has got a sense of humour and, the more I think about him, the more I realise, he's not that bad looking. He just needs to do something with his teeth, and have his hair cut.'

'Hey! Don't you start falling for the vicar, Fifi.'

She smiled at him. 'No chance. I wonder if there's something we can do to speed things along. I mean, if she likes him and he likes her ...' Becky's mind wandered. 'You could probably find a way Max; you seem to be able to do everything else without much effort. I'd really like her to be happy. And then there's Jess of course.'

'Dear God. So now I'm the local matchmaker too. Okay, I'll give it some thought.'

Becky snuggled up to him. 'I'll thank you in advance, if you like.'

'Fifi Cooper, I'm beginning to think you're addicted to

sex.'

'That's what the vicar thinks but the truth is – I'm addicted to you, and there's no chance of a cure.'

The preparations for Lizzie's wedding were progressing nicely. Susie had been asked to make the bride and bridesmaids' dresses and Stephanie was organising the flowers. Jess would be doing hair and make-up for the wedding party, and the fireworks, band, cake and menus had all been agreed. The refurbishment of Beckleston Hall was way ahead of schedule – to everyone's surprise but Max – and the pond was repaired and refilled and the ducks, returned.

'Sometimes, I think I'm living in a fairytale,' Becky said one evening when she and her friends were having a curry at her house. 'Max and I have been dating for six weeks and things just seem to be getting better and better.'

'It's so good to see you happy,' Susie said. 'Life can be full of surprises can't it?'

'We're all living in a fairytale,' Jess said. 'You only have to see the vicar to realise that. He's gone from a buck-toothed frog to a prince and even I have to admit – albeit reluctantly – that he's not bad looking now.'

'That's not very nice Jess. He was never a frog!'

'Oh Susie, love really is blind. Anyway, my point is who would've believed that he could turn out to be handsome?'

'I know!' Becky giggled. 'I hardly recognised him.'

'That was a truly providential accident – or an act of God, as the vicar no doubt believes,' Jess laughed.

'It wasn't funny!' Susie said. 'He could have been killed when he was knocked off his bike! He had to have four of his front teeth replaced and surgery to his upper jaw and nose. He was in a lot of pain.'

'That's true Susie. Sorry,' Becky said suitably chastised.

Susie smiled. 'Actually, I suppose we even have to thank Max for that. It was good of him to arrange for a friend of his to do the surgery.'

'Too right!' Jess said, 'If it'd been done under the national health, I'm pretty sure the vicar would have false teeth instead of implants and there's no way they would have done the cosmetic, rather than purely reconstructive, surgery on his jaw and nose – although, I never thought I'd see the day when a vicar had a face-lift,'

'It wasn't a face-lift! His jaw and nose were broken in several places and anyway, why shouldn't he take the opportunity to improve his looks ... oh,' Susie saw both Jess and Becky grinning at her, 'you're teasing me.'

'To be honest,' Becky said, 'the vicar would have gone with the NHS but Max told him that his friend was trying out a new procedure so they'd be doing each other a favour. He also told him that there was no harm in making a slight adjustment, because vicars are red blooded males too and pretty girls like nice teeth – although I probably shouldn't have told you that. Oh well. Even the vicar conceded that God moves in mysterious ways.'

'Max said what?' Susie shrieked.

Jess just laughed. 'Good for him. Don't get all high and mighty Susie. It's an improvement, let's leave it at that. Of course, the haircut I gave him is what really made the difference.'

Susie sighed deeply. 'I hate to admit it but that's partly true. Perhaps you should do something about your own.'

'Meow! Actually I'm going to. I'm bored with pink and blue hair. I'm going to dye it purple and black instead.'

Spring was in the air; the weather had turned unseasonably warm and the parkland of Beckleston Hall was filled with daffodils and tulips.

Lily would be five in two days' time, on Saturday March the 31st and Becky felt that everything seemed right with the world.

So did Max, until six o'clock that Thursday afternoon, when he got a phone call from Lizzie.

'What do you mean the wedding's off?' Max couldn't understand what Lizzie was saying; she was crying and talking at the same time and the television volume seemed rather loud. 'I can't hear you Lizzie. Turn down the television, try to stop crying and tell me what's happened.'

'He's having an affair!'

Max almost laughed. 'Jack! I don't believe that for one minute. He loves you far too much and, to be honest, he's not the two-timing type.'

'He doesn't and he is! All men are. Don't forget, he was engaged when he slept with me and that's what makes it worse Max. Guess who he's having it with?'

Max had a dreadful feeling he knew but he still couldn't believe it. 'Tell me.'

'Only Kim bloody Mentor, his ex-fiancée!'

Max slumped onto the sofa. He was in the sitting room at his mother's and was just about to leave for Becky's. 'I know who she is Lizzie, although she's not Kim Mentor now, she's Kim Briarstone remember? Ross' wife. But anyway, he wouldn't. What on earth makes you think that?'

'Because she told me!'

Max almost dropped the phone. 'Who told you? Kim? And you believed her? When? When did she tell you?'

'This morning and when I called Jack and asked if he'd been seeing her – he said "yes"!'

'Okay, this is crazy. There must be some mistake. Is Jack still in town? When is he coming up to you?'

'He's not. I told him not to. I told him I was going away for the weekend and I wouldn't tell him where.'

'That wasn't a good idea Lizzie. What did he say, exactly?'

'He said he had been seeing her but it wasn't like that but he was furious that I didn't trust him because he wouldn't be unfaithful so I reminded him that he was unfaithful – with me and ... and then he said things and I said things and ... and then I called off the wedding and slammed the phone down.'

'Okay, well he'll obviously come and see you and talk it out and I'm sure you'll find it's all a big misunderstanding. I assume you're not really going away for the weekend.

Lizzie, will you please turn the television down, it's deafening.'

'It's not the television. I'm at the airport.'

'The airport. Which airport? Where are you going?'

'Inverness airport and I'm phoning to ask if I can come and stay with you.'

This time, Max did drop the phone. He hurriedly pulled himself together.

'You said I could, if I ever needed to, you said you'll always be there for me. Well I need to and I need you. Please say yes Max. Please!'

'Where're Jane and Iain?' He couldn't understand why she hadn't gone straight to her best friend.

'They went away this morning. It's their wedding anniversary on the 31st, remember. They won't be back until Sunday.'

'So, who's going to be looking after Alistair and the animals if you come here?' Why he should be thinking about Lizzie's dog at a time like this he wasn't sure but he still couldn't quite get his head around any of this.

'Iain's son Fraser. Yes or no Max? I need to know now. My flight closes in fifteen minutes.'

'Becky, I'm really sorry but I'm going to have to cancel this evening.'

For the first time since she'd known him, Max actually looked flustered.

'What's happened Max? Is Margaret all right. Come in.' She held the door open for him.

'Actually, I can't stop. I'm on my way to Gatwick.' He went inside nevertheless.

'Oh! Is everything okay? I've never seen you like this. You ... you look really worried.'

'I am really worried. I've just had a phone call from Lizzie. She's called off the wedding and she's coming to stay for the weekend!'

Becky was astonished. 'W... why?'

173

'She thinks Jack is having an affair.'

'Why?'

'Because the woman called her and told her he was.'

'Good grief! And ... and she believes it? Is it true?'

'If you knew the woman and their history, you'd probably believe it too. I don't think it is but ... I don't know for sure.'

'I don't understand, this is making no sense. Why ... why is Lizzie coming to stay with you? What can you do about it?'

'She just wants to talk to someone about it and have a shoulder to cry on.'

'And you're the shoulder? Doesn't she have friends?'

'Yeah but her best friend's away for her anniversary so I'm the next best thing.'

'Oh. And you're going to pick her up from the airport? I wish you'd called me earlier, I've made dinner for us.' Becky turned away and poured herself a glass of wine from the bottle she'd opened. She felt as if she'd been hit by a truck – and it was carrying several tonnes of jealousy.

'I've only just found out. She called me just before the flight was leaving, only a few minutes ago. She'll be landing in less than an hour.'

'What? She just assumed she could call you and you'd drop everything for her. Well, obviously she was right.'

'What? Look Becky, I'm sorry about dinner, really I am but she's in a bit of a state and I can't expect her to make her own way here.'

'No. Of course not.'

'Okay. What's wrong? Clearly you're upset and it's not just about me having to miss dinner is it? You're not having doubts about me again are you? Just because I'm doing a friend a favour.'

'She's not a friend Max; she's your ex-wife. An ex-wife you spent two years trying to get back and almost as long to get over when she met someone else.'

She saw the look of disbelief on his face.

174

'Look Becky, I don't know why you're so upset about this. She is a friend, a good friend and she really needs me at the moment. But the points you make are correct. She is my ex and I am over her. Completely. You're my present and I love you. I'm hoping you'll be my future too but there's something we need to get clear here and now. I care about Lizzie and she's asked for my help. I intend to give it. If you can't handle that and don't trust me, then we have a serious problem.'

'I ... I do trust you. It's ... it's just so sudden that's all. Such a surprise.' Panic began to take hold of her.

'Tell me about it. I dropped the phone when she said she was coming to stay.' He took a step towards her and pulled her into his arms. 'I'm sorry if that sounded harsh but she does need me. If you had to cancel dinner because Jess or Susie needed you, I wouldn't mind.'

'That's completely different Max!'

'Not to me it isn't. I care about her in the same way as you care about your friends. That's it. Just because I'm going to pick her up and just because she's staying at my mum's house for a few days doesn't mean I'm going to fall back in love with her.'

'How do you know?'

He held her slightly away from him and looked her directly in her eyes. 'Because if I did that would mean what I feel for you isn't real.'

'That's what worries me. You said you thought you loved her yet you had an affair because you didn't love her enough – and you were married to her. We've only been dating for six weeks. How do I know you won't suddenly realise that you don't love me enough either?'

'This is crazy. Either I love you or I don't. And you either trust me or you don't. Perhaps it's time we really found out. I've got to go. I'm sorry Becky, truly I am. Are you going to kiss me goodbye?'

She stared at him, with tears pricking her eyes. She wanted to grab him and stop him but she knew that was

175

insane.

'Fine,' he said giving her a quick peck on the cheek. 'I'll call you later.' He turned and left.

She was furious. How dare he walk away from her? Then she realised what she'd done and ran after him.

They almost knocked one another over as they crashed into each other just outside the door. He'd turned round and come back.

She fell into his arms. 'I'm sorry Max! I'm really sorry.'

He held her away from him. 'I'm sorry too. And I do understand. You're right, it's different from you and Jess and Susie. If our roles were reversed and you ran off to see an ex-husband, I'd be eaten up with jealousy too, I just realised that – but I would trust you. I do have to go and get her but I don't want to leave like this.'

'I know. I'm being totally unreasonable. I'm ... I'm just jealous. I do trust you and you're right, you have to go. Drive safely and ... and call me when you get a chance.'

He relaxed for the first time since Lizzie had called. 'You don't know how good it is to hear you say that Fifi.' He pulled her into his arms and kissed her long and deep. 'I should have told her to get a cab here,' he said when he finally let her go.

Becky smiled up at him. 'No, if she's upset you should be with her. You were right to say you'd collect her. It's who you are, and it's one of the reasons I love you. You do things for people you care about. Now go. I'll see you soon.'

Despite what she'd said, Becky spent the next hour and a half worrying. Twice the phone had rung and she'd grabbed it, without looking at the caller display, hoping it was him, then been disappointed when first Jess then Susie had called. They'd agreed, Max was right to go but they didn't think Lizzie should have just assumed she could arrive on his doorstep, virtually unannounced and they were all beginning to feel, they might not like her after all.

Finally, he called.

'Hi sweetheart. We're just leaving Gatwick and should be home in about an hour. Have you had a good evening?'

His voice sounded calm but more importantly, it sounded full of love and Becky felt the tension drain from her. That, at least was the first hurdle over.

'Not bad, all things considered but hearing from you has made it better. How's Lizzie?'

'Okay, I think. She wants to talk to you. I'll pass you over.'

'Hi Becky. Listen, I'm so sorry about this. Max just told me you had plans this evening. I'm sorry to have ruined them. He told you about Jack. I ... I was just so devastated and, I did tell you, Max was the person to have around in a crisis didn't I? I wasn't really thinking straight, to be honest. I just wanted to get away. But, now that I come to think about it, coming to the place where I was intending to hold my wedding, may not have been my best idea. I may go to my grandparents tomorrow. I'm in a bit of a state, emotionally, as you can imagine but I'd love to meet you. Is there any chance we could have a cup of coffee tomorrow morning, assuming I haven't drowned in my own tears by then?'

Becky could hardly say no. 'Yes, of course. I ... I hope you ... well, I hope things work out for the best.'

'Thanks. Max has been giving me a lecture, of course, and he's sure there's nothing going on with Jack and that bloody woman but ... well, I'll talk to you about it when I see you. Good night Becky. I'll pass you back to Max.'

'Hi love. Is Lily in bed?'

'No, she's a bit late tonight. She wanted to finish a jigsaw puzzle and, to be quite honest, I needed the company.'

'Give her a hug for me. I'll call you later. Bye.'

'Well, well,' Lizzie said when Max had rung off, 'unless I'm very much mistaken Max Bedford's in love.'

Becky pottered in the kitchen. She felt much happier having spoken to Max but she wouldn't feel totally at ease until he was safe at home. She had really wanted to ask him to pop in and see her later, once Lizzie was settled but she knew that was being ridiculous. He'd said he'd call, that was good enough. But Lizzie hadn't sounded quite as upset as Becky had expected her to be and, as hard as she tried not to, she still couldn't help wondering whether Lizzie wanted Max back.

It was nine-thirty and she'd cleaned the oven, cleaned the sink twice and rearranged the cutlery drawer. She realised she was being silly and decided to go upstairs and read.

She was just about to lock up when Max knocked on the door and poked his head round. 'You really should lock your door at night; you never know who might be around. May I come in?'

She ran to him and threw herself in his arms in the doorway.

'I take it that's a yes.' He kissed her tenderly and when he pulled away he said, 'Lizzie's settling in and pouring her heart out to Mum and Victoria. I've left them to it. I'm starving. I don't suppose there's any dinner left is there?'

Becky laughed ecstatically. 'I'll make you something. I'm so happy to see you, Max. I know this sounds really silly but it feels as if you've been gone for a lifetime.'

'It doesn't sound silly at all. It's good to know you miss me as much as I do you. On second thoughts, forget dinner, let's just go to bed.'

When Max spent the night at Becky's, he either left by seven, or made sure he was dressed and downstairs by then. Lily woke up around that time and whilst they were happy for her to see them kissing or holding hands, letting her know he slept in Mummy's bed was a step too far. Not that she would have understood, of course but somehow, acknowledging to her that they spent the night together, gave their relationship an air of permanence and, it seemed neither of them were ready for that.

'Why don't I take you and Lily for breakfast at Mum's?' Max asked when he got out of the shower. 'That way, you can meet Lizzie and, if you hit it off, I can nip up to town this morning as I'd originally planned and be back in time for lunch. Then, we can all drive down to drop Lizzie at her grandparents, if she still wants to go. What do you think?'

'That sounds good to me. Will your mum – or Lizzie mind?' Becky said.

'Mum won't, and I'm sure Lizzie won't either but I'll call and check, if you like.' He dialled the number and when Margaret answered, he said, 'Is it okay if the three of us drop in for breakfast? How's Lizzie? Is she up to company?'

Becky couldn't hear Margaret's reply but Max was nodding and smiling at her so she went into Lily's room and helped her put on a pair of jeans and a dark red sweater then she showered and dressed in a pair of black trousers and a navy sweater whilst Max took Lily downstairs to play.

By eight o'clock they were all seated around the breakfast table in the kitchen of Beckleston Hall.

'It's lovely to meet you at last,' Lizzie said, smiling warmly at Becky. 'And Lily's beautiful; you must be very proud.'

'I am,' Becky said returning the smile. Despite her

reservations and doubts, Lizzie appeared to be as lovely as Max and Margaret had said she was and she clearly had no interest in Max as far as romance went. She obviously cared for him as much as he did her but, Becky soon realised, their relationship actually wasn't very different to the one she had with Jess and Susie, after all.

'So, any news from Jack?' Max asked buttering his third slice of toast.

Lizzie shook her head and cast her eyes down to the half-eaten egg on her plate.

Max glanced at Becky then at Margaret then back to Lizzie. 'Let me rephrase the question; are you going to answer any of his calls and discuss this like adults?' He took a fourth slice of toast and started buttering it as everyone in the room stared at him in astonishment – except Lily.

'Wh ... what makes you think he's been calling?' Lizzie asked, her voice raised by several octaves.

Max poured himself more coffee and refilled Becky's mug, smiling and winking at her as he did so. 'Because I know Jack ... and I know you. You've turned your phone off haven't you?'

Lizzie scowled at him. 'I don't want to hear his excuses and lies. I – '

'Oh for heaven's sake Lizzie! Give the man a break will you? How do you know he'll lie or make excuses unless you actually listen to him? I said it last night and I'll say it again. I don't care what Kim told you; I don't believe it – and neither should you.'

'That's easy for you to say! But when I asked him if he'd been to see her – he said he had!'

'Yes. Because he wanted to tell you the truth. But seeing someone doesn't mean you're screwing them. If it did, imagine what he'd be thinking about you coming to see me! Oh! Sorry Becky.' He put his arm around Becky and kissed her on the cheek.

'Max!' Lizzie hissed.

'He's got a point,' Margaret said.

'What do you think Becky?'Lizzie asked.

'Er ... ,' Becky wasn't sure what to say, especially since she'd been thinking along similar lines. 'I think ... I'd feel as you do but Max is right. Perhaps you should hear what Jack has to say.'

Lizzie held eye contact with Becky for several seconds then looked away. 'I'm just not sure I could go through all that again,' she said quietly, lifting her eyes to Max's face.

'Okay,' Max said hurriedly getting to his feet. 'I need to go. I'll drop Lily off on my way to the station but I'd like a quick word Becky.' He grabbed her hand and gently pulled her to her feet. 'Excuse us.' He led her out of the kitchen, down the hall and into the sitting room in silence.

'Right,' he said sitting her down on the sofa and sitting next to her, holding both her hands in his. 'You're all going to be discussing Jack's alleged affair when I've gone and there's something I should tell you; something you should hear from me. I told you I had an affair with my secretary but I didn't tell you her name.'

'I don't need to know her name Max. It was before we knew each other and it really doesn't matter. Why do you want to tell me this now?'

'I think it might matter, when Lizzie starts telling you about Jack, how they met and who his ex-fiancée was.' He saw the shadow of suspicion slowly creep across her eyes.

'You ... you don't mean ...?'

He nodded in confirmation. 'I'm afraid so. It came as quite a shock to all of us at the time, believe me. When Lizzie ... found out about my affair with Kim – that's her name, Kim – I ended it. I didn't know Jack then but it seems she immediately got her claws into him. I say claws, not out of spite but because of the type of woman she is.'

'It takes two to tango Max,' Becky said a little shakily, clearly trying to absorb this latest revelation.

'I agree. I'm not for one minute suggesting I didn't play as big a part in it as she did; I'm just saying, when Kim gets

181

a man in her sights, it takes more than bullet proof glass to keep her from taking him down – no pun intended.'

'I ... I've met women like that.'

He was relieved she was taking it so well. 'Anyway, about two years later, Jack turns up at Lizzie's on his stag weekend. He's already having serious doubts about Kim; even the engagement and forthcoming wedding seem to have been staged and controlled by her so, when he meets Lizzie and they fall for one another – big time, well, let's just say he goes against type and sleeps with Lizzie even though he's still officially engaged to Kim, although Lizzie doesn't know it's Kim he's engaged to. Are you with me so far?'

'God, Max! Hold on. I've just realised what you're saying. Lizzie had an affair with the fiancé of the woman who had an affair with her husband – you!'

'Er. That's about it – I think. It's still confusing, even to me and I was involved in it! But it gets worse!'

'How could it possibly get worse?'

'It seems Kim had found another target, Jack's best friend, Ross. When Jack was away on business, she got her clutches on him and they also had an affair.'

'Good grief! Margaret told me a bit about that but not about your involvement with Kim. So, you had an affair with Kim who then got engaged to Jack and she then had an affair with his best friend Ross. Is there anyone the woman didn't sleep with? Then Lizzie fell in love with Jack not knowing he was engaged to the woman you had an affair with!'

'Er...Yes. You couldn't make this stuff up could you? I didn't know Mum had told you about Jack and Lizzie and I'm not sure whether I ever told her that Kim was the woman. Anyway, Ross married Kim – a big mistake in my opinion but there it is – and Jack could be with Lizzie, so it all worked out well in the end – until now that is.'

'And now Lizzie thinks Jack is having an affair behind her back just like he did when he was engaged to Kim and just like you did – with Kim?'

'Well, yes, but it's worse than that. Lizzie thinks Jack is having an affair *with* Kim.'

'What? Why?'

'Because Kim apparently called her yesterday and told her he was – and like the complete and utter idiot that Jack can be sometimes, he didn't deny it.'

He saw the odd look in her eye.

'So ... you think Jack should have denied it? You think he should have lied?'

'No! I told you, I did that once, I certainly wouldn't suggest anyone else try it. He should have denied it because, no matter what Kim says and now matter how difficult the woman is to ignore, I don't believe Jack's guilty.'

'Is she difficult to ignore, Max? Would you be able to –'

'Stop right there.' He kissed her on her nose. 'Been there, seen it, done it, got eaten for breakfast. Not only would I be able to ignore her, I have. She came on to me just before Christmas last year and I told her in no uncertain terms, that dog won't hunt. Why are you grinning?'

'Because I love the things you say. But ... is she still married to ... Ross, was it?'

'Yep. Although Lizzie told me last night that Jack had said they were having problems. Ross and Kim that is. They've got a young child. Ross is crazy about him but Kim apparently, not so much. No big surprise there. She always has to be centre stage. She seems to be looking about for a new starring role.'

'Thanks for telling me. How long did the affair last? Yours and Kim's I mean?'

'Six months.'

'Six months! Would it have continued if Lizzie hadn't found out?'

He studied her face. 'If I'm honest. Yes, it probably would.'

'Would you have left Lizzie for her?'

183

'Good God no! I never had feelings for Kim, it was just sex! Oh. Wrong thing to say I guess. What I mean is, I was never in love with Kim and if I'd really loved Lizzie as much as I thought I did, I'd have been able to resist her, even though she is sex on legs. Was sex on ... Sorry. I think I'll shut up now, I'm not really doing myself any favours am I?'

He saw her smile reach her eyes.

'I think you are. I don't like the image that description conjures up – it's difficult for us ordinary women to compete with – but you're being completely honest and I like that.'

She kissed him and he wrapped her in his arms.

'There's nothing ordinary about you Fifi and forty Kim's could cross my path and I think I can say, with all honesty, I'd probably trip over them – because I wouldn't even notice they were there.'

Fifteen minutes later, Becky, Lizzie, Margaret and Victoria were indeed discussing men and marriage, love and betrayal and exactly why it was that tall, buxom, blondes could lure men to the rocky bed of infidelity with their Siren song of sex.

'I just don't understand it,' Lizzie said, 'Jack does love me, I'm absolutely certain of that. But then, I thought Max loved me and he did the same thing. Maybe it's me! Oh God. I'm sorry Becky; it must be weird hearing me say things like that about Max.'

Becky shook her head and said truthfully, 'We can't pretend it didn't happen. You're his ex-wife. If I can't deal with that then clearly Max and I won't last very long. I will be honest though. I did feel a bit jealous when I heard you were coming to stay.'

'You really don't need to worry about me Becky. You must know this, you'd have to be blind not to see it but I'll say it anyway, Max is crazy about you and Max doesn't get crazy about many women does he Margaret?'

Margaret smiled warmly at Becky. 'He certainly doesn't.'

Becky felt her heart soar and yet she had to be realistic. 'But you've said it yourself, that didn't stop him from cheating on you, when he loved you.'

'That's true. And of course, there are never any guarantees but Max has changed since then. I don't think he'd make the same mistake again. You're right though. We never really know. Take Jack. After everything that happened, how we met, that woman and Ross, I would never have believed in a million years that he would get involved with her again and yet – here we are.'

'Do ... do you really believe her though Lizzie? I mean, from what Max has told me about her, she doesn't sound a very nice woman.'

'She's an absolute cow! And no, part of me didn't, even though she gave me dates and times and places but Jack didn't deny it so ... '

'What did he actually say and what did you actually ask him?'

'I said I'd heard that he had been seeing K ... that woman, sorry but I can't bring myself to say her name again, and I asked if it were true. He hesitated for just a second then he said that he had. I was stunned. I really couldn't believe it. I asked how many times and he said "five".'

'Just like that?' Victoria said, 'he didn't try to lie or make some excuse?'

'Not at first. Then he said, as casually as you like, "It's not like that". I said "Oh really, that's not what she says. She says, it's *exactly* like that." He didn't answer for ages then he said "And you believe her?" And when I said he hadn't denied it so it was clearly true, he said something about being really hurt that I didn't trust him; that he'd never cheat on someone he loved, so I reminded him about us and how we met and he just said, "That was different". I ... I can't really remember what I said then to be honest but

185

I don't think it was very nice.'

'Then what happened?' Becky asked.

'He said we could talk about it when he got home at the weekend and I said not to bother coming home because I wouldn't be there and I wasn't going to tell him where I was going. Max says that wasn't very bright but I was just so hurt and angry! I couldn't believe it was happening to me again and with that bloody woman too! God I hate her!'

'And that was it?' Becky said.

'No. I said that clearly he had a phobia about marriage. Every time he got engaged and the date was set, he ran off and screwed someone else! That he needn't worry, because the wedding was off and that I'd send his things down to him because I never wanted to see him again. And then I told him to fuck off and I slammed the phone down.'

'Well,' Victoria said, 'I think we can safely say he knows you're upset.'

'But he has tried to call you?' Becky said.

'A few times, yes; but I wouldn't answer the phone and Max was right; I've turned it off. He says that I've got to face Jack sometime and that I should, at least listen to his side of the story but I can't face it. I'm sorry to bring this up again Becky but I can remember how awful it felt, after I found Max and that bloody woman together. When he told me his side of the story, it didn't make me feel any better, in fact, if anything it made me feel worse. I didn't really know what she looked like – all I saw was the long, blond hair but when he said that she hadn't meant anything and that it was just sex, I kept asking for a description. He clearly didn't want to tell me but one day, I think when we were having yet another row, I remember he said she was sex on legs! And that, believe me, did me absolutely no favours in my battle to pretend she didn't matter.'

Becky fiddled with her coffee mug and cleared her throat. 'I know what you mean. He said the same thing about her to me – and I didn't find it very comforting either.' She didn't say what else he'd said though and that she had found that comforting. Very comforting indeed.

Lunchtime came and went. Max called Becky to say he was running very late and to ask if it was possible for her to stay with Lizzie and to make sure she didn't get a cab to her grandparents. Becky needed to collect Lily from playgroup so she suggested Lizzie go with her and then to meet her friends Jess at her salon and Susie at her shop and by the time Max arrived at Becky's at six o'clock that evening, all the girls were in Becky's sitting room drinking wine and eating chocolates.

'I hope you didn't mind,' he said after getting Becky to follow him into the kitchen, 'I had a few things to do and it took much longer than I'd expected.'

'Not at all. We've actually had a lot of fun.'

'I need to get Lizzie back to Mum's now. I've managed to get Jack here and they really need to sort this out.'

Becky was astonished. 'Jack's here!'

'I've dropped him at Mum's. I didn't think Lizzie would come with me if she saw him in the car.'

'I don't think she'll talk to him Max. She's still really hurt and very angry. What does he say about it?'

'He says she should trust him but he can, finally, see why there might be a little problem with that and he's willing to talk things through. To be honest, I've never seen him like this. Every time I've met him he's always been too laid back and easy going for his own good but for some reason, this has really made him angry. He loves her though so I'm hoping they'll both see sense.'

'Well, Lizzie clearly loves him too. The problem is, she just can't see any reason for Kim to lie or any reason for Jack to see Kim unless they are having an affair.'

'I know and there's going to be some fallout from this little bombshell, I can tell you but that can't be avoided.'

'So is he? Having an affair I mean?'

Max shook his head. 'No. The idea never even entered his head and that, funnily enough, is why he's found

187

himself in this position. I'll explain it all to you tomorrow. I think I should stay at Mum's this evening, just in case things don't go as smoothly as I hope they will. Do you mind?'

'Of course not. Will ... will you be here tomorrow?'

'Of course I will. It's Lily's birthday. Oh. I've got a little surprise for her by the way. You're still going to be bringing her and her friends up to the Hall for cake after her birthday lunch aren't you?'

'Well, I did mention to a couple of the mums that we may just be staying here. I wasn't sure what with everything that's happened but if it's still okay with you and Margaret then yes, please. Lily has told them all about the secret passage I showed you all and they were looking forward to that more than anything else if I'm honest.'

Lizzie saw Jack the minute she walked into the hallway and spun round to leave. 'What the hell is he doing here Max?'

'Not so fast madam.' Max grabbed her by the shoulders and ferried her towards the sitting room door where Jack was hovering nervously. 'He isn't having an affair Lizzie and if you let the man speak instead of throwing a temper tantrum, you may actually be able to save your wedding. And I really think you should.' He gave her a final shove in Jack's direction. 'No shouting the pair of you. Be nice.'

He walked off and headed to the kitchen where Margaret was pouring him a very large scotch.

'Keep those coming, Mother. I think we're going to need a lot of them before tonight's out.'

'You look lovely Lizzie,' Jack said, 'and this is a great house. You were so right to choose it for the wedding.'

'There isn't going to be a wedding.'

She saw him clench his fists and it took her totally by surprise. In all the time she'd known him, he had never lost his temper – until Thursday – let alone shown physical violence but the flush in his cheeks and the glint in his sapphire blue eyes made her wonder if there was a side to Jack that she hadn't seen.

'I know I was engaged to Kim when I met you so I suppose I deserved the jibe you made on the phone, about infidelity not being a concern for me but really Lizzie, in the two years we've been together have I ever given you any cause to doubt my love for you or my loyalty?'

'Not until now, no.'

'Have I so much as looked at another woman?'

'No but –'

'So the only reason you think I've been unfaithful is because Kim phoned you and told you so?'

'And because you admitted it!'

'You didn't ask me if I was having an affair with her. You asked me if I'd seen her and I said yes – which was true and you hadn't, at that time, told me what she'd told you. Would you rather I'd lied?'

This wasn't going along the lines she'd expected. 'Of course not but –'

'So, in fact, the only reason you said the things you did and called off the wedding is because I told you truthfully that I had seen Kim five times?'

'Precisely! You've been having an –'

'I have not! I've seen Kim on five separate occasions because she asked me for advice and help, which I now realise was an excuse but at the time, I thought was completely genuine. I went because Ross was away on business and Kim said she needed help. I did it for Ross as much as Kim and I had no idea that she was, in fact, playing a nasty little game to hurt you, and me and Ross.'

Lizzie stared at him. 'But you ... I don't understand.'

'Ross told me a few weeks ago that they were having problems. I met him for a drink one night, remember? I told you what he said.'

She did remember. 'Ross said he thought she was seeing someone behind his back and that she wasn't happy and wasn't really interested in their son and –'

189

'That's right. He was going away on business and because he knew he could trust me – in spite of what he'd done to me with Kim, he knew I'm not the sort of person to get my own back, so to speak – he asked me if I would, sort of, keep an eye on her while he was away. I didn't mention that part to you because, well, he asked me not to and because, strangely enough, I thought it might upset you, which clearly it has.'

'But –'

'Let me finish. Kim called me and asked if I could help her move some heavy boxes – which I did. She then called and asked me to read a document through for her mum – which I did. Three more times she asked me to do things for her, all of which I did and I began to think that Ross was imagining things at least as far as her seeing someone else was concerned. If she had another man around, she would have asked him, not me.'

'So you're saying it was all innocent. Why then did she call me and tell me you'd had sex with her five times? Well, on five different nights. She actually said you had "rampant sex" to use her exact words. But that's what clinched it for me, you admitted seeing her five times when I asked, not knowing what she'd told me!'

'Because, on the night before she called you, the last of those five times I'd gone there, she made it clear that she wanted to have sex with me and I told her that, not only was I not interested but that I would have to tell Ross because I wasn't going to let her treat him like that. It didn't even occur to me that she would do something as shitty as call you and make up lies just to get back at me. If it had, I would have told you immediately.'

Lizzie felt as if the stuffing had been knocked out of her. 'If ... if that's true then why didn't you just say so when I called you?'

'Because it also didn't occur to me that you were going to be accusing me of having an affair and frankly, when you did, I was so hurt and angry that I couldn't really think

190

straight myself. I'd been worrying how I was going to tell Ross and it hadn't occurred to me that I might need to explain myself to you or to convince you that I was faithful. You seemed to believe the affair so easily and instantly wanted to call off the wedding, that part of me wondered if you'd actually been having second thoughts and were looking for a way out yourself. I've tried to call you several times but you won't answer my calls. To be totally honest, if Max hadn't come to the office today and told me where you were and explained things, I think I ... well, I may have thought you didn't love me anymore.'

She saw his eyes water, saw the forlorn expression, saw the look of total dejection in his usually stunning, sapphire blue eyes and realised that she was an absolute fool. She had very nearly lost the one thing that mattered most to her in the world and all because of a nasty, manipulative woman who would clearly never be happy with her lot, no matter how good it was.

She ran to him and he opened his arms wide for her, scooping her up and kissing her with such fervour that they almost forgot they were in Max's mum's house.

'Can you ever forgive me for being so stupid Jack? I love you so much.'

'You're not stupid, Lizzie. I suppose with our history, we should have expected at least one little hiccough. I ... I assume that's all this is now; at least I pray it is. You ... you will still marry me won't you?'

'Tomorrow, this instant! Six years from now. I'll marry you whenever you like, if you forgive me.' She covered his face with kisses.

'I forgive you – and I think August is still a good time, especially as this place is so incredible.'

'Shall we go and tell everyone the good news? And thank Max, of course.'

She saw the light of passion fill his eyes and the devilish smile that she knew and loved so well, return to his lips.

'In about half an hour,' he said pulling her even closer,

'we've got a lot more kissing and making up to do first.'

Max arrived at Becky's at seven-thirty the next morning laden with presents for Lily.

'Happy birthday Lily,' he said depositing them on the floor near the sofa.

'Max! You shouldn't have bought so many!' Becky said, her eyes filling with tears.

He pulled her into his arms and kissed her softly. 'I know. But it's not every day a little princess turns five, is it Lily?'

Lily beamed up at him, a look of astonishment on her cherubic face. 'Are they all for me?' she asked in disbelief.

'Yes. They're from Mummy and me,' he said winking at Becky.

'No they're – 'Becky began.

Max shook his head at her. 'Yes they are.' He knew what she was going to say and he didn't want Lily to think that he had bought her more presents than her mother. He wasn't sure if little girls really noticed things like that but he didn't want to risk it.

'Oh Max!' Becky said wrapping her arms tightly around him. 'Thank you so much. I don't know what to say.'

'Don't say anything. There's no need. A very large mug of coffee will be ample thanks. I've got the "hangover from hell". And a couple of headache tablets would be good too.'

Becky grinned at him. 'Oh dear. One of those nights was it? How did things go with Lizzie and Jack? Were you drinking in celebration or commiseration?'

She headed into the kitchen and he followed her.

'Celebration. The wedding's back on.'

'Thank heavens for that.' Becky poured him a mug of coffee, handed him two headache pills then slid her arm through his and led him back into the sitting room.

Lily had just unwrapped a toy pony and her screams of excitement tore through Max.

He winced. 'You were right,' he said. 'We shouldn't

have bought her so many. I'm not sure my head will take more than two of shrieks of delight.' He smiled, in spite of the pain in his forehead.

'You have no one to blame but yourself – on both counts. The presents and the headache.' Becky grinned at him. 'But because you were wonderfully kind,' she whispered, 'and said the presents were from both of us, I'll lavish you with sympathy.'

Jess and Susie arrived at eight-thirty, also bearing gifts for Lily, who was using Max as a jump for her pony, when they opened the door.

'That's what I like to see,' Jess said, 'a man on his knees.'

'The cavalry's arrived,' Max said, grinning up at them. 'Good morning you two.'

'You look rough; long night?' Jess asked.

'Too many bottles,' Max replied. 'But the wedding's back on, so it was a small price to pay.'

'Thank God for that,' Jess said picking Lily up and swinging her around in the air. 'Happy birthday darling.'

'You look gorgeous Lily,' Susie said, noticing the princess outfit she was wearing.

'I'm a princess. Mummy and Max bought me a princess dress!'

'So I see.'

'I'll be off then,' Max said, getting to his feet. I'll see you all later. Have fun.' He kissed Lily on the head, lifting her tiara up to do so then he gave Becky a quick kiss on the lips.

'I'll see you out,' she said walking to the door with him and giving him a long, lingering kiss after pulling the door shut behind them. 'Thank you so much for all this Max. You don't know how much it means to me.'

He held her eyes with his and smiled. 'It means a lot to me too,' he said then strode off down the path, his headache clearly long forgotten.

Becky watched him get into the Range Rover and waved to him as he drove off then she dashed back into the sitting room to see what new presents Lily had received.

'Did Max buy all these?' Jess asked looking at the pile of presents scattered all over the floor, whilst Lily was opening presents from her and Susie.

Becky nodded. 'Yes. But he told Lily they were from both of us. Wasn't that wonderful of him? Money is still tight, even though I no longer have to repay the banks, and the dress and shoes I'd bought her were really practicalities. I bought her a few little gifts: a toy kitchen set and some colouring books but they were nothing compared to Max's.'

'That was good of him,' Susie agreed. 'But Lily wouldn't have made comparisons Becky; you know that.'

Becky nodded. 'I know. And I was a little worried that she might think every birthday will be like this one but Max said it was a special birthday because she is five.'

'Oh dear,' Jess said, 'we're not back to thinking he's not going to stick around are we? Has something happened?'

'No!' Becky said. 'Quite the opposite really – but that's the problem. It's all too good to be true.'

She saw the look pass between Jess and Susie and held up her hands. 'I know; I'm being maudlin. I'm sorry. But you know Lily's birthday always does this to me. It brings back so many memories and ... I always wish my mum could be here and ... okay! I'll shut-up.'

'Please do!' Jess said, giving her a playful shove. Your life has turned a corner Becky. The bad times are over. Memories are lovely but today is about having fun, right?'

'Right,' Becky said, watching Lily tear open her presents with unbridled delight.

Max returned in the afternoon to help ferry Lily's party guests up to the Hall. Becky knew that, despite her protestations that it was too much, he'd organised party games including a Treasure Hunt, a Bouncy Castle – Lily was a princess today after all – and a Magician.

195

Lizzie and Jack joined in the fun; they'd bought Lily a pair of "magic" red shoes, from Susie's shop, and Gerald Merriton who'd arrived that morning, for the weekend, bought Lily a magnificent Doll's House. Margaret gave her a silver, charm bracelet and Victoria gave her a musical jewellery box.

Lily pronounced that this was the "bestest" birthday she had ever had and that she was such a lucky girl 'cos not all little girls got presents, so when the Magician called Becky and Lily up to help with his final trick and a real pony appeared for Lily from behind a black and silver screen, it wasn't just Lily who burst into tears of joy.

'Max! This really is too much!' Becky was almost annoyed.

'I've told Lily several times that it's only because she's five that she's getting so many presents and that may not always be the case.'

'It's not just the amount of presents Max. A pony!'

'It'll be stabled here as soon as the stable block is restored, until then, it'll be kept at the stables I bought it from and I'll take Lily there when she wants to go. And, as I know this will have immediately jumped into your head despite the fact that everything is going perfectly between us – if you dump me, the pony will still be hers and remain here with everything paid for by me. It's a lifelong present.'

'The thought hadn't even occurred to me!' she said, even though it had. She knew she should have been thrilled, but she was a little disappointed that he had made provisions for the pony in the event of them splitting up, especially as she knew, it was unlikely to be her doing the "dumping".

She watched as Lily threw herself into his arms, watched him lift her in the air and spin her around, watched him put her on the pony and lead them in a small circle to the shrieks of delight and envy of her friends and she felt her heart slowly breaking. She'd been so deliriously happy for the last few weeks, so completely and utterly in love and although she kept reminding herself that it could end, she

196

hadn't fully appreciated the impact it would have if it did. All her past sorrows would pale into nothing compared with the total and utter devastation she'd feel if Max Bedford walked out of her life and not just her, Lily would feel it too.

'I never thought I'd see the day when Max would be so happy leading a little girl on a pony.' Lizzie was standing beside her and she slipped her arm through Becky's as if they'd been friends for life.

Becky quickly wiped away the tear that trickled down her face but not before Lizzie had clearly spotted it.

'It's all very emotional,' she said. 'I even sobbed a bit myself.'

'Yes. Yes it is.' She didn't want Lizzie to know what she was really thinking. That being with Max made her feel part of a family again and she hadn't felt that in a very long time. That she was terrified of the thought of losing him and that even Lily wouldn't be able to fill the gaping hole his absence would leave.

'Mummy! Mummy! Look!'

She saw Lily's beaming smile and shook herself from her depressing thoughts. There were no guarantees in life but today Max was there, her child was safe and well and ecstatically happy and for now, that was all that mattered.

CHAPTER TWENTY-FIVE

Easter came and went. Becky organised a giant Easter egg hunt at Beckleston Hall, at Margaret's request, and the entire village attended, which firmly established Margaret and Max as "the Bedfords of Beckleston Hall".

May Day festivities were held, then a Midsummer's Day party and Becky began to feel that the house and grounds had been restored to the happy days of her childhood. Only the Summer Fete in July, the Witches Bonfires in October, the Fireworks on Guy Fawkes Night and the Christmas Eve Ball remained and, when she mentioned it to Margaret in passing one day, she was both surprised and pleased when Margaret said, 'What a good idea. I'll leave all the arrangements to you'.

It was the end of June so getting a Fete organised and held in less than a month was a bit of a challenge, even for Becky and there were still a few things to do for Lizzie's wedding in August but she pulled out all the stops, got Jess, Susie and Max fully involved and on Saturday the 28th of July, the Fete was in full swing.

'Another successful event by my favourite Events Organiser,' Max said, holding her in his arms whilst the prizes for "the best hat" were being awarded.

Susie won and Becky and Max clapped and whistled in support, matched only in their enthusiasm by the vicar, who was standing close by.

'Why don't you do us all a favour Ben and take the woman on a date,' Max said.

Becky was astonished, not just because Max should speak to the vicar in such a way but also because she didn't even know his name was Ben.

'I'm sure Susie wouldn't have the slightest interest in going out with me,' Ben replied.

'Well you'll never know unless you ask her and, I think I can almost guarantee, you're wrong. In fact I can guarantee it, and so can Becky.'

Ben's eyes shot to Becky's face and she was surprised to see the vicar blush. She nodded in agreement. 'Ask her; she'll say yes.' She had never seen him move so fast.

'Well,' Max said a self-satisfied grin on his face, 'only Jess to go now and then I think I can safely say my demigod powers are still working.'

'Why didn't Horace formally adopt you?' Max asked the day after the Fete.

He and Becky were sitting on the terrace at Beckleston Hall sharing a bottle of wine and watching the sunset.

A warm breeze danced around them to the songs of chirping crickets and ribbons of red, pink and purple unfurled across a darkening blue-grey sky.

Lily was at a sleepover at a friend's in the village. It was her first and Becky had been nervous about letting her go but Max reminded her that they were only minutes away; she may be five but she was going on fifteen; and she was spending the night with three other five year olds and two very responsible adults, not going to a rave, so Becky had relented.

'Sorry Max, I was wondering if Lily was asleep by now, what did you say?'

He smiled, reached out his hand and gave hers a squeeze, then repeated the question.

Margaret had just given Becky Horace's diaries back and they'd been flicking through them comparing the parties of old, to the recent ones.

'I don't know. I was still young at the time, maybe seven or eight so I wasn't involved in any of the conversations but I can remember him talking about it to both me and my mother. He seemed very keen but she was holding back for some reason and, although they didn't actually argue, I did hear one rather heated discussion where he said something about it feeling as if Mum didn't want him to be my father. They both got upset, I remember. A few months later, they changed my surname, legally but that was it.'

'And the diaries don't give a reason?'

'No. And that's really weird, because he writes so enthusiastically about the possibility of adopting me – it was obviously as he thought of it and before he discussed it with Mum. He mentions the night of the "row" and says he was shocked and hurt but that he loves us both and that's really all that matters but he doesn't say what the "row" was about or why he can't go ahead with the adoption. After that, he never mentions it until he writes about changing my name and he says, that'll have to suffice. He thinks of me as his daughter. I love him as my father. That is enough. And that's it.'

'How odd. What was your surname?'

'Grant. I was christened Rebecca Lily Grant.'

Max raised his eyebrows in surprise. 'I didn't know your middle name was Lily! So, your mum was Lily, you're a Lily and Lily's a Lily. Was your grandmother a Lily too?'

'Don't make fun of me Maximillian Royston Pollard Bedford.' She saw his questioning look. 'Margaret told me, and yes, my grandmother was a Lily too. Julia Lily.'

He grinned. 'It seems our forebears believed in keeping it in the family, as far as names go. I'm named after my paternal grandfather, Dad, and Mum's surname. You do realise don't you that this means that at least one of our twenty children is going to be called either Royston Pollard Maximillian or Pollard Maximillian Royston.'

'I'm not sure she'll be pleased,' Becky joked.

He leaned across grinning and kissed her on the lips. 'Our son, Margaret Rebecca Lily will persuade her to get used to it. So, does the Rebecca come from your father's side?'

Becky studied the contents of her glass. 'I ... I don't know. I don't know anything about my father's side of the family.'

'Really? Nothing at all? Didn't your mother ever talk about them? Didn't your grandparents send you birthday cards or anything? I can understand – well I can't, but you know what I mean – your father not sending them, if he abandoned you and your mother, but surely your grandparents ...?'

Becky shook her head. 'All I know is my father's name – and that's only because it's on my birth certificate. He was Peter Robert Grant. Mum wouldn't talk about him – ever. I didn't push it, to be honest. It made her unhappy when I asked and she'd say that I had a father and I shouldn't dig up the past, so I didn't. I loved Horace and to all intents and purposes, he was my father. Jeremy did suggest I should try and find him once but ... for some reason, I didn't want to.'

'You thought you might find something you didn't like?'

'Or someone. There was something about Mum's face when I mentioned him, a cross between fear and sorrow. I can't really explain it. She said she had no idea where he was and my paternal grandparents were dead. I know we lived abroad though. I was born in England, Brighton to be precise but when we came here – to live with Mum's great-aunt – we came on a ship, and it was a long journey. Of course, to a five year old everything seems bigger and to take longer than it is in reality but we were on board for several nights, at least.'

'Wow! It seems there's still so much I don't know about you, Rebecca Lily.'

Her eyes shot to his face.

'Don't look so worried Fifi; it means we'll still have plenty to talk about when we're in our eighties.'

He took her hand in his and rubbed his thumb across her fingers. 'We could do a search on the internet if you like; see if it throws up anything. It's entirely up to you.'

CHAPTER TWENTY-SIX

The following weekend Lizzie and Jack; Jane, Lizzie's best friend and bridesmaid, and Phil, Jack's best man, came to stay at the Hall.

Becky had arranged a mini wedding rehearsal for the Saturday and Lizzie and Jane were also having their dress fittings with Susie. Final decisions had to be made about the flowers and the menus, and guest rooms selected for those of the wedding party staying at the Hall.

'I don't remember there being this much fuss for my wedding,' Max said rather tactlessly on Friday morning as Becky checked and re-checked her list of things to do.

'That's probably because Lizzie and her parents no doubt organised the entire thing leaving you with just the tasks of arranging the honeymoon and of turning up,' Becky said without taking her eyes from her iPad – something Max had bought her to "help with her business".

He responded by pulling her into his arms and kissing her then he said, 'You have no idea how relieved I am that this time, all I have to do is sign the cheques. What time are Lizzie and her entourage arriving?'

'Around six-thirty.'

'Did you know Mum's also invited Gerald and Victoria to stay? She told me she's having an informal supper party tonight and a dinner party on Saturday to which she's also invited Jess, Susie and Ben.'

Becky nodded.

'And you and Lily of course but that goes without saying – although I've said it anyway.' He grinned. 'I hope I'm on that list of things to do today.'

Becky raised her eyes to his. 'Haven't you got any work to do? You haven't been to your office all week.'

'Mum and Dad's property business runs itself – well our manager does and he doesn't need me around – and the Venture Capital company is ticking over nicely, so no; I can help you instead.'

'Oh good,' Becky said sarcastically. 'Do you know Phil, Jack's best man? You obviously know Jane, the bridesmaid.'

'Yes to both. I'll make some coffee just to prove I can be helpful,' he said heading for the kitchen and switching on the kettle. 'I've known Jane for years. She's been Lizzie's best friend since way before my time. And Phil works at Brockleman Brothers Bank, where I used to work, so I've known him for several years, although it was only since Lizzie and Jack started dating, that Phil and I became friends. We were just work colleagues before.'

'So ... they knew you when you were with Lizzie?' Becky asked after a few minutes.

'Yes. Oh ... I know what you're thinking.' He came back into the sitting room and handed her a mug of coffee then sat next to her on the sofa. 'Don't worry, they won't be comparing you; they are really nice people. And even if they did – you'd come out on top in my eyes.' He put one arm around her shoulders and smiled lovingly at her. 'Speaking of you being on top ... '

Lizzie was thrilled. She'd told Susie, by email and phone, the sort of dress she wanted and the sketches Susie sent her were spot on. The material, ivory satin and organza, she'd seen when she had come down for the weekend in March and she'd seen the photos Susie emailed her but she wasn't prepared for the real thing.

It was a close fitting, satin shift dress overlaid with a film of fine embroidered organza. The dress swept across the top of her arms, off the shoulders and low down at the back where it trailed to a point just below her waist. The sleeves were the finest organza, and came to a point at her wrists at the front. The skirt fell to the floor with a small flick of a train at the back. Simple but beautiful and Lizzie was lost for words.

'Try on the organza veil,' Susie said. 'That'll be held in place by a band of fresh, white rose buds but for now, we'll use combs.'

Susie attached the veil then handed Lizzie a pair of ivory coloured, embroidered satin, slippers, with a softly pointed toe.

'Your bouquet will be white roses and two dark pink roses, the only splash of colour other than ivory but for now try this, just so that you can see the effect.' She gave Lizzie a bouquet of dried rosebuds.

'Oh Lizzie!' Jane said, her eyes filling with tears. 'You look even more beautiful the second time around.'

Little alteration was needed so Susie packed the outfit away and Jane tried on hers. It was a simple close fitting, emerald green, satin dress with the same scooped shouldered neckline but the skirt fell to just above the knee and the sleeves ended just above the elbow. It showed off her copper-coloured hair to perfection.

'Oh. It seems a little too close fitting,' Susie joked. 'Don't worry though; it's not a problem to let it out as I always make allowances when working from measurements alone.'

'That's the problem with being happily married,' Jane said a wistful look in her eyes, 'contentment makes you forget to watch what you eat.'

Lizzie studied her friend's profile and her eyes burst open like a camera shutter. 'Jane! Are you sure that's the reason you've put on weight? The only places that dress is tight are your tummy and your boobs!'

Jane did a half turn to see her profile then spun round and stared at Lizzie in disbelief. 'Oh my God, Lizzie! I can't be! Do you really think ...?'

'I think we need to get to a pharmacy and find out!' Lizzie said enthusiastically.

They fell into each other's arms, laughing and crying whilst Jess, Becky and Susie exchanged bemused looks.

Jane was pregnant, the test confirmed it and when she sat down in Susie's kitchen and worked it out, she realised that she could be anything up to ten weeks. Her cycle had never been particularly regular and she hadn't even considered that she might be pregnant. In her everyday clothes, no one would have noticed, although she did say that her jeans had felt tighter of late, but in the bridesmaid dress, her usually flat stomach had shown a slightly more rounded look.

'I can't wait to tell Iain. Oh God, Lizzie, he will be pleased won't he? I mean Fraser's twenty-six now and I don't know whether Iain even wants another child. We've never discussed it and we've only been married for two years and –'

'Will you stop panicking! Of course Iain will be pleased. He loves you and whether you've discussed it or not, he knows you want a family. He's heard us talking about children enough times to know that. I will admit, he'll probably be surprised but I'd stake my future happiness with Jack, on Iain being pleased.'

'Of course he will. I'm being ridiculous it's ... it's just such a shock. Wonderful, marvellous, incredible but a shock nonetheless. I just don't know how it happened.'

Lizzie laughed. 'It happened because the two of you haven't been able to keep your hands off each other since the night of that ceilidh two years ago!'

'Are you going to phone and tell him?' Jess asked.

'No. As hard as it's going to be to keep this to myself when I speak to him, it's not something I want to say on the phone.'

'Definitely not,' Lizzie said, 'this sort of news has to be delivered in person.'

'What did your husband say when you told him about Lily?' Jane asked. Being the only one of them to have had a child, Becky had first-hand experience. 'Was he excited?'

Becky's jolly demeanour faded slightly and she shook her head. 'Jeremy ... wasn't exactly thrilled,' she said truthfully, 'but don't go by my experience. He ... he didn't really want to be with me. He left us just after I told him.'

'Oh God, Becky! I'm so sorry, we didn't know.'

'It's okay. I ... I thought Max or Margaret might have told you something about it.'

'No. Max told me you were a widow,' Lizzie said, 'He said that you might tell me about it one day and that was it.'

'Yeah,' Jane said, 'that's one thing I have always liked about Max. He is discreet.'

None of them were quite sure though, by the inflection in Jane's voice, whether she meant that as a compliment or not.

'I ... I'd like to tell you about it, if ... if you'd like to hear it,' Becky heard herself saying.

'We'd love to,' Lizzie and Jane said simultaneously.

Becky didn't know why she wanted to tell them her sad story, she didn't want their sympathy or their pity but they both felt like friends, good friends and good friends tell one another their deepest, darkest secrets. 'It's a bit depressing, I'm afraid.'

Saturday night's dinner wasn't going to be a grand affair but it was going to be a celebration of sorts because of Jane's news. She had intended to keep it quiet until she'd told Iain but the minute she and Lizzie arrived back at the Hall at five o'clock, she blurted it out to Margaret and Victoria.

The shrieks emanating from the dining room, where the women were setting the table, brought the men running, so Jane decided to tell them too, although she swore them to secrecy.

'This calls for champagne,' Max said opening a bottle, 'and it's a good thing that you can't drink Jane; you're so high on a wave of euphoria already that one glass would send you smashing through the ceiling, and Mum's just paid a considerable sum to have the ornate plasterwork restored.'

Max drove down and collected Becky, Lily and Jess; Susie and Ben had said they wanted to walk. They'd only been dating for a week and cherished any time they could have to be alone together.

'They look really happy don't they?' Becky said as they pulled up at the front door of the Hall just as Susie and Ben were arriving.

'I'm going to be a gooseberry tonight aren't I?' Jess said.

'No!' Not everyone's a couple,' Becky reminded her, lifting Lily out of the rear seat and into her arms.

'Gooseberry's don't have black and purple hair Jess,' Max said putting an arm around her and giving her a friendly hug. 'Besides, my demigod powers are clearly back to full strength and you may be surprised how tonight turns out.'

'What do you mean by that?' Becky asked as they headed towards the terrace for aperitifs.

'You'll see,' he said kissing her on her forehead.

They stepped onto the terrace where the other dinner guests were assembled and Lily ran over to Margaret – who was holding up a particularly colourful drink for her – as soon as Becky set her on her feet.

'Phil,' Max said, 'may I introduce Becky's friend Jess. Jess this is Phil, Jack's best-man. May I leave you to get Jess a drink Phil, there's something I want to have a quick word with Becky about?'

Before anyone could speak, Max dragged Becky back into the house and wrapped her in his arms kissing her passionately.

'What was that for?' she asked smiling at him.

'I needed a reason to leave Jess and Phil together. Saying I wanted a quick word with you seemed a pretty good one.'

'Well,' she said a trifle breathlessly, 'if that's a quick word I can't wait for the time you need a lengthy conversation.'

'It just so happens,' he said a mischievous grin spreading across his mouth, 'there is something I've been meaning to discuss.'

But he didn't say another word for at least fifteen

minutes.

'So,' Becky said much later that night when she and Max were in bed, 'it seems your work on this earth is done and you can return to Mount Olympus or wherever it is you demigods reside. First solving all my problems, then getting the vicar' – she still found it weird calling him Ben – 'to ask Susie out, now Jess and Phil. It was clear tonight that that's a love affair waiting to start. How did you know they'd hit it off so well?'

'Because when Phil, Jack and I nipped into the village: we went to the pub for a pint this afternoon, we saw you all coming out of Susie's shop. We were going to come and say hi but you all looked so engrossed, we thought we'd leave you to it. Anyway, Phil stopped dead and just stared at Jess. She was a bit of a distance away but still clearly visible. He asked who the stunning woman with purple and black hair was.'

'And that was it? You just assumed they'd hit it off.'

'I wasn't certain but he liked the look of her and he's a great guy so I couldn't see why Jess wouldn't like him. Besides, she was open to offers, she said so herself.'

'Max! That's sounds as if she would have jumped at anyone. She wouldn't.'

'I didn't say she would. I just meant she was ready to meet someone special and so was Phil.'

Something was still eating at her. 'So, what is there left for you to do, oh great one?' She was only partly joking. Try as she might, she couldn't get rid of the final niggling doubt that Max would, one day leave her, just as everyone else had done.

'Ah Fifi. My task here isn't done. Jess and the others were mere trifles; your ongoing happiness is my real assignment.'

She couldn't help herself, 'Ongoing happiness – that sounds as if there isn't an end date.'

'There isn't, some assignments are for life but don't

worry, it's a labour of love.' He kissed her deeply and his right hand teased its way down to her breast. He lifted his head from hers and grinned at her. 'And it's back to work for me.'

Becky, Jess and Susie were sitting at their favourite table in The Coffee Cake Café having lunch on what was turning out to be an exceptionally wet, August day.

'Can you believe that only six months ago we were sitting at this very table discussing how perfect Max would be for you – although you were very anti the whole idea at the time – and now look at us,' Jess said.

Susie nodded. 'So much has changed since then. You've got Phil, I've got Ben and Becky's virtually living with Max.'

Becky almost choked on her coffee. 'I am not, "virtually living with Max"! He just spends the night sometimes.'

'Yes, about five out of seven nights each week. It's nothing to be ashamed of Becky, although Ben did say that he hoped you would get married and not just end up living together.'

'Oh he did, did he? And I'm not ashamed, believe me; if he asked to move in with me I'd go and pack his cases for him. I just don't want him to think that people are saying that sort of thing about us.'

'Max couldn't care less what people say,' Jess said.

'I know. I just don't want him to think that's what I'm expecting.'

'Why not? Surely that's the next step isn't it? Well, either that or Ben's way. Get married,' Susie said.

'It may be the next step but it's not one we're ready for.'

'But you just said –'

'Okay! It's not one *he's* ready for. If he ever will be.'

'Ah. Now I see the problem,' Jess said. 'You're back in your "everyone leaves me and so will he" mindset. I thought you'd got over all that. The guy's crazy about you – everyone can see it. Mary Parkes and Connie Jessop have already discussed how wonderful your wedding will be – don't look at me like that – I heard them in the Stores the other day. The vicar ... Ben ... even assumes you'll end up together in fact every single person in this village and their dog, thinks you will. You're the only one with any doubts.'

'I just don't want to take anything for granted, that's all. I've done that too many times in the past and been wrong. I'm very happy with things the way they are and besides, it has only been six months. You can't expect people to make such a major decision about their lives after only six months.'

'Really? I decided I wanted to marry Ben after our first date last Sunday.'

'And I'm marrying Phil, and I only met him on Saturday.'

Becky was astonished. 'What?'

'Well, it's true, and there's no point in pretending it's not,' Jess said. 'When you know, you just know.'

'What if they don't feel the same?'

'But what if they do? Think about that Becky. Maybe Max thinks you're the one who isn't ready.'

Becky sighed and sipped her coffee, watching the rain bounce off the pavement. Were they right, she wondered, did Max think she wasn't ready? He'd said in the beginning that he thought she was the one holding back but now? They were always talking about the future as if they would be together forever; they joked about the twenty children. Should she say something? Tell him that she was ready to commit to him. But was he really ready to commit to her?

'Who's that?' Jess asked, dragging Becky from her thoughts and nodding towards the man standing under the tree across the road from the café.

Becky glanced at him and thought she recognised him but she couldn't think from where.

'No idea. He's probably waiting for someone.'

'Well he's been staring at us for the last ten minutes or more. If you still owed money to the banks I'd start thinking they'd sent in the heavies. Do you know him Susie?'

'No but you're right. He's been there for a while.'

'He's probably just thinking how cosy it looks in here and how wet it is out there,' Becky said.

'But he's staring at *us*. Perhaps he's thinking how gorgeous we all are.' Jess grinned.

'Perhaps he's wondering why you've got purple and black hair and he can't take his eyes off it,' Susie quipped.

'Or perhaps, Susie, the Diocese or whatever it's called has sent someone to see if you are suitable to be dating a vicar.'

'Or perhaps he's just a man standing in the rain, trying to decide whether he wants a coffee or not.' Becky glanced at her watch. 'Is that the time? I've got to go and pick up Lily. I'll see you later,' She jumped up and threw on her raincoat.

'Yeah. See you,' Jess and Susie said simultaneously.

Becky dashed out and ran across the road. She saw the man move but she was going in the opposite direction, away from him. She didn't see him turn and follow her down the street.

'He's following her!' Jess was on her feet in a second, grabbing her raincoat with one hand and Susie with the other.

'Hey you, stop! We're calling the police!' Jess yelled.

'Becky!' Susie shouted.

Becky heard the commotion and looked round. She saw Jess and Susie frantically waving and running towards her. Then she saw Jess pointing at something. She spun round and sucked in her breath in surprise. The man who had been watching them was just a few feet away and from the expression on his weather-beaten face, he wasn't happy.

He glanced back at Jess and Susie then made a final sprint towards Becky grabbing her by the arm. She screamed and tried to wrestle her arm free but he was too strong. He pulled her towards him.

'Rebel! ... Rebecca! I won't hurt you! Don't be

frightened. Please!' He released her and stepped back.

Jess and Susie caught up and were about to pummel him with their bags and fists but Becky stopped them.

'No!' she yelled stepping between the man and her friends. 'Don't hurt him! He's ... he's my father.'

She didn't know how she knew but she did. There was something about the way he had said her name, something about his features, even something about the way he'd grabbed her arm and she instantly knew who he was – and that he wouldn't hurt her. As Jess had said, "When you know, you just know."

CHAPTER TWENTY-SEVEN

'I didn't mean to scare you Rebecca, and I'm sorry if I hurt your arm. I ... I didn't want you to get away from me again. I wasn't thinking straight. I'm sorry.' He spoke with a faint Australian accent and though his voice was gravelly it was kind.

They were in Becky's sitting room and Jess and Susie were hovering in the kitchen. Becky had called Jenny, the mother of Lily's friend, Emma, and asked if Lily could stay for another hour or so, and she'd invited her father back to her house, against both Jess and Susie's advice.

'You haven't seen him for years. Your mother was terrified of him. He walked out on you. Don't take him home. Take him to the café or something. Better still, call Max and see what he says,' Jess had said.

'He won't hurt me. I know it Jess. I'm taking him home and I'm not calling Max – yet. I want to hear what he has to say.'

'Well then we're coming with you.'

'I'll be fine.'

'Us or nothing,' Jess said emphatically.

They had walked back to Becky's in silence. Becky and her father kept glancing at one another but no one spoke until they were in the sitting room.

'You didn't hurt me, but you did scare me, until I recognised you.'

'I ... I didn't know if you would. It was so long ago. You were five when your mother took you.'

'When Mum took me – when you abandoned us you mean!'

He shook his head and his huge brown eyes filled with tears. 'I would never have abandoned you Rebel, you were my life.'

'Rebel!' she repeated. 'That's what you used to call me. I ... I can't remember why but I do remember the name.'

'Because you always did the exact opposite of whatever

your mother told you to. She said you were always rebelling and that it was my fault. So ... I called you Rebel.'

'And I loved it, didn't I? I ... I loved you too, didn't I? More ... more than Mum!'

He nodded. 'We were inseparable you and I. Until ... '

'What happened? Why ... why did Mum – take me, you said? And, why did she tell me you'd left us?'

'I can't answer the latter but I guess because she thought that way, you might not try to find me, might not try to come back when you were grown.' He shrugged his shoulders. 'As to why she took you well, that ... that was partly my fault – and I'm not proud of it but ... I think I'd better start from the beginning.'

'Please.'

She couldn't stop staring at him and he smiled at her for several seconds before he began.

'It was a whirlwind romance. We met in Brighton when Lily was on holiday – she lived in Essex with her parents but she wasn't very happy. We fell in love and after she went home, we would meet in London or I'd go to Essex and stay in a bed and breakfast and she'd come to me. Then she discovered she was pregnant. She came to live with my family in Brighton. My parents were moving to Australia and I was going with them, but I said I wouldn't go unless you both came with me. We were young; you were born just days before Lily's nineteenth birthday and she wasn't sure about Australia but I persuaded her it would be a good life so she agreed and everything was rushed through. We actually married on the ship going over.' He stopped and drank some of the coffee Jess had made.

'I knew I was born in Brighton because of my birth certificate. I can remember coming here by ship but I couldn't remember where we'd lived in between times.'

He nodded. 'It was a mistake. I should have realised Lily would hate the life. We lived with my mum, my dad and my grandparents on a sheep station, miles from anywhere. The nearest town was several hours drive. No life for a vibrant, nineteen year old girl from Essex. She said she wanted to go home but ... I loved it there. I could never have given you both such a good life here. I ... I suppose I was selfish but I kept thinking if she would just make the effort, she'd love it too. She didn't. We rowed all the time. She said she wanted a divorce, to go home to her parents – not that they wanted her back, particularly. I said she could go, but she couldn't take you. From the minute you could walk you were always out in the dirt with me, you loved the outdoors. You ... you can't remember the station at all?'

Becky shook her head. 'No. Strangely I don't, but a few seconds after I saw you, just now, in the rain, it triggered something, a memory. I could remember you grabbing my arm and ... and I felt safe.'

He nodded. 'I pulled you from a river during the rainy season. It was a day a bit like today only the rain was worse.' He grinned crookedly. 'When it rains in Australia, it rains.'

'Lily was furious, said you could have died, said this hell hole was no place for either of you, said ... well, said some things about me, said she was taking you back to England and I'd never see you again. I ... I lost my temper and ... I'm not proud of this but she wouldn't stop screaming and she lashed out at me. I pushed her away and she fell and cut her head. I had stopped loving her a while before but I'd never hurt her, not intentionally.'

Becky saw the pain and shame in his eyes and reached out her hand to him. 'I know you wouldn't. It wasn't your fault.'

He sniffed and brushed a tear from his eye. 'Lily thought it was and things got worse. I told her she could have her divorce and go but you were staying with me and she just said, "we'll see about that" I ... I said that if she tried to take you, I'd come after her and ... and I'd kill her. I wouldn't have Rebel – killed her I mean or ... or anything else but I think she thought I would. I don't know. Anyway, things seemed to calm down for a few months. She ... she'd become friendly with one of the pilots who stopped by now and then and one day when I got back to the station, you'd both gone. No one saw you go but they had seen Hank, the pilot. I found him and he said she'd told him they were just going to town overnight and that I knew about it. She only took a small bag. No one saw her leave town and I still have no idea how she got from there to England although one of her friends from Essex did work on a cruise ship so maybe ... I don't know.'

'I don't know either. The only thing I can remember is the ship and being very unhappy. And yet. I'm sorry if this upsets you but, it's just so strange because, after we came here, I can remember being happy and ... and I didn't remember you! How can that be?'

He shook his head. 'I don't know. Perhaps it was such a wrench, such a traumatic experience that ... that you shut it out. Maybe, if Lily told you enough times that I'd abandoned you, you believed it.'

'Possibly I suppose. That would explain how I knew you wouldn't hurt me just now. A suppressed memory or something. I ... I can't believe that all these years, I thought you'd left me and really, we'd left you. Did ... did you ever hear from her again?'

'No. I came to England to try and find you. Her parents told me she'd asked them for money which they'd given her but they hadn't heard from her since. I searched everywhere I could think of, found her old friends, no one knew where she was – or if they did, they weren't saying. We didn't get the internet till years later – not a high priority on a sheep farm – but when I realised it could help find you, I started looking.'

'And ... and you've only just found me!'

'I found a photograph of you and your daughter, my granddaughter, taken at Easter. It was in your local paper. I've been searching for anything with a Lily, for your mum and Rebecca, for years and there are hundreds. I recognised you instantly and little Lily is the spitting image of you at her age. So here I am. Twenty seven years late but here just the same.'

Jess and Susie were dumbstruck. They'd been listening to every word – they knew she wouldn't mind, the privacy was for her father's benefit, not hers.

'All those years, her mum lied to her!' Jess said.

Susie just nodded; she couldn't find any words to say.

'What I don't understand is, she must have contacted you for the divorce. Didn't she give you an address then or was it just via solicitors?'

He looked confused. 'We're not divorced. Lily's still my legal wife.'

Becky, Jess and Susie all gasped in unison and she spun round to look at her friends. 'That means ... Oh my God! No wonder he couldn't adopt me!'

'Who couldn't adopt you? What do you mean Rebel? Why ... why did you think we were divorced?'

Becky held his hands tightly. 'Because – prepare yourself for a shock – Mum married someone else just over a month after we arrived here. They were married until ... Oh! You don't know that either! Mum ... Mum died, over sixteen years ago!'

The colour seemed to drain from his tanned and weather-beaten face. He blinked several times and his brows knit together. 'Lily re-married immediately? Just like that! But ... she couldn't have. We weren't divorced. And ... and ... she's been dead for all these years.'

'I'm so sorry, that was really thoughtless of me. I shouldn't have just blurted it all out like that.'

He shook his head. 'That's okay love. I stopped loving Lily long before she left me. It was never about finding her; only about finding you but ... it does feel strange to know that she's dead. I can't understand how she could have remarried so quickly though.'

Becky shook her head too. 'I don't understand either. Perhaps ... perhaps she used another name or something or ... no, I have no idea either. My fa ... Horace, the man Mum married, wanted to adopt me and I can remember them having heated words about something. He never did adopt me – just had my name changed to his and I never knew why. Perhaps that was why. Perhaps it would have then all come out and ... maybe she was worried you'd find me and ... try to take me back.'

He shrugged. 'I would have tried but even I knew there was little chance of me getting custody. Perhaps she was worried of going to prison for bigamy or ... or maybe she took my threat seriously. Maybe she thought I ... well, I suppose we'll never know; she's not here to ask.'

'No, I suppose we won't.'

'I ... I'm not sure what happens now. Is Lily's ... husband still around?'

'Oh no. They died together, in a car crash.'

'And Lily's parents? Do you ever see them?'

'Both dead.

'And your husband? Or partner. I ... I noticed you don't wear a ring.'

'My husband ... died.'

'Oh Jeez love! I'm so sorry.'

'It's fine. I'll tell you about it sometime. It was just before Lily was born.'

'So ... apart from Lily, you have no family here?'

'No ... but I have a boyfriend! He ... he lives locally.'

'And you're happy?'

'Yes. Very. He's a truly wonderful man.'

'I'm glad. I've got to go back, my life's in Aus. but I'd really like to spend more time with you and ... may I meet Lily? I don't have to leave for another week and –'

'Of course! She'll be thrilled to know she has another grandfather.'

'You'll tell her who I am?'

'Yes! Unless ... unless you'd rather I didn't.'

'No! I mean, I'd love her to know. I just ... it's been twenty-seven years. I wasn't sure what to expect. I didn't even know if you'd remember me – or want to see me. I just wanted to see you again. Talk to you. I wasn't expecting anything.'

'You're my father! I've spent twenty-seven years of my life thinking you abandoned me, that you didn't want me, that ... you didn't love me. Today I've discovered all that was a lie. You don't know how much this means to me. To find out that you did want me, you did love me ... '

'I still do want you Rebel and I'll always love you. You're my daughter.'

Becky burst into tears and her father hugged her close and stroked her hair. In the kitchen, Jess and Susie were crying and hugging too.

There was a knock on the door and Max marched in but he stopped in his tracks when he saw Becky in the arms of a man in his fifties and her friends sobbing. A cold sharp knife pierced his heart.

'What's happened? Where's Lily? Is she hurt?' he shrieked, terrified that something had happened to the precious little girl he'd come to love.

Becky raised startled tear-laden eyes to his. 'Oh Max! No! No! Lily's fine. She's at Jenny's.'

His eyes searched the room and came to rest on the man. 'Then ... what's going on? Who's been hurt? What's happened? Will someone please tell me before I go mad with worry?'

Becky sniffed and reached out her hand to him, pulling herself slightly away from the man she hugged. 'Sorry Max. This is ... I'd like you to meet ... my father.'

'Well I have to say, you're one person I never expected to meet,' Max said thirty minutes later.

Jess and Susie had left and Becky had gone to pick up Lily. Max had offered to take her but Becky said she wanted to explain to Lily that she was about to meet her grandfather and that was a conversation they needed to have alone – which both Max and her father understood.

'I expect not but I'm very pleased we have. You'll

219

probably feel it's none of my business as I haven't been around for the last twenty-seven years of my daughter's life, but I am her father just the same and I would like to know – do you love my little Rebel?'

Max grinned. They'd already explained to him the reason for her father's pet-name for her. 'That suits her, Rebel, I mean. I call her Fifi and in answer to your question, yes I do. More than she seems to believe, in fact. I love your granddaughter too.'

'And ... does this have a future, do you think?'

Max held Peter's eyes. He could see the genuine concern of a loving father. 'It does if I have any say in the matter. I can't speak for Becky but ... I'd like to think she feels the same. I believe she does. To tell you the truth, your coming here may have an even greater impact than reuniting father and daughter, although that's pretty spectacular. Becky believes ... she expects actually, that everyone whom she loves will either abandon her or die. I can understand why she feels that way and so will you when she tells you more about the past twenty-seven years. It's a deep seated fear, made worse by the fact that her mother, step-father and husband all died but it seems it stems from you abandoning her –'

'But I didn't! I've –'

'That's precisely the point I'm making. Not only did you *not* abandon her, you've continued to love her, for her entire life – even if you haven't actually been around to tell her so. I think you may be the best thing that's happened to Becky in a very, very long time.'

Peter smiled warmly at Max. 'From the little I've heard so far about you, I got the distinct impression that was you.'

Lily was almost as thrilled to discover she had another grandfather as she had been when Max had given her the pony for her birthday. She didn't really understand why she was only getting this one now as she'd had her other grandfather for her whole life and she was five, so she was very old.

They told her that he lived a long way away, so she assumed it must have taken him all those years to get here, although her friends often went on holidays to places they said were a long way away and it didn't seem to take them very long at all.

She did get a little more excited when he said that one day soon, if she and Mummy wanted, he would pay for them to go and see where he lived and, as it was a long way away he said they would have to go on an aeroplane to get there. She liked that idea a lot, especially because she would then be able to tell her friends that she had been on an aeroplane.

Mostly though, she liked the cuddly toy sheep he had brought for her. It was soft and warm and she could carry it on her back because it wasn't just a cuddly toy sheep, it was a bag too.

'Where are you staying?' Max asked when Becky took Lily up to bed.

'At The Beckleston Inn. I arrived this morning.'

'It's nice there; Trisha and Terry are lovely but unless you'd prefer to have your own space, which I completely understand, I'd be really pleased if you came and stayed at my mum's. No. Don't worry, I'm not still living with my mum at thirty-seven, I have my own place in town, I just stay at Mum's to be near Becky – although most of the time I'm here.'

'Most of the time?'

'We're adults – and we're in love,' he said, grinning but not entirely sure he should be. 'As I said, it's up to you but you're very welcome at the Hall. Mum'll be happy to have you. Trisha and Terry won't mind either. Discuss it with Becky and let me know.'

'Discuss what with Becky?'

'Ah Fifi. I've suggested your dad might like to stay at my mum's. I've got to pop out for about an hour, there's something I need to discuss with Ben but I'll be back by nine and you can let me know then.' He kissed her briefly on the lips and left father and daughter to catch up on twenty-seven years of one another's lives.

Peter decided that, as his bags were already in his room at the Inn, and as he was beginning to feel the effects of jetlag, he'd spend his first night there but warmly accepted Max's offer to stay at the Hall for the remainder of his stay.

'I still can't believe it,' Becky said when she and Max were lounging together on the sofa after her father had gone. 'How Mum managed to convince me, so completely, that Dad had abandoned us. I always thought my mother was the victim and that dad must have done something horrid when he left and all the time, it was Mum who'd lied and done something horrid and Dad who was the victim.'

'Actually sweetheart, you were the victim. Your mum shouldn't have left like that and she shouldn't have lied – and I'd still like to know how she managed to marry Horace when she was already married; I must ask Gerald about it – anyway, neither should she have kept you from your real father but, your dad didn't help himself by saying she couldn't take you or making false threats. Unhappy women do very nasty things, we've seen it ourselves with Kim and what she did to Lizzie and Jack and her own husband, Ross. The point is, they were adults, and you were a child. They should have thought how their actions would affect you but they didn't. You were the victim and it's affected your life more than they could ever have imagined.'

'You're right. Just think how different my life would have been if they'd separated amicably.'

'Very different. At least now though, you know that not everyone you love leaves you. That must surely be a good thing.'

'It's a very good thing. A very good thing indeed. What's happened with Kim and Ross by the way? Last time I asked you said you hadn't heard anything. Lizzie and Jack didn't mention it either, other than to say Ross was trying to sort things out.'

'That's all I know too. When Ross got back from his business trip, Jack told him what she'd done. Needless to say, Ross wasn't too pleased. The last I heard was that Ross was thinking of leaving her and trying to get custody of their son. That should, in theory be straightforward; Kim's not really interested in the child but if Ross leaves her, she is just as likely to try and get custody just to spite him. Unhappy women doing nasty things, as I said and another child's life affected by adults who should know better.'

Becky was feeling even happier the next day – and only twenty-fours before, she would have said that wasn't possible. But she now had a father who loved her and that made her part of a real family; it wasn't just her and Lily any more if Max did leave her. She wondered why it should make such a huge difference, after all, he lived thousands of miles away so it wasn't as if she was going to have him just around the corner, but it did make a difference and a very big one. Because Max was right. Not everyone she loved left her.

She thought about Max and her heart seemed to swell in her chest. She loved him so completely, so utterly and yet she rarely told him so. He knew she loved him, of course, she realised that, and you shouldn't have to constantly tell people you love them but neither should you constantly tell people that you thought they would leave – and that she did say – often.

She sat in her garden drinking coffee, listening to the birds chirping and a soft early morning breeze rustling the leaves of the trees, and wondered why she did that. Why she constantly thought he would leave her. She knew it was because of her past experiences but now, sitting here with the sun playing hide and seek through marshmallow clouds, she realised how absurd that notion was.

Yes, he might leave her and if he did, there was nothing she could do to change that; constantly worrying about it wouldn't help, constantly expecting him to go, wouldn't make him stay. And wasn't it also true that she could leave him? She wouldn't of course, because she loved him so much – but he didn't know that. There were no guarantees and yet he didn't automatically assume she would end their relationship one day.

She watched a butterfly land on the purple buddleia and thought about how fleeting time is, how none of us can know what life has in store for us and worrying about what the future may hold is not a good way to spend your present.

Max brought his coffee out and joined her at the table. His thick blond hair was still wet from the shower and little drips of water marked his T-shirt where they fell. He smiled at her and his eyes were full of love; pure unquestioning, undoubting, trusting love.

'It looks like it might be a lovely day,' he said nodding towards the sky.

She smiled and turned in her chair to face him. 'Yes it does,' she said. 'And it's the perfect day to tell you I love you – completely, thoroughly, utterly – I love you.' Then she kissed him just to make sure he understood.

'Wow!' he said when she finally moved away. 'It really is going to be a lovely day. Perfect in fact.'

The day just kept getting better. Her father arrived at nine a.m. and as it was such a gloriously sunny day and Peter was now going to be staying at the Hall, Max suggested they all go there and get him settled in.

'We can have a picnic at the pond,' Max said. 'If the grass is still wet from yesterday, we've got matting and blankets so it won't be a problem. Lily can ride her pony and I'll watch over her while you two get to know one another a little better.

'A family picnic,' Peter said, 'I'd like that very much.'

Margaret and Victoria were in the kitchen and Max did the introductions then took Peter to his room to settle in. It didn't take him long; he was anxious to spend as much time with his daughter as he could.

Just over an hour later, they were settled near the pond, feeding the ducks and basking in the sunshine. Lily was giving Max and her pony, which she'd named Magic – because it was – precise instructions as to where she wanted to go, and where she wanted to go was for a ride right around the grounds of Beckleston Hall.

'It seems she wants to survey her empire,' Max said. 'We may be some time.'

In their absence, Becky told her father everything that had happened to her over the past twenty-seven years and he was furious to learn of Jeremy, his suicide and more importantly in his eyes, the theft of her inheritance.

'Well,' he said when she'd finished, 'I wish I could have been here for you but there is one thing I can do for you. I called my solicitor last night to tell him I'd found you. You've always been in my will but as I didn't know where you were, a trust was set up until you could be found.'

'Dad! I don't want your money! I mean ... I didn't mean it like that but you know what I mean. Just having you in my life again is the best thing you could ever give me.'

He reached out and took her hand in his. 'I know love but you've always been provided for, I just need the terms changed because I've now added Lily. I'm not a millionaire but we're not badly off. Not that I think you'll need it.'

He glanced towards Max who was some way off with

225

Lily and Magic and his implication was clear.

'That's really lovely of you, Dad. Thank you. And thank you for telling me.'

'I'm telling you because ... there's something else you need to know. I didn't mention it yesterday because I thought you'd had enough surprises for one day. I told you I stopped loving Lily long before she left. Well, it gets lonely on a sheep station especially for a young man and about four years after she left, someone moved in with me. Her name's Gilly, Gillian and she's a lovely woman; I love her dearly.'

'Dad that's great. I'm so happy for you!'

'We never married because I thought I was still married to Lily and although I know you can eventually divorce someone even if you can't trace them, I didn't want to because ... I thought it might affect my claim on you. Silly, but there it is; and Gilly never complains. She's taken my surname and she knows I love her so that's good enough although when our ...' he stopped and looked Becky directly in the eye. 'We have three children, Gilly and I. Two boys and one girl. Your half brothers and sister.'

Becky couldn't believe her ears. Not only had she got a dad again; she'd also got brothers and a sister.

'Brothers and a sister! I ... I have brothers and a sister! How old are they? What are their names? Do ... do they know about me?' She fired questions like a repeater rifle.

'Yes Rebel, they know about you and they know I've come to see you. They've been helping me search for you for years.' He pulled out an envelope from his pocket and handed her the photograph inside.

She saw a picture of a very pretty woman in her late forties and two boys and a girl all smiling happily with their arms around each other.

'That's Gilly,' he pointed out 'and that's Bethany, she's twelve; that's Robert, the eldest, he's twenty and that's Paul, he's sixteen. They're great kids – and they're really looking forward to meeting you one day. Gilly too. You'll like her. Some women would have told me to stop looking for you; would have said "enough is enough". Not Gilly. She knew how important you are to me and she never once said I should be content with the family I've got. I don't think I realised, until this day, sitting here with you, just how special that makes her.'

Becky saw his eyes fill with love and squeezed his hand. She studied the photograph. Gilly had a friendly, homely look about her but Becky was more interested, at the moment, in her brothers and sister. They looked so much like her father it was uncanny – and, just a little like her too. They all had the same curly brown hair and brown eyes. Becky had always thought she got those from her mother; she too had brown hair and brown eyes but Becky now remembered, her mum's hair wasn't naturally curly.

Peter handed her a letter, also from the envelope. It was a letter from her brothers and sister. It read:

"Hi sis! We're so pleased we've finally found you and we hope this letter reaches you soon. We're not sure what we're supposed to say to a sister who doesn't even know of our existence so we'll just say "Hi and welcome to the family". We hope it won't be long before we can say that in person, face to face and we can't wait to hear all about your life in Blighty and for us to tell you all about ours. Dad said we may be able to speak to you on the phone once he's told you we're here so we'll save everything 'till then. If you want to though, you can look us up on Facebook – although on second thoughts, maybe not; you'll then see we're all a bit crazy and might decide you don't want to meet us after all! Only joking (we hope). Details below. Well, we'll sign off for now. Speak soon. All our love, Beth, Rob and Paul. xxxxxxx P.S. Our mum says "Hi" and she's looking forward to meeting you too. Xxxxx"

Becky was laughing and crying at the same time. It was such a friendly letter; a letter that said nothing really and yet so much. She instantly knew she'd like them and she couldn't wait to talk to them. She also knew that Gilly would make her feel welcome.

'They sound really wonderful, Dad. Can we call them?'

He beamed with love and pride. 'I think we'd better wait awhile love, they're about nine hours ahead so they'll all be in bed right now. We can call them late this evening when they'll just be getting up, if that's okay with you.'

Becky nodded enthusiastically and studied the photograph again picking out little things like Bethany's freckles and the way Robert's smile curved crookedly, just like their father's. 'You have a really lovely family, Dad,' she said 'and, I know it's none of my business but, you do realise don't you, that you're completely free to marry Gilly now – if you want to.'

His eyes shot to hers in a look of total surprise then a huge smile spread across his face. 'Blimey love, you're right! I hadn't thought of that. I should have done it years ago to be honest. And the timing couldn't be better. We just found out that we're having another child.'

'Dad! That's wonderful news!'

'Yep! It's a bit of a surprise to be honest love but we're thrilled. We haven't told the kids yet; we wanted to wait until I got back. We thought that, if things didn't go well here and you didn't want to see me, it would soften the blow for them when we told them that they might not have you but they were going to have a new baby brother or sister.'

'God, I'm starving,' Max said returning with Lily and Magic and lifting Lily down, 'I feel as if I've been walking for days without food.'

Lily ran to her grandfather and pulled him to his feet dragging him off to feed the ducks.

'You'll never guess what Max,' Becky said.

He fell onto the blanket beside her, gave her a quick kiss on the lips then collapsed on his back with his head in her lap. 'I'm too tired to guess sweetheart, your daughter's a slave-driver,' he joked, 'but by the look on your face I'm assuming you've had more good news. Tell me.'

'Dad's just told me I've got two brothers and a sister and I'm about to have another one.'

He suddenly wasn't so tired after all.

Far too soon for either of them, it was time for Peter to return home. He and Becky had grown close in just a few short days and it was a difficult parting for them both.

'It's a long journey, especially for someone Lily's age,' he said, 'but we'd be happy for you to come and stay whenever you want to.'

'Lily will be starting school in September,' Becky said, 'but I'm so eager to meet everyone. We must make it soon.'

'There's always Christmas,' Max suggested 'or Easter. Your new baby is due around then so Becky and Lily would be able to see the baby too.'

'That's a brilliant idea Max!' Becky said, 'although Easter does seem so far away as it's only August now.'

'When you've waited twenty-seven years to see someone, a few months is a drop in the ocean love,' Peter said, 'it'll be here in no time.'

Max held Becky tightly in his arms as she watched her father walk through the departures gate.

'He's not leaving,' Max said, 'he's simply popping home for a while.'

She waved her father a last goodbye then turned to face Max. 'When did you get so smart?' she said smiling at him.

'I'm a demigod; I was born smart. Although, I have to confess, even I didn't foresee the arrival of one father and several siblings.'

'Isn't life amazing? Seven months ago the only family I had was Lily. Now I've also got you and Margaret, a father and a step mother, three siblings and another on the way. I can't believe it.'

Max held her away from him and looked deep into her eyes. 'Did you just say Mum and I are your family?'

She hadn't realised she had; the words had just come naturally. She nodded. 'Well, you are ... sort of ... to me.'

'That's one of the nicest things you've ever said.'

CHAPTER TWENTY-NINE

Life was good in Beckleston.

Becky hadn't realised how much fun having a family again could be. She spoke with her dad and her brothers and sister every day and she soon felt as if she had been a part of the family for her entire life, which as far as they were concerned, she had.

Susie and Ben were clearly in love and Jess and Phil seemed to be following close behind.

Beckleston Hall was looking even better than it had when Becky grew up there and preparations were almost complete for Margaret Bedford's first real event – Lizzie and Jack's wedding.

Even the weather seemed to get on board the Beckleston ship of happiness. For three days there hadn't been a cloud in the sky and the forecast for the weekend was equally good.

But ships on maiden voyages need to watch for icebergs, and an iceberg was heading towards Beckleston Hall – in the human form of Kim Briarstone.

Lizzie, Jane and Iain, Iain's son Fraser and his girlfriend, Annie arrived at Gatwick on Friday morning and Max went to collect them whilst Becky did a final run through of her list for the big day.

Susie had the dresses for Lizzie and Jane, waiting at the Hall so they could have a final fitting and she could do any last minute alterations.

The rosebud head band and bouquet would be delivered by Stephanie on Saturday afternoon together with the buttonholes; the flowers for the pergola would arrive that morning, to be twined around the frame and the poles lining the aisle.

The bar for the terrace was set up and the chairs were stacked just inside the French windows so that they could be carried out by the staff in the afternoon.

Margaret and Victoria with Connie Jessop's assistance were preparing dinner for Friday evening and the catering company had the celebratory dinner for Saturday and the wedding brunch for Sunday firmly under control.

Jack, Phil, Ross and Lizzie's parents were arriving early Friday evening. Lizzie's grandparents and Gerald weren't arriving until Saturday morning. Everyone else would be arriving on Saturday afternoon.

The villagers had been invited to watch the firework display on Saturday evening but the house and the lawns were being "roped off" so that no one would intrude on the wedding party itself. Margaret had asked Becky to arrange for everyone to be served with a glass of champagne or soft drink for the children so that they could all feel they were at least involved in some small way, by toasting the bride and groom's good health.

Everything was in place and even Becky thought that nothing could possibly go wrong by the time Max came to collect her for dinner on Friday night.

'Wow! You look incredible,' he said when she opened the door. 'We could call and say we'll be a little late.'

She smiled and kissed him then grabbed his hand and pulled him out towards the car. 'We could but we won't, although I am happy to come home early.'

'That sounds good to me.'

'I've got things to check for tomorrow,' she grinned.

He reached into his pocket and pulled out a box from Tiffany. 'I bought you this.'

For just one second, her heart skipped a beat and she stopped in her tracks but she soon realised it wasn't the right shaped box. She hoped he hadn't seen the look of disappointment she was sure had flashed across her face. She opened it and found a gold locket. Small, delicate and very beautiful. Opening the locket she saw on one side a picture of her and her father that Max had taken on the day of their picnic. On the other was a picture of her and Lily and Max.

'Oh Max it's beautiful! Thank you so much. Will you put it on me please?'

He put it around her neck and fastened the clasp, kissing her neck then her shoulders and trailing a finger down her back.

'Stop it,' she said then turned and gave him a quick kiss. 'I'll thank you properly later.'

'I thought you had things to check,' he said in a mocking tone and his smile was wicked and tempting.

Jack was banished to The Beckleston Inn after dinner because it was unlucky for the bride and groom to see one another on their wedding day and the men joined him there for breakfast, including Max, once he'd dropped Becky at the Hall. He was given strict instructions to keep Jack away until half an hour before it was time for the ceremony to start.

Becky and Lily were staying the night at the Hall and she'd taken their clothes to change into for the wedding; for now, she just wore jeans and a T-shirt.

She double checked her list as the flowers for the pergola arrived and the chairs were set out either side of the aisle – which would be strewn with white rose petals just before the bride's arrival.

Margaret and Victoria kept Lily amused so that Becky could deal with any last minute details – not that there seemed to be many.

The catering staff set up in the kitchen and the rest of the staff were hanging ribbons and flowers, setting the tables, polishing the glasses and generally trotting hither and thither carrying out their appointed duties.

The hours marched on, to the melodies played by the rehearsing string quartet as the sun rose higher peeking over a solitary candyfloss cloud to spread its golden rays like a giant stage light, over the scene being played out in Beckleston Hall and its grounds.

Everyone stopped for a light lunch at two in the

afternoon and Max popped back to the house at three, to see if there was anything Becky needed.

'Other than a kiss, no,' she said smiling triumphantly, 'we're actually ready ahead of schedule.'

Max obliged by kissing her deeply and then he held her in his arms without speaking for several minutes.

She raised her eyes to his and saw that he was clearly lost in thought. She couldn't help wondering if his mind had wandered back to his own wedding day and in spite of everything, she felt a tiny twinge of jealously.

'You're miles away,' she said, 'what are you thinking about?'

Her words seemed to startle him. 'Sorry sweetheart. I was just thinking what a wonderful day this is going to be. You've made the place look really beautiful. Lizzie must be thrilled. I hope she's told you how sensational, talented and gorgeous you are.'

'Not in those words but she is very pleased. Jess is doing her hair and make-up after her pedicure and manicure so I've left them to it for now. Her dress is stunning Max; Jack will realise he's a very lucky man when he sees how beautiful she is.'

He held her slightly away from him. 'Jack knows he's a very lucky man Fifi and he already thinks she's beautiful.' He looked deep into her eyes. 'You could be soaking wet, covered in mud and have bits of old newspaper in your hair and you'd still be the most beautiful woman on the planet in my eyes.' And he kissed her in a way that proved she was.

He was referring to the time he'd saturated her, all those months ago, she realised and her heart soared. Even then, when she'd looked her worst, Max Bedford had thought she was beautiful. Could her life get any better than this?

Her life couldn't get much worse than this, Kim Briarstone told herself as she got in her car and headed towards Beckleston Hall. Every man she loved seemed to dump her and she couldn't understand why. First Max then Jack and now Ross. It just wasn't fair; it just wasn't right.

There had been men before them of course, many men in fact but she'd been the one to do the dumping with them. Max was the first man to finish with her; the first man to toss her aside like an old carrier bag and she didn't like that feeling, didn't like it at all.

Then Jack, although she'd seen that coming and had already moved on to Ross. Now he was leaving her and that meant she'd be alone and she didn't like being alone. She didn't want to end up like her mother who pretended to be happy even though she hadn't had a man in her life for years. She couldn't be alone, she simply couldn't.

She took a large swig from the vodka bottle she'd put on the passenger seat. She'd show them. Max and Jack and Ross. They'd all be at the wedding today and she'd show them they couldn't just forget her. She'd give them something to remember her by. She'd give them the surprise of their lives. She glanced at her handbag and sneered. Lizzie Marshall's wedding would go off with a bang but it wouldn't be from the fireworks she knew they were having, it would be from the present she'd brought them.

'You look absolutely beautiful,' Becky said when she went to check if Lizzie was running to schedule. 'All the guests have arrived and are on the terrace with champagne and canapés; we'll get them all seated soon. I've just seen the men headed back this way and yes – they're all dressed and they all look perfectly sober so don't worry about a thing. How are you feeling?'

Lizzie looked radiant and she dashed to Becky and gave her a hug. 'Thank you so much for everything you've done Becky and you Susie for this magnificent dress and you Jess for today. Thank you all so much. This is the happiest day of my life. I feel absolutely wonderful!' She spun around several times just to prove it.

'Please don't do that Lizzie,' Jane said, 'it's making me

feel a little nauseous.'

'I need a drink,' Lizzie said, 'I've suddenly got butterflies!'

Becky poured them all some champagne and Jane a glass of non-alcoholic wine and they toasted to Life and Love and Happiness.

'I'll go and make sure the men are ready, get the guests seated and everyone in position. I'd say that'll take about twenty minutes so you can start making your way down any time after that.' She squeezed Lizzie's hand. 'Good Luck Lizzie. See you down there.'

She headed back downstairs and took a final look in the ballroom. The tables were set, the floral centrepieces were in place, the "disco" was ready for after dinner. She rang the pyrotechnic team on her mobile and they confirmed they were setting up the fireworks and would be ready in plenty of time for the nine-thirty p.m. blast off. She checked the caterers in the kitchen – all running to schedule and finally she saw Ben – she had at last got used to calling the vicar Ben – dressed and ready to officiate.

She stepped onto the terrace and asked the guests to begin to take their seats informing them that the ceremony would start in about twenty minutes. Slowly people started making their way to the chairs set out on the lawn just a short way from the terrace at the back of the house.

Becky looked around for Jack and saw him chatting and laughing with Max and Phil and Ross. She had met Ross for the first time yesterday but when they were introduced, she found herself wondering why any woman would be unhappy with him. He was good looking, he was friendly, he was thoughtful and he talked of his son at every opportunity. Clearly, his wife, Kim Briarstone, was a fool.

Max cocked his head to one side when he saw her and waved his hand to call her over. He put his arm around her when she reached his side and told her she looked even more beautiful than usual.

'Right,' she said, 'we're all set. If you gentlemen want to

start taking your places, the bride will be with us in ten to fifteen minutes.'

'Thank you so much for this Becky,' Jack said. 'You've done a fabulous job. And Max, mate. Thanks for this day, for paying for all this, I mean. It's really great. Thanks.'

Max grinned. 'Don't get all mushy Jack, it's my pleasure – and Mum's of course. And the money was nothing; it's Becky who's made today what it is. Oh – and the fact that you'll soon be married to the woman you love, of course. Now come on, let's not keep the bride waiting.'

They all turned to head towards the pergola but stopped in their tracks. Kim Briarstone stood in their path, waving a vodka bottle in one hand and a gun in the other.

Max pushed Becky behind him with one hand and held his other out towards Kim.

'Don't do anything you'll regret later Kim,' he said his voice surprisingly calm. 'Why don't you put that down and we can all have a chat.'

'I don't want a chat Max! I wanted you but you dumped me like ... like I was nothing. Someone you just screwed then tossed aside when wifie found out.'

He took a step towards her but Becky grabbed his arm to hold him back. Without taking his eyes from Kim he gently removed Becky's fingers. 'Don't worry,' he said, 'I'll be fine.' He took another step forward. 'It wasn't like that Kim. I was just trying to save my marriage that's all. Just as you should be trying to save yours, not doing this.'

'Shit Kim!' Ross said finally getting to grips with the situation.

'Don't be stupid Kim!' Jack said also taking a step forward.

Phil said nothing but gradually started edging towards her.

'Stop! Stop right where you are or ... or I swear I'll use this,' she shrieked.

They all stopped.

'What do you want Kim?' Max asked, indicating to the

others to stay where they were. 'What do you want us to do?'

She seemed unsure and took another swig from the bottle as Max took another step forward.

'I mean it Max! Stay there.'

'Fine. I'll stay. Just tell me. Why are you here? And ... what exactly are you planning to do with that?' He nodded at the gun she waved maniacally around. 'You could hurt someone you know.'

She laughed drunkenly. 'That's the whole point Max. I want to hurt someone. I want to hurt you Max. Just like you hurt me. And you Jack. And you Ross. All I wanted was a man to love me. Really love me.' She lowered the gun a fraction.

'I love you Kim,' Ross said, 'in spite of everything, I love you.'

Her eyes shot to his face, hopeful but not quite believing. 'You don't love me! You just love our son. That's why you married me. Because I was pregnant. All you wanted was him!'

'That's not true Kim. If you remember, I didn't even know about the baby when I came to you in hospital. And then we thought he was Jack's. I had no idea he was mine when I asked you to marry me. I wanted you Kim. I've always wanted you.' He moved slowly towards her.

She seemed to relent and her eyes filled with tears then she suddenly raised the gun again. 'No! You don't want me. You've left me and you're going to divorce me.'

'I thought you didn't love me anymore. I thought that was what you wanted.'

'You're lying! You're all liars. All you want from me is sex. All you ever wanted was sex. You never loved me. None of you! Stay there. I won't say it again.'

'Okay Kim. You're very upset. Let's just put the gun down and talk shall we?' Max took another small step towards her.

She looked unsteady on her long legs and she blinked

several times as if trying to focus. 'It's too late for that Max,' she said. Then she raised the gun and took aim directly at Max's head.

CHAPTER THIRTY

Everything seemed to happen in slow motion. Becky heard herself scream. Felt herself dive forward in a futile attempt to save the man she loved. She felt Jack catch her and stop her from falling then spin her around out of harm's way. She saw Phil and Max dash forward, out of the corner of her eye and Ross put himself between Kim and Jack and herself. Then nothing. Silence. No bang. No gunfire. Nothing. Then a crack like a fist hitting bone and the sound of smashing glass.

Jack released her and she spun round half expecting to see Max sprawled across the terrace covered in blood. She blinked several times in disbelief. Kim hung in his arms like a rag doll, her head lolling back and her arms limp at her sides. The vodka bottle was smashed on the ground and Max passed the gun he'd taken from her, to Phil. Then, as if she were a sack of potatoes he threw her over his shoulder.

'The gun's a fake. Excuse me,' he said to Jack, Ross and Becky then, 'Sorry about this Ross but she clearly needs sobering up.' He strode off with her and minutes later, threw her in the pond.

They all raced after him and watched as she came to the surface and splashed frantically in the water.

'She's your wife Ross,' Max said, 'I think you're the one who's going to have to get her out. Here,' he handed Ross the life ring from a post beside the pond, 'use this, that way you won't get wet. And I know it's not very gallant but I strongly suggest you tie her up in your room until the ceremony's over. That'll give her time to sober up and think about her actions. Jack, don't keep your bride waiting. I'll give Ross a hand. You and Phil go and take Becky with you.'

'No!' Becky snapped, standing her ground.

Max gave her a curious look then turned back to Ross.

'I can manage her Max. She won't be much trouble now I don't think. You go too. I'll be along later.'

Max hesitated for a second. Looked at Kim sobbing quietly in the water and clinging to the ring Ross had thrown her then he grabbed Becky's hand. 'Okay. See you later. Yell if you need me.'

He marched a still bewildered and furious Becky back towards the guests.

'I thought you were dead!' she screeched. 'What were you thinking? Will you stand still and look at me Max?' She dug her heels in.

He stopped and looked her directly in the eye. 'I was thinking that Kim was very drunk and that the gun was either fake or unlikely to be loaded. And forget about me. What were you thinking? I saw you try to dive in front of me. If that gun had been real, you could have been hurt. Don't ever do anything like that again.' He wrapped his arm around her and resumed walking.

'Max stop! I thought I'd lost you! You're behaving as if nothing's happened!'

He stopped again but looked a little irritated. 'Nothing did happen. Just a very drunk and unhappy woman doing nasty things. She clearly needs help. And how many times do I have to tell you? You are not going to lose me Rebecca Cooper. Not today. Not ever. Now will you please stop making a fuss. We can talk about this later if you want. For now we've got a wedding to go to or have you forgotten?' He kissed her quickly on her forehead then linked her arm through his and marched her reluctantly to the wedding.

'Everything all right Max?' Ben asked dashing forward to meet Jack, Phil, Becky and Max as they reached the pergola. 'It looked as if there was a little bit of a commotion going on.'

'Yeah Ben. Everything's fine. Just a guest who's had a bit too much to drink. You know what weddings are like.'

They took their places as the string quartet began playing Felix Mendelssohn's "Wedding March" and Lizzie Marshall, looking every bit the blushing bride walked down an aisle strewn with white rose petals to meet her soon-to-be husband, Jack Drake, blissfully unaware of anything save how happy she was.

The sky was a kaleidoscope of colours as Lizzie and Jack said their vows; a canopy of rose pink to blood red, soft lilac to deep purple, azure to cobalt blue, pale gold to silver then baby blue chased by indigo as the evening crept stealthily across the heavens.

Confetti was thrown, congratulations given then Lizzie and Jack led the way to the ballroom for the celebratory dinner and dance to begin.

Ross had followed Max's suggestion and taken Kim to his room. He hadn't tied her up but he had locked the door.

'If she's sobered up and can behave herself,' Max said when Ross came down, 'she can join the wedding but make it clear that just one word and she goes back in that pond for good. She'll have to borrow something of Mum's to wear until we can get her dress washed and dried but it's up to her. Either that, or she can sleep it off.'

'Thanks Max. I think I'll let her sleep it off – just in case.'

Max turned to Becky. 'Well, that was a rather beautiful ceremony wasn't it? Did you see the colours of that sunset – no wait – you probably arranged that too didn't you?'

'Very funny.'

'I detect a slight chill in the air,' he said wrapping his arms around her.

She pulled away from him. 'How can you be so blasé about this Max? I ... I really don't understand. I was terrified and you're just dismissing it as a joke! What's more, you're inviting her to the wedding reception as if she's a friend. Have you forgotten what she did to Lizzie and Jack?''

His brows knit together. 'I can't see why it's such a problem. The woman was drunk and we weren't in any danger. It's over. Forget it. As to what she did to Lizzie and Jack, yeah, that was awful but we all know she's unhappy and it all turned out fine in the end. She's still Ross' wife and I have no idea why but he loves her. We can't ostracize the woman just because she has a few issues. Let's go and have some dinner. I'm starving.' He reached out for her.

'Max!' she stamped her foot like a child in a temper.

He raised his eyebrows but didn't speak and they stared at one another in silence for several seconds. Then Becky burst into tears.

He wrapped her in his arms and hugged her.

'I was terrified Max! Terrified!'

He stroked her hair. 'I'm sorry sweetheart. I hadn't realised it had upset you so much.'

'I told you it had!' she said between sobs.

'Yes but ... I didn't think you meant it had terrified you this much. I think you're in a state of shock. We'll be laughing about this tomorrow, truly we will. We're all safe. Kim's a bit wet and probably smells of pond water but when you actually think about it, no real harm was done. Oh, she's got a bruised jaw too. I've never hit a woman and I didn't mean to hit her but I caught her on the chin when I grabbed the gun from her.'

He rocked her in his arms until her sobbing ceased and he heard a little giggle.

'She deserved it Max. Okay. I ... I think I feel a little better now. God! I need a drink. My legs feel like jelly. I'm not sure I can walk.'

Without a word he swept her up in his arms and carried her to the ballroom.

Despite telling Max she felt better she was still shaking and the only thing that seemed to calm her frayed nerves was champagne. She drank rather a lot because her nerves were very frayed and then she drank some more, just because she could. By nine-thirty p.m., when the fireworks began and they all moved to the terrace to watch the display, she was 'oohing' and 'ahhing' with every firework.

Max asked Jess and Susie to keep an eye on her whilst he took Lily up to bed. They had let her watch the fireworks but she was half asleep in Max's arms before they had finished.

'We nearly died!' Becky said when Max had gone. She didn't see Lizzie standing behind her talking to Jane. 'That Kim woman came here with a gun and threatened to kill us all. Well, Jack and Phil and Ross and Max and me. Then Max threw her in the pond as calmly as you like and says everything is fine and I'm being silly for thinking we almost died! Can you believe it? Nothing worries Max!'

'What are you talking about Becky? Lizzie said, then to Jess. 'Is she drunk?'

Jess nodded. 'Yeah. Ignore her.' She'd heard a vague rumour herself but she didn't want Lizzie to worry.

'That's right! Ignore me. Max ignored me when I thought he was dead. Just ignore me. I need a drink.'

'What is she talking about?'

'I'm talking about Kim! She came here with a gun. Just before the ceremony. A gun! To shoot us.'

'Jack! Is this true?' Lizzie called to her husband who was chatting to Iain a few tables away.

'Is what true darling?' he said joining them and slipping his arm around his wife's waist.

'That Kim was here – and she had a gun!'

His eyes shot to Becky who was leaning against the table with two of her fingers pointed at Jack like a gun.

She made "pow, pow" noises then flopped onto a chair.

'Um,' he hesitated. 'She was very drunk and it wasn't a real gun. She just wanted to scare us. Max got the gun and then he threw her in the pond to sober her up. She's upstairs now I think, sleeping it off.'

'That woman is under the same roof as me on my wedding day!'

'Ross is with her. There's ... there's nothing to worry about, honestly Lizzie.'

'Oh really! Max! I want a word with you.' She saw him returning and headed in his direction.

'Oops!' Becky said and poured herself some more champagne.

Whatever Max said to Lizzie must have placated her because thirty minutes later she looked perfectly happy, dancing in her husband's arms. Max on the other hand, did not.

'I think you've had quite enough of that for tonight,' he said, taking Becky's glass away from her and sitting down beside her. 'Maybe you should go and lie down.'

'I don't want to lie down. I want to dance.' She pulled him to his feet and dragged him to the floor where she fell into his arms and he effectively carried her around for a few minutes.

'Okay, you've danced. Why don't we go and sit down now or better still, why don't we go and get some fresh air?'

'Okay,' she said allowing him to lead her out onto the terrace.

'I wish you hadn't said anything to Lizzie,' he said after a few seconds, 'it would have been better if she hadn't found out about today until they were on their honeymoon at least. You obviously had too much champagne. I know you wouldn't have upset her on purpose.'

'Obviously!' she snapped. She was being told off and she didn't like it. 'I need a drink.'

'You've had several. Let's sit out here for a while.'

'I want to dance.'

'We have danced. Now let's sit.' He led her to a chair and sat her down then sat down next to her.

'You're cross,' she said glancing at him from under her lashes.

'I'm not cross.' He didn't look at her but stared out at the night sky.

She sat in silence for a few seconds then as several guests tumbled out onto the terrace she saw her chance, jumped up and ran back inside to the middle of the dance floor. She began whirling around then as the music took her she stepped onto a chair and climbed onto a table. She kicked off her shoes and began gyrating to the beat. Several of the guests gathered round and applauded her.

Max got to her just as she toppled over and he caught her in his arms. 'Okay,' he said, 'I think someone needs to sober up a bit.' He carried her towards the door.

'Help me!' she shrieked at the top of her lungs. 'He's going to throw me in the pond!'

She struggled but he held her firm and people stepped aside to let him pass.

She realised her attempts to free herself were futile so she gave in and pleaded with him instead. 'Please don't throw me in the pond Max. I promise I'll be good.'

'I'm not going to throw you in the pond,' he said, 'I'm taking you up to bed.'

'That's nice,' she said snuggling up against him then seeing Ben step aside, she called out to him, 'Max is taking me to bed now vicar and we're going to have hot sex. Lots and lots of hot sex, because he's a sex god!'

'Okay, thank you,' Max said in a voice as smooth as silk.

That was the last thing she heard as she sank into a champagne induced oblivion.

CHAPTER THIRTY-ONE

Shafts of sunlight pierced Becky's eyes like red hot pokers and the distant gurgle of laughter from beyond the window sounded like Niagara Falls. She lifted her head an inch from the pillow but it was too heavy so she let it drop back down.

She tentatively opened her eyes and the walls of the Yellow Room were like sheets of bright sunlight. She slowly turned her head and buried it in the pillow.

The knock on the door was a procession of drums and she managed a faint 'Argh!' before wrapping her pillow around her ears.

Jess and Susie poked their heads round the door and came in. 'Morning Dancing Queen,' they sang out in unison.

She managed to drag a hand from the pillow and hold it in the air in a "stop" gesture.

'We come bearing gifts,' Jess said dropping onto the bed and yanking the pillow away.

Becky could smell the coffee and she turned gingerly. 'I ... I can't move,' she said, 'will you help me sit up?'

They helped her then Jess passed her the coffee and Susie handed her the headache pills.

'Industrial strength.'

'I need the entire factory this morning. God, I must have had a lot to drink last night. I feel like death warmed over.'

She saw Jess and Susie exchange looks. 'What?' she said.

'You don't remember anything?' Susie asked.

Becky tried to shake her head and realised it wasn't a wise move. 'No. Oh, God. Did I do something really embarrassing?'

'Well,' Jess said, 'let's just say you've given everyone a great deal to talk about. Where shall we start? Telling Lizzie there was nearly a massacre at her wedding. Dancing on the table to "Do you think I'm sexy?"

'I think everyone did,' Susie said nodding.

'I think so too. Or telling everyone that Max was going to throw you in the pond. Of course, when I say "telling" what I actually mean is screaming at the top of your lungs.'

'No,' Susie said, 'it has to be when you again shouted at the top of your lungs to Ben and everyone within a five mile radius that Max was taking you to bed to have lots and lots of hot sex because he is a sex god. Did we miss anything Jess?'

'No. I think that just about covers it.'

Becky had gradually been slipping down in the bed. Each thing they said flashed before her eyes as she saw herself doing all of them, one by one, in minute detail. And then she suddenly realised, she'd woken up alone.

'Max!' she said in a strangled voice.

'He's outside playing with Lily.'

'Oh my God! How am I ever going to face him again? How am I going to face anyone?' she let out a little sob. 'Oh! What must Margaret think? And Lizzie and Jack. I ruined their wedding. And Ben! Oh Susie I'm so sorry. And ... and everyone heard it? Definitely?'

'If the stunned silence was anything to go by, I'd say yes,' Jess said.

'Don't worry Becky. Everyone laughed about it afterwards.

'I bet they did. Oh hell! I can't go to the wedding brunch. I just can't. I'll die from embarrassment.'

'No one dies from embarrassment. Anyway, you can't, not go. That would be worse,' Jess said.

'You could say I'm ill – which is true actually, I feel sick.'

'No way honey. You're getting out of this bed and into that shower and you're going to face everyone.'

'Is ... is Max really cross? Have ... have I ruined everything? Is ... is he going to dump me?'

'No, no, and I doubt it very much,' Jess said. 'He seems in a very good mood and he's been chatting to Ben without the slightest hint of embarrassment so I don't think he's cross.

'Then ... why isn't he here?'

'Because he thought you'd need a bit of a lie-in and he didn't want Lily to wake you up,' Susie said.'

'Oh,' Becky whimpered.

'Don't be pathetic Becky Cooper. You've faced almost certain death at gunpoint, danced on tables, exposed your sex life to the world, after accusing your boyfriend of trying to drown you; you can handle this.'

'I'm glad you find it so amusing, Jess.'

'Oh I do. And not just me either. I think I can safely say the entire village will have heard about it by now. Now get up and get in the shower.'

Becky didn't know how she managed to stand up let alone get showered and dressed but she did. She heard the door open just as she was bending down to tighten the buckle of her sandals and thought Jess and Susie had come back for her.

'For heaven's sake can't you leave me in peace for five minutes!' she snapped. 'I'm coming!'

'It's a good thing the vicar didn't hear you say that,' Max drawled.

Becky's head shot up. He was leaning against the doorframe, his arms folded in front of him and his legs crossed casually at his ankles. His blond hair was dishevelled and his face was tanned from the sun. Little flecks of gold dust danced in his green eyes and his generous mouth was curved into a grin.

'Max!' she shrieked. Inwardly praying that he still loved her just a little bit.

'The very same,' he said still leaning against the frame, 'and no longer just a demigod but also a sex god now it seems – at least, that's what the entire village of Beckleston is saying this morning – or words to that effect.'

She lowered her head in shame but couldn't find the words to apologise.

249

'And for someone who told me they never dance on tables, your performance was extremely, shall we say, professional – until you fell off, that is.'

'Okay Max. I get it. I behaved appallingly. I embarrassed you, the vicar, your mum, everyone it seems and I ruined Lizzie and Jack's wedding. I'm sorry. I don't know what else to say.' She stood up straight even though she felt as if she were on board a ship. 'I'll make sure there are no problems with the wedding brunch and then I'll leave.'

She was trying to be brave. He clearly didn't love her anymore. She'd humiliated and disappointed him and he was angry. He had every right to be.

She headed towards the door but he barred her way.

'Leave?' he repeated. 'Why would you want to leave?'

'Because you're clearly disgusted and ... and cross – and you have every right to be, I'm not suggesting you don't. All I can say in my defence is that the incident with the gun scared the life out of me and I had a few drinks to calm my nerves and then I had a few more. I've never behaved like that in my life and ... what's the point? You obviously don't love me anymore after what I did –'

She was in his arms before she had even seen him move and he was kissing her passionately.

'More hot sex Max?' Phil said as he approached the open doorway from his room along the hall.

Max lifted his head but still held her firmly in his arms. He grinned at Phil. 'I hope so,' he said, 'tell the vicar we may be some time will you?'

'Sure thing,' Phil said grinning, 'morning Becky.'

'Now, where were we?'Max said.

'Wait! Aren't ... aren't you angry with me?'

'Do I look angry with you?' he leant forward.

'Hold on. I told Lizzie about Kim. I got drunk. I danced on the table. I ... I told everyone about our ... sex life – again. I ... what else did I do?'

Max grinned. 'Wasn't that enough for you?'

'Yes! I mean no! I mean. I didn't mean to do any of it. I really didn't. So ... you're not angry? Not even a little bit?'

His lips brushed hers. 'No. Not even a little bit.'

'But just now, you were leaning against the door as if ...'

'As if ...? he prompted.

She shook her head. 'I don't know.'

'I was leaning against the door thinking how incredibly beautiful you are and trying to stop myself from ravaging you because, unfortunately, we need to be downstairs in fifteen minutes and what I had in mind will take a lot, lot longer than that.'

'Oh!' she said raising her eyes to his.

'Oh indeed.'

'You're really not angry? You ... you still love me?'

He lifted her chin with his fingers. 'Why would I be angry? My girlfriend loves me so much that she is willing to throw herself in front of what she believes is a loaded gun to save me, she dances like a professional and she has the entire village convinced I'm a sex god. On the whole, I'd say I'm a lucky man. Now come along Fifi, your public awaits.'

She hadn't expected to be tarred and feathered exactly but she had expected at least someone to say something unpleasant – which she would have understood. She deserved it after her behaviour. Margaret should be just a little bit annoyed that her son's girlfriend behaved so badly and in front of so many people too. Lizzie and Jack should be cross that she'd made a spectacle of herself on their big day. The vicar should be shocked, at the very least. She took a deep breath and with her hand in Max's, she stepped out onto the terrace where everyone had congregated for coffee and biscuits.

'Morning,' she said sheepishly.

'Morning,' everyone carolled cheerfully, then continued with what they were doing.

'How are you feeling? Bit of a hangover I expect,'

Lizzie said grinning and giving her a hug.

'I'm so, so sorry Lizzie, Jack I –'

'Don't be silly,' Lizzie said. 'It's a wedding, everyone gets drunk at weddings. You did nothing to be ashamed of. Thank you again for everything you did yesterday. It was an absolutely marvellous day Becky. Jack and I will remember it for the rest of our lives, won't we Jack?'

'Yes. It was the perfect day. Thank you so much Becky.'

'Ah Becky dear. How are you this morning?' Margaret came over and kissed her on the cheek.

'Fine thank you. I'm sorry about –'

'No need to apologise dear! I've done a lot worse I can tell you. You had a good time, that's the main thing. The whole day was wonderful, wasn't it Lizzie?'

'Yes. We were just saying that. Absolutely perfect.'

Ben and Susie approached, hand in hand and Becky flushed crimson.

'Ben, Reverend, I'm really sorry. I'm truly ashamed.'

'Nothing to be ashamed about Becky, although my official stance is, if you're going to have hot sex, you should be married.' He winked at her and smiled.

She caught a glimpse of long, blond hair. 'Is that ... Kim?'

Lizzie nodded. 'Yeah. It took some doing but Jack and Max finally made me see that she has problems and needs help. Throwing her out wouldn't solve anything. She's apologised most profusely actually and whilst I can't say I'll ever like her, or trust her further than I'd still like to throw her, I'm prepared to bury the hatchet if only for Ross' sake.'

'Are ... are they getting back together then? Even after everything she did?' Becky couldn't quite believe it.

Jack shook his head. 'Only time will tell. The thing is Ross really does love her. He's crazy about her in fact. He only left her in the hope that she'd see sense. He realises that's not going to work and he's persuaded her to go and see a shrink. Not sure how much good that'll do to be honest but it's worth a shot I suppose.'

'And they have a son to think about,' Phil said.

'Wow! I'm not sure I'd be so forgiving. Oh! I'd better check with the caterers that everything's set for brunch,' Becky said glancing at her watch. 'We should be ready in about twenty minutes if we're still on schedule.'

The wedding brunch went off as smoothly as the celebratory dinner had then Lizzie and Jack cut the cake, had some more photographs taken and were ready to set off on honeymoon by one-thirty p.m.

Lizzie got all the single women assembled so that she could throw her bouquet and when Becky saw it heading in her direction she quickly moved to the left so that Susie could catch it instead. She smiled at Susie as she held it up triumphantly and then from the corner of her eye she spotted Max looking at her oddly.

She made her way to him and slid her arm through his. 'Well I have to say I'm glad it's all nearly over. It's been wonderful but so exhausting. I think I could sleep for a week.'

'That's all the dancing on the tables – and the hot sex of course,' he said.

'Actually, I haven't had much of that this weekend. We've got some catching up to do.'

'Your wish is my command. Speaking of catching, I noticed you dodged the bouquet. I hope I'm not supposed to take that as some sort of hint.'

She glanced up at him. 'I thought you'd be pleased. Most men would panic if they thought they were next on the marital list. But that wasn't why I did it. It was actually because I was the organiser for the wedding and I didn't think I should be the one to catch the bouquet – especially after my little performance last night.'

Max smiled. 'I'm not most men but I can see why you did that. And, about your performance last night, the table dancing one in particular, I wonder, is there any chance of a repeat but private showing, only before you fell off the table, you were really rather hot?'

The guests had finally left with the exception of Victoria and Gerald and peace descended once more on Beckleston Hall. Lily fell asleep from sheer exhaustion and Max took her upstairs and put her to bed whilst Becky made sure everything was restored to the way it was before the wedding.

By seven-thirty everything was ship-shape and Becky and Max joined Margaret, Victoria and Gerald on the terrace for more champagne.

'Not too much for me,' Becky said, 'just in case.'

Gerald laughed. 'I can tell you some stories about these two,' he nodded towards Margaret and Victoria, 'that would make what you did seem boring.'

'Not in front of the children Gerald,' Margaret said. 'I'd hate my little boy to think his mother is a wanton woman.' She laughed and winked at Max.

'Your little boy already knows you are, Mother,' he said.

It was another glorious sunset. A rainbow of colours filled the horizon and the slipstream of jet aircraft looked like a meteor shower trailing across the cornflower blue sky.

'Let's take a stroll over to the pond Fifi,' Max said. He stood up and held out his hand.

Becky was slightly surprised but she got up and slipped her hand in his.

They reached the post where the life ring hung and Max flipped a switch that Becky hadn't seen before. Strings of multi-coloured fairy lights encircling the pond twinkled before her eyes and three coloured under water lights threw up beams of green and yellow and red like little fountains.

'Do you like it?' he said. 'I wasn't sure if it made it seem more magical or less, in your eyes.'

'Oh more Max! Definitely more! It's ... it's beautiful. When did you have this done?'

'A few weeks ago. I thought the ducks might like to party so I gave them party lights.' He grinned.

She noticed a blanket and two cushions on the ground.

'Is this in case the ducks want to have a picnic?'

'No. I brought that over a couple of hours ago. I wanted you to see the lights and I thought we could sit here for a while.' He knelt down and grabbed a rope tied around the post. On the other end was a bottle of champagne. 'The glasses are under the cushions.'

'Well, it seems you've thought of everything.'

'This has been a pretty spectacular weekend,' he said sitting down and staring into the water.

'It certainly has.' Becky sat down beside him.

'In fact it's been a pretty spectacular seven months since Mum and I came here. I didn't want her to buy this place you know. I did everything I could to put her off it. Of course, I didn't know its history then or why she wanted it so much but she was adamant and nothing I did or said changed her mind.'

'She seems so at home here that it's hard to imagine her living anywhere else. It's ... almost as if she belongs.'

'That's just what she said. I thought I belonged in London. I've always loved living there, so much to see, so much to do but when I came here I felt, well, as if I belonged here too.'

Becky found herself hoping and watched his every move. The way he shoved his hand through his hair, the way he kept licking his lips as if his mouth was dry, the way he kept his eyes averted from hers.

He gulped his champagne and refilled their glasses.

'Silly though of course,' he said.

Her hopes shattered like a thousand broken fairy lights.

'Oh, I meant to give you this.' He handed her a large folded envelope, 'it's about another wedding Mum thought you might like to arrange.

'Okay, thanks. I'll read it later.'

'I think you should take a quick look at it now. They

need an answer pretty quick as to whether you're interested or not.'

She sighed. This evening wasn't going at all the way she'd hoped. She tore open the envelope.

'I think the plan is to have it around Easter. They're hoping to go to Australia for the Easter holidays – the bride to be's got family there and the groom's hoping they'll all come over for the wedding and then travel back together.'

She was only half listening. The envelope just seemed to be full of little bits of paper and when she tipped it up, handfuls of confetti spilled out onto the blanket. She glanced up at him. He was still staring into the water.

'Max. Is this some kind of ...' Then she saw it, twinkling up at her like the North Star.

'He's also hoping the in-laws will look after the couple's daughter for a few days so that he and his wife can nip over to Bora Bora, but that bit's negotiable ...' His voice trailed off and he twisted round to face her.

She was staring at the diamond ring, unable to speak.

'And he's really hoping she'll say yes because he loves her with all his heart and all his soul and all his mind. Will she? Will she say yes? Will you marry me Rebecca Lily Cooper?'

Her lips parted but she still couldn't find her voice.

'And he's running out of things to say and panic's setting in and he's praying that she loves him even half as much as he does her.'

She threw herself into his arms and cried.

'Is that a yes? Please Becky I need to hear it. Will you marry me – or are you crying because I've upset you somehow?'

She pulled herself away from him, tears streaming down her face. 'Yes!' she said, finally finding her voice. 'Yes she'll marry you. I'll marry you! I love you Max. More than I ever thought it possible to love someone, I love you. I love you. I love you!' She covered his face in kisses.

He held her away from him, his eyes filled with love and

happiness. 'Well you'd better have this then,' he said picking up the ring and sliding it on her finger.

'Oh Max. It's beautiful. I love you so much.' She wrapped her arms around him and pressed her body against his.

'And my body! I forgot my body,' he said his lips just touching hers, 'I love you with all my heart, all my soul, all my mind *and* all my body – and it's all my body I'm going to love you with right now.' He pulled her tighter into his arms. 'And the vicar won't mind, I've already told him I was hoping to make an honest woman of you.'

The end

***

THE GOLF WIDOWS' CLUB

Love doesn't play by the Rules

Jenna Baker needs a job but work isn't easy to find in the small seaside town of Claremont so when she's offered a position at the prestigious, Green Miles Golf Club, Jenna should be thrilled but she isn't – until she discovers she'll be working for thirty-four year old, Robert Miles.

Despite opposition from his father, Robert intends to turn the stuffy, elitist club into a place to bring the entire family and whilst he would hardly have chosen a pretty, thirty year old, former estate agent as his personal assistant, she certainly seems to have some good ideas. With her help, he's sure to succeed, if he can just keep his mind on his plans and not on Jenna and her irritating new boyfriend, Tom – who has plans of his own.

But when the past encroaches on the present and rumours start to fly, involving Robert, his parents and Jenna's, the ensuing conflict affects the lives of everyone involved, and things are about to change in ways none of them would ever have imagined.

*

Thanks for reading Lizzie Marshall's Wedding. I really hope you enjoyed it. To see more of my books or to contact me, pop over to my website.

http://www.emilyharvale.com

16767090R00147

Printed in Great Britain
by Amazon